RIGHT KIND OF WRONG

KATARINA MARTINEZ

To anyone who relates to any of these experiences.
I see you.
♥

✦ AUTHOR'S NOTE

Right Kind Of Wrong is a grumpy x sunshine, rockstar(ish) romance, where two opposites end up together. Before continuing I'd like to let you know a few things: this book absolutely contains **an accidental pregnancy.** It is one of my favorite tropes, but I realize it's not for everyone so please do not continue if it's not for you. She is pregnant from chapter seven until chapter twenty-eight. So basically the whole damn book.

When she does finally have their baby, it is by **emergency c-section.** So please keep that in mind. As someone who has experienced a traumatic emergency c-section, I realize it can be triggering for some to read. **If you cannot read that scene, please skip chapter twenty-eight.**

It is also so important that I inform you for a few chapters, she is involved with a man named Holt. There is love bombing, degrading (subtle and not the kinky kind), and eventually physical abuse. The abuse does happen while she's pregnant, so please make sure to check in with yourself while reading this book and if for any reason you need to DNF, I absolutely understand and love you anyways. Your mental health is and always will be the most important thing.

These experiences wrote in this book are inspired by events that I went through. It has been very healing to write and I hope it reaches who it needs to.

You are not alone.

IF YOU OR ANYONE YOU KNOW IS IN
A DOMESTIC ABUSE RELATIONSHIP,
DON'T HESITATE TO UTILIZE THE
DOMESTIC ABUSE HOTLINE.

NUMBER: 800-799-7233

TEXT: "BEGIN" TO 88788

OR LIVE CHAT: WWW.THEHOTLINE.ORG

BORN WITH A BROKEN HEART - DAMIANO DAVIA

LOVE ME LIKE YOU DO - ELLIE GOULDING

TONGUE TIED - GROUPLOVE

I WANNA BE YOURS - ARTIC MONKEYS

SAILOR SONG - GIGI PEREZ

DISTRACTION - SLEEP TOKEN

SECOND SIGHT - ARANKAI

PAPER RINGS - TAYLOR SWIFT

THE SCIENTIST - BEA AND HER BUSINESS

THE ONLY THING LEFT - VINCENT LIMA

WALK THIS WORLD WITH ME - THE HOME TEAM

CONTENTS

Chapter 1	1
Chapter 2	9
Chapter 3	18
Chapter 4	25
Chapter 5	35
Chapter 6	48
Chapter 7	55
Chapter 8	66
Chapter 9	74
Chapter 10	82
Chapter 11	91
Chapter 12	98
Chapter 13	111
Chapter 14	124
Chapter 15	134
Chapter 16	143
Chapter 17	155
Chapter 18	165
Chapter 19	173
Chapter 20	181
Chapter 21	194
Chapter 22	205
Chapter 23	214
Chapter 24	227
Chapter 25	236
Chapter 26	245
Chapter 27	252
Chapter 28	259
Chapter 29	266
Chapter 30	274
Epilogue	281

Acknowledgments 285
About the Author 287
Also by Katarina Martinez 289

Olivia

1

The last bell of the day rings throughout my classroom. All of the students in my advanced level art class stand up and say their goodbyes as they all rush to leave through the door. I'm thankful that they're my last class because they leave the least amount of mess for me to clean up before I get to leave for the day.

I go to my computer, pull up my cleaning music playlist, and start to wipe down the tables. I've been an art teacher for the last three years and I have loved every moment of it so far. I didn't set out to be an art teacher when I started at Dryer University. Actually, it would have made more sense for my identical twin sister, Daphne, to be an art teacher.

Me? Not so much.

I needed an elective, so I decided to take art. I didn't expect to fall in love with it the way I did, but I truly found a piece of myself in that first class. What started out as that one elective ended up in me going to museums and taking any additional courses I possibly could.

I've never done *anything* as fast as when I switched my major.

Mom was stressed, to say the least. She had no idea what I was going to do with a degree in art history, but I ended up getting my credentials and now I'm here teaching at a high school level. Out of the four of us kids, I've always been the most dependable and definitely the most studious. Lists, schedules, and routines are basically engraved in my DNA. I'm *technically* the oldest, but Daph refuses to acknowledge the ten minutes between our births. Matilda is six years younger than us and has been counting down to her twenty-first birthday since she turned sixteen. Out of all of us, it's her that enjoys partying the most. Daphne is really, *really* close to stealing that spot from her, though. It's always Daph who commands the attention of everyone in the room.

I'm much more *go with the flow*. I don't ever expect to be the center of attention, but I don't do anything to hide from people either. My best friend, Gracie, is much more standoffish. Aside from me and my sisters, she doesn't really like anyone. We were put in the same dorm room when we went to Dryer University and have been inseparable ever since.

I finish cleaning up what I can of the mess my kids left behind, then head to my desk to pack up my stuff. My brown laptop bag makes a *thud* when I set it on my chair. I close down my laptop and take my phone off of the wireless charger, only to see all of the missed text messages from my sister group chat.

> Daph: What are we doing tomorrow?

> Mattie: Twenty-One Babbby!

> Daph: We're gonna fuck shit up.

Mattie: That new club, The Grind, just opened up on main street. I think that might be cool.

Mattie: Pregame at your place?

My sisters go on to make plans to meet at the apartment Daphne and I share around six tomorrow evening to celebrate Mattie's twenty-first birthday. I roll my eyes at the obscene amount of cursing Daphne does throughout the thread and shove my phone into the front pocket of my bag. I may not be excited to go to a club, but I am really looking forward to spending time with my sisters.

I flick off the lights in my classroom and shut the door behind me. The sun is setting across the campus, which is basically empty as I walk across it. An occasional teacher exits their classroom and joins me on the walk to the office. I make sure to smile and wave at everyone. Some of them give me dirty looks, but I swear there's power in smiling at someone. You never know if they're having a bad day or not.

"See you tomorrow, Rhonda. Have a wonderful night!" I wave to the office manager and make my way out of the front. I take a deep breath of the crisp fall air as I walk towards my car.

I adjust my bag over my shoulder and push the small button on my door to unlock the car. After placing my bag on my passenger seat, I pull myself into my driver side seat. My phone connects to the car on the center console, so I scroll through and start up the newest episode of my favorite true crime podcast. The voices of the hosts fill the space and ease settles into my chest at the familiarity of this part of my routine.

I pull out of the parking lot, into the midday traffic, and towards my apartment. My sister will be home since she is not currently booked for anything. Her last modeling job paid her well enough that she could not work for the next four months and be fine, but she enjoys the work too much to sit still.

I drive across town and turn off into the parking garage beneath my apartment building, parking at one of the two spots that are labeled *apt 13*. I lock my door behind me as I exit my car, making sure I hear the *beep* echo in the garage before I head over to the elevator.

It travels in silence to the first floor of apartments, which is the second floor of the building, the sound of music from my apartment fills the hallway as soon as the doors slide open.

"Daph, you can hear that down the hallway. Mr. Goldlin is going to complain again." I groan, stepping inside. It takes me a moment to realize I'm talking to an empty room.

I hang my keys on the hook, kick my shoes off by the door, and go to my room to put my purse away in its spot. My room is always kept the same. The queen sized bed is set in between two bedside tables just beneath a window that leads outside. I chose to keep décor very minimal, making sure to still include some color. On one of the tables is a sunshine yellow lamp and on the other, a stack of books next to a vase full of sunflowers and baby's breath.

Besides that, there's nothing out on the surfaces.

I can't *stand* when there's clutter.

After putting my bag on its hook inside of my walk-in closet, I grab a change of clothes and meander into the shared bathroom to start my after work routine. First, I start the shower to let the water warm up while I wash my face in the sink. Piece by piece, my work clothes fall to the floor before I toss them in the hamper. When I step in the shower, the water runs over my skin and washes away my long day.

As much as I love my job, *this* is my favorite part of the day.

Once I've finished, I dry off and put on my favorite pink lounge set. When I first saw it at Costco, I wasn't sure if it would be comfortable. But after I wore it once, I loved it so much I went back and bought three more. I grabbed another pink one, the baby blue, and then the gray.

My stomach gurgles as the smell of dinner hits my nose. The best part of having Daphne as my roommate? Man can that girl cook.

"What's for dinner?" I ask as I sit down on the couch, tucking my legs beneath me.

"Just some noodles, nothing fancy." She smiles over her shoulder.

"Whatever it is smells delicious." It takes my brain a moment to process the absence of music. "You didn't have to turn the music completely off. Sorry for snapping at you. I just really don't want him to complain about us...again."

"I turned it off when my," she clears her throat, "friend left."

Friend.

"Oh."

I always envied that of Daphne. Her freedom with exploring her sexuality. There was always a shyness I felt when it came to sex. I've had a couple of partners over the years, but never friends with benefits or one night stands like Daph.

"It was Derek. You've met him a couple of times."

"Right. Derek."

Truth be told...I can't remember who he is, but I'll pretend like I do.

"His band is actually playing at The Grind tomorrow. So, it'll be really cool to watch them."

"For Mattie's birthday?"

"Yes! Sis, you have *got* to let loose tomorrow. Let your hair down, babe!"

Without thinking about it, I run my hand over my low pony. When mom let Daphne and I start expressing our individuality, she dyed her strawberry blonde hair dark brown, but I couldn't do anything *that* drastic. Aside from adding some highlights here and there to make the blonde stand out, I don't mess with it often. I've never really even cut it aside from the occasional trim every few months.

"I'm literally only going for her birthday. I don't like clubs." *Too much noise,* I think to myself. I love meeting new people, but clubs are so crowded and loud.

"We have *got* to get you out of the house more, Livy. You can't sit here on the couch with your matcha and smutty romance books forever." *Can't I?* I just shrug in response, knowing at the end of the day Daphne will get what she wants. She always has. "Let me dress you and do your make-up! I know you refuse for me to do your hair too, but let me at least do everything else. Especially get you out of your graphic tees."

I don't hide the groan as I toss my head backwards, landing it on the back of the couch. "I'll compromise with you. You can do *some* of my make-up and you can *help* me with my outfit."

"You're impossible, but I will take what I can get." She shimmies and walks around to hand me my bowl of noodles.

It's my favorite comfort food, angel hair pasta tossed in garlic, butter, red pepper flakes, and topped with fresh parsley and parmesan cheese. Mom used to make it for us frequently. It wasn't until I was an adult that I learned it was because we often didn't have the means for anything more.

Daphne joins me on the couch and turns on the T.V., going straight for Netflix so that we can watch the next couple of episodes of *Bridgerton*. It has quickly become a nightly thing for us to watch at least an episode before we go to our bedrooms.

I WAKE up before the sun, like normal, and head down to the gym that's a couple of buildings from my apartment. It's important to me that I start the morning with *some* kind of movement. I put my headphones on and turn on my workout playlist, consisting mainly of a mix with Sabrina Carpenter, Taylor Swift, and Paramore.

The gym is typically quiet this time of day. Aside from me, there's just a couple of other people working out and like two or three employees. That's one of the reasons I prefer coming this early, the solitude.

I get off my machine, clean it off, and wipe my forehead and neck, removing as much sweat as I can with my personal towel. The sun is beginning to rise, the pastel purple and pinks coming in through the window as I walk towards the front of the gym. After waving goodbye to the person at the front desk, I turn to walk a street over to get my morning coffee from my favorite coffee shop, Solid Grounds.

My favorite barista, Bodhi, has recently left after starting a new company with one of his friends. Even though I am super disappointed, I understand why he'd want to go and pursue his dreams.

"Good morning," I say to the new barista. "I'd like a large iced white chocolate mocha with no whip and with oat milk, please. Oh. also a large, iced caramel macchiato, upside down."

"Okay, great. Your total will be $13.21."

"Perfect." I tap my phone to pay and sit at one of the small tables near the front of the coffee shop. Ever since I moved to this part of Dryer Hill, I fell in love with the atmosphere of this place. In the back corner is a small bookshop that specializes in books of all sorts, but only recently they decided to showcase more independently published authors.

"Olivia, your order is ready."

I smile to the nice barista and take my coffees, cursing myself for not bringing a jacket when the crisp fall air bites at my skin. *Of course* I get an iced coffee at the end of October so by the time I get into my apartment building, two streets over, my hands are frozen.

I struggle to open the door to my apartment.

"I brought you a macchiato," I announce.

"You are an *angel* sis." Daphne yawns from the couch. "You ready for tonight?"

"Ready to celebrate our baby sister? Yes. Ready for the crazy night I'm sure you have planned? Not even a bit. I've got to get ready for work," I walk over to her and hand her the iced coffee.

"It's going to be so, *so* much fun to get you to finally let loose, big sister," she yells from the living room as I walk through my doorway, shutting the door behind me.

2

I turn off the last light in the workshop and make sure the door closes behind me. Even though I locked it from the inside, I shake the handle to ensure it's locked. Grant would have my ass if someone stole any of the equipment because I didn't make sure it was secure. Besides Blaire, Grant is the only person whose opinion really matters to me. So, the fact that he taught me carpentry and trusts me enough to work for him, *with* him, means a lot.

If it weren't for him, carpentry, or Celeste... I don't know where Blaire and I would have ended up. You hear horror stories, ya know? Kids in the system talk and you always hear about foster homes that seem good, but beneath the surface it's worse than the houses we left. Nothing could have been as bad as living with dad though.

I could have killed him the moment he laid hands on Blaire for the first time. Watching the light dim in her eyes when he hit her...made a fire erupt inside of me.

I'd take it all to protect her.

Every hit. Every smack. Every yell.

And I did.

Mom was too busy searching for her next high to give a shit, and if she wasn't using, she was getting hit, too. At first the bruises were hidden by my oversized jackets and clothes, but soon they couldn't be hidden anymore. My high school English teacher, Ms. Hazel, didn't think twice about reporting my piece of shit dad to social services. It didn't take long for him to be arrested, charged, and ultimately sentenced to time in prison for the abuse. Since Mom was nowhere to be found, Blaire and I were put in the system.

We really lucked out with Grant and Celeste, especially taking a sixteen year old and his eight year old sister. They never gave up on us, on *me*. When I pushed against them, they gave me space. When I resisted, they showed me I was worthy of love. Celeste insisted that we go to counseling, both independently and as a new family. Eventually, they legally adopted Blaire. They gave me the option, but I was already almost eighteen at that point.

I found my mom when I was twenty-three. It had been at least seven years since we had seen one another. She was sitting in front of a local coffee house. I recognized her right away, but for her, it took longer than it should have. She seemed like she hadn't eaten, so I went into the coffee shop and ordered her water and something to eat. It didn't take long after that for her to finally really recognize me. It was like she had no understanding of how long it had truly been since the county took us from her. She didn't ask about Blaire, and I think that made me madder than her taking forever to recognize me. After she scarfed down the chicken wrap, she asked me for money. By the state of her body and the sores that covered her arms, I knew exactly where the money would go.

I told her I refused to pay for her addiction. She yelled at me and said she was glad, *glad*, they took me away.

I haven't seen her since.

My phone chimes with an alert as I cross the parking lot to my truck. I unlock the door to my hand-me-down, beat up red Chevrolet, crawling into the driver's seat before I look at my phone.

Sis: Pizza for dinner, pleassse!

Sis: I'd love you forever!

Me: Pepperoni and sausage?

Sis: You know me so well.

Me: Be home soon.

Sis: Love you!

Me: Love you too

I close my phone and start up the truck. The familiar roar of the ancient engine rattles throughout the cab. I plug my phone into the Bluetooth, which was the first thing I bought with my *adult* money, and switch on my favorite playlist. Our pizza spot, Messina's, is about halfway between the workshop and home, so it's not out of the way. But even if it was, I'd stop there for Blaire, and she knows it. The music fills my cab, and I let it blur my thoughts as I pull onto the highway and head towards Messina's.

The parking lot is empty for a Thursday night, which is when they offer free garlic bread with the order of a large pizza.

I park in the spot closest to the front door and walk in, a *ding* alerts them that I'm here.

"Ah, Beck! How are you tonight?" The owner, Dante, yells from behind the counter.

"Hey, Dante. I'm good. You?"

"Good. Good. The usual?"

"You know it."

"I'll throw in extra garlic bread, eh?" He winks as he turns around and walks towards the kitchen area in the back.

"That would be great, Dante. I appreciate you."

"You and Blaire keep our lights on."

The double door swings behind him and I sit in a booth. Only four other tables are occupied. I find myself staring at the family, a man, woman, and two children, longer than I should. Something about the way the man looks at the woman across from him while she plays with the little girl with pigtails, makes my chest ache in longing. I don't know that I *want* kids, or a wife for that matter, but sometimes the one night stands and booty calls leave me feeling emptier than before.

But I don't *do* relationships and everyone knows it.

Besides from my foster parents, Blaire, Adrian.... don't really talk to anyone. Adrian is Grant and Celeste's only biological child who lives in a different state for work. They wanted to have more, but they weren't able. That's one of the things that led them to open their home to foster. Celeste gets *pissed* when she hears me say that Adrian's their only son because she's never seen me in any other way *but* as her son.

"Beck. Your pizza and bread are ready." Dante says behind the counter, raising up the pizza box in emphasis before putting it down. "See you next time."

"Of course. See you." I wave and pick up my order.

For whatever reason, I look over my shoulder to look at that family sitting in the booth one last time before shutting the door and going to my car.

I PULL into my parent's neighborhood. The streetlights line both sides of the road leading towards their house. Everyone's car is parked outside, so I pull up behind Blaire's sedan and put the truck in park. I check the clock on my phone. I only have about an hour before I have to meet the guys for practice. Our band, Skarred, has a gig at this new brewery in town. Rumor has it there's going to be people from a record company in the crowd.

Skarred doesn't mean nearly as much to me as it does to Derek, Tieran, and Hayes. This was just something I did to let loose, but the other guys consider it their ticket out of Dryer Hill. Hayes is on guitar, Tieran is bass and backup vocals, and Derek is our lead singer. Since high school, it's been the four of us. Even after children's services took me out of my house and put me with Grant and Celeste, the guys have been there with me through everything.

I walk into my parents' house, Blaire is laying on the couch. "Hey Beck," she mutters without looking up from her phone.

"Squirt." I reach across the back of the couch and ruffle her hair, carefully balancing the pizza in my other hand. She squeals in response and jumps up off to storm into the kitchen and gripe at Mom.

"Beckett, do you *really* have to antagonize your sister the moment you walk in through the door?"

"Yes."

"Well, there you have it, Blaire. Now can we eat our pizza, cause I'm starvin," my dad says as he joins us in the kitchen.

Blaire, as if we're still children, sticks her tongue out at me. I let out a low laugh and slink nearer to her, closing the space between us and wrapping her into my arms. She's always been my soft spot, and she knows it.

"Got band practice tonight?" Dad asks. He tries to act like he understands the band, the we make music, and the genre but he is more of a folk country kind of guy.

We play alternative.

"That's the plan. We have a gig tomorrow night and Derek wants us to be ready."

"Are you ever going to let us watch you play?" Mom's voice is soft, she raises her eyebrows in hope.

"I don't think you'd like the crowd, Ma."

"One day you guys are going to be up on the stage, and everyone will travel from all over to see you." She opens the box of pizza and starts to hand out slices.

"Maybe, but I'm pretty happy at the shop right now."

"I know you are, baby, but I don't want you to be stuck in Dryer forever."

I shrug, unsure of what to say. Dryer Hill is *home*. I don't even know where I'd go or what I would do if I wasn't here. The band is a good way for me to let loose, but I've never thought it would go further than playing at dive bars and breweries on Friday nights.

Blaire starts talking about her new job. She is an assistant to a woman who runs social media for a publishing house that opened earlier this year. I listen to her as she gushes about how cool everyone is and how much she's enjoying it.

My phone vibrates in my pocket, bringing my attention away from the conversation. I know who it is even before I pull it out of my pocket.

> Derek: I'm on my way. Who's grabbing the beer?

> Tieran: I've got a twelve pack.

> Derek: That won't be enough for the four of us, plus anyone else who might come.

My eyes roll involuntarily, and I try to tamp down my annoyance when I type up my response. Derek is notorious for having groupies come to our practices and shows, even more so any after parties we have.

> Me: Tell your groupies to bring their own alcohol, D.

> Hayes: Agreed.

I ignore the incoming text messages and slide my phone back into my pocket. The band really likes to party. They've *always* liked to party.

Me? Not so much, but I always show up. Sometimes it gets to be too much. All of the alcohol, drugs, and women throwing themselves at all of us. I know exactly how that fucking sounds, too. *Oh, poor Beck.* I've just been around enough alcohol and drugs to last me a lifetime.

We finish up our pizza and I say my goodbyes to my parents and sister, hopping in my truck to drive to practice. Tieran's shop, where we play, is about twenty minutes across town. He lives closer to me in the inner part of Dryer, while my parents live in the suburbs. I pull into the small parking lot and find a parking spot between Derek's Crossover and Tieran's truck.

The gravel of the walkway crunches beneath my feet as I walk around towards the back entrance.

The sound of Derek's laugh, followed by the sultry chuckles of a couple of women floats through the air. I can tell that one of them belongs to Michelle, who I *really* can't fucking stand. I stop at the edge of the wall, out of view, and take a deep breath to prepare myself for practice.

"About time you showed up," Derek announces when I step through the open door. Michelle and the other woman, I think her name is Willow or some shit, whip their heads around to look in my direction.

"Heyyy Beck." Michelle saunters over in my direction, running her unnecessarily long red fingernails along my chest. The scent of cheap tequila and awful perfume fills in my nostrils as she tries to whisper something in my ear.

"Get off me, Michelle. I told you it's never going to happen."

"Come on, baby. You know you want me."

"Everyone's already *had* you, honey. I know I'm not missing out," I whisper low in her ear, making sure only she hears.

"You're such an asshole." She storms back over to Willow, crossing her arms and whispering to her friend. I can tell she's angry, probably embarrassed. I should feel like an asshole, but I don't.

I go over to my drums behind where Hayes and Tieran are standing.

"Earth to Derek, can we fucking play?" Hayes throws his hands up in the air, frustration lacing his face.

He rolls his eyes and says something in Willow's ear,

resulting in her cheeks flushing a deep pink, and finally manages to get to his guitar.

I count us in and we start playing our first song in the set list, *Only Yours For Tonight.*

After we finish running through the five songs we're playing at The Grind tomorrow, we all say our goodnights and go our separate ways. I wipe the sweat that's running down my face and neck and hop into my truck. There's a knock on my window that makes me jump. I turn and look to see Willow standing at my door.

I roll down the window. "Yeah?"

"You going home?" She bats her long eyelashes.

"I am."

"Can I come with you?"

"No." I roll up my window and put the truck in reverse, leaving Willow standing in the gravel and dust that fill the air.

Olivia

3

I go through my every day, after school, routine but instead of a lounge set, I get dressed in jeans and my sister's lacy emerald green shirt that leaves *little* to the imagination. Hoping it covers more of my stomach, I pull down on the hem with rough tugs. If anything, all it did was expose more of my breasts.

"Damn, sis." Daphne comes up behind me. "I didn't realize you had those under your t-shirts."

I roll my eyes and bite my lip to hide the fact that I want to giggle.

"You look great, sissy," Mattie says from my bed. She's sitting with her legs crossed on the edge. Unlike Daphne and I, she has our mother's naturally curly brown hair and green eyes. Whereas Daph and I inherited our dad's blue eyes and straight blonde hair.

"Thanks," I mumble, my face now feeling warm. I can hear my lounge set crying my name from the dresser drawer. It's a

Friday night and I'd much rather be curled up on the couch with a good book and trashy TV on in the background.

"Okay. Now, sit down so I can do your make-up." Daph motions to the chair in front of my vanity. There's no use in arguing with her, so I don't even try.

"Just don't do it too dark, please." She scoffs as I beg. "I'm not used to wearing dark makeup." I sit down on the chair and close my eyes.

My stomach drops when she starts to apply the eyeshadow. Knowing my sister, it will absolutely be too dark. I typically like to keep my make-up minimal, especially at school, with just light eyeshadow, mascara, and lip gloss or chapstick. But as my sister says sentences with words like contour, lipstick, and blush, I realize it's not going to be anything like my typical day to day look.

"Hey bitchesss!" My best friend Gracie sings as she enters my bedroom with a gift bag in one hand and her make-up bag in the other. She hands the gift to Mattie and kisses her on the top of the head. "For you, Princess."

Mattie squeals and tears into the gift. She practically leaps off the bed to wrap her arms around my bestie when she realizes what it is. Of course, I already knew it was an e-reader, and I know my sister will *love* it. She's been absolutely dying for one since she started getting into reading and Gracie didn't second guess snagging it for her.

Gracie and I have been friends since second grade, so she was basically adopted into our family. Her parents are great too, but they were a lot stricter than Mom. It wasn't a surprise when we spent the majority of time at my house.

"Well, don't you look hot as fuck." She kisses my temple. "Hey hoe," she directs to Daphne.

"Slut," Daphne hisses back. There's a moment of silence before the two of them erupt into laughter. The two of them spent their share of time together when they partied in high school, and after, while I stayed home.

"Is everyone ready to partaaaay?"

"No," I respond while the other two shout, "Yes!"

"Okay. You're done." I slowly open my eyes. Relief instantly floods my chest when I see Daphne didn't go *too* dark and kept it fairly casual with a brown smokey eye and mauve matte lipstick. "And please do us *all* a favor and get laid."

"I'll cheers to that!" Gracie chimes in.

"I hope we all get laid," Mattie shrugs.

"Let's do shots! The Uber will be here in..." Gracie checks the app on her phone. "Ten minutes!"

Everyone leaves my room to head towards the kitchen, but I linger back to stare at my reflection. I try to recall the last time I actually had physical contact with someone other than my sisters or best friend. I've always been envious of the confidence both Daphne and Gracie have to just *go for it*.

"Liv! Get your ass in here!" Gracie yells from the kitchen.

I stand up, adjust my shirt one last time, and check myself out in the full length mirror that hangs by my door. It may just be the shot, but I'm feeling *good.*

I close the door behind me to meet my best friend and sisters at the kitchen island. Gracie is pouring tequila into four shot glasses on the counter while Daphne cuts up a lime beside her, handing each of us a small slice with a smile.

"To Mattie!" Gracie raises her shot glass, and we all follow. "Happy birthday, bitch!"

"Happy birthday, Mattie!" Daphne and I say together. We all

toss the shot back, the tequila burns as it glides down my throat.

Gracie's phone chimes and she pulls it out of her pocket, removing the lime only to say, "Our rides here! Let's go fucking party!"

I run into my room and grab my purse and jacket, making sure to lock the front door behind the four of us as I leave.

The others left it wide open.

DAPHNE AND GRACIE both know the bouncer at The Grind, so we get to go right in when we arrive. The four of us go straight to the bar while we wait for the band to start. After we get another shot, I order a cosmo and decide once I've finished it, I'm done with alcohol for the night.

"What's the name of this band again?" I ask the group.

"Skarred. They're so good!" Daphne replies over the music.

"You mean Derek is so good in bed." Gracie laughs. "Hayes is pretty great, too."

"You?" My sister's eyebrows rise.

"Oh, yeah. A few times actually!" I stand there and listen to my sister and best friend go on and on about the bandmates they've *enjoyed time* with.

"They went to high school with us, actually!"

"Who did?" I ask, furrowing my brows.

"The band, duh!"

"You didn't tell me that, Daph."

"I think they were all a year or two ahead of the three of us."

She points between herself, Gracie, and me. "You didn't really hang out with the same crowd as us, so I didn't think you'd know them."

"Who are they?"

"Derek Hale, obviously. Tieran Summers, Hayes Wright, and Beck Haven."

Beck Haven.

I stumble back as if someone hit me in the face with a stack of magazines.

"Wait, oh shit. I forgot you had a thing for Beck!" Gracie exclaims and covers her mouth.

"I did not." *No. I absolutely did.*

I remember the first time I saw him in biology. Of course, I was in a class with a majority of sophomores and juniors as a freshman, and there he was, Beck. He was a bad boy, everything that was the opposite of me in every way, and I would've done anything to get a chance with him. For him to even *look* at me.

But even in high school, Beck didn't date. I would hear the stories of parties they went to, and it always included people sleeping around, which is why I stayed home. But he never had a serious relationship.

"Shut the fuck up. Why didn't I know this?" My sister looks back and forth between me and Gracie. I've never been more grateful that it's dark than I am at this moment. I am crimson from the chest up, I can feel it.

"Because I didn't."

"Oh, she so fucking did!" Gracie insists to my sister. I try to shoot her a *can you shut the fuck up* look, but the crowd starts to cheer and the band takes the stage.

Thank the heavens.

We make our way towards the small baracade in front of the

stage and watch as the band gets to their spots. I watch each of them, only slightly recognizing the other members. Obviously, they've all aged, but they all look great.

That's when I see him.

Beckett.

The noise quiets down around me as he takes his place and I swear his eyes lock onto mine. His dark brown hair is cut shorter on the sides but kept longer on top. His baby face is now chiseled, and the light reflects off the hoop in his left nostril and the ring in the middle of his bottom lip. I let my eyes keep wandering down his torso, which is exposed because *of course,* he's shirtless. Tattoos cover his body, starting at his neck and down his left arm, ending just below his chest.

"Oh, babe. You want to fuck him *so* bad," Gracie whispers in my ear. "I say get some because the way he's looking at you says he feels the same."

I lift my eyes and meet his gaze. A smirk plays on the corner of his mouth as if he just *knows*, and the butterflies in my stomach multiply at a rapid rate.

"Thanks for coming out," the lead singer says into the mic. "We are Skarred."

Without breaking eye contact, Beck taps his drumsticks together and the band erupts into music. Slow at first, but it isn't long before the tempo picks up. When Beck finally looks away, I find myself longing for him to look at me again.

As soon as the first song ends, they continue onto the next one and the next. Gracie and Mattie head back to the bar for more drinks, but I just ask for water.

Does Gracie have choice words about my choice not to *partaaaay*? Yes, she absolutely does.

Beck is intoxicating enough that I don't need any more alcohol.

"I say go for it. You haven't stopped watching him the whole time. If I would have known *sooner* I could have hooked you up with him through Derek," my sister says in my ear as the others shuffle through the crowd.

"He was really cute in high school and that whole bad boy thing did it for him," I respond, keeping it as vague as possible.

"Honey, that bad boy thing is *still* doing it for him."

I nod in agreement as I watch his skin glisten underneath the lights of the stage. Should someone sweating so much as they hit an instrument with sticks be making me *this* hot and bothered? Probably not, but I can't stop watching the sweat drip from him.

The logical side of my brain is telling me to stay away, *far* away from Beck. I know he doesn't do relationships and typically, that's all I want to do. I've never done a one night stand or casual fling, but I'm feeling brave and I think I'm going to go for it.

Tonight, I'm going to have sex with Beck.

4

"Okay guys, this show is important. There's a chance that there's agents in the crowd." Derek looks each of us in the eye as he makes his announcement.

I stifle the annoyance on my face and give Derek a fist bump. This is important to him and the other guys. But me? Not so much. I love playing in the band, just not the pressure of getting signed. Music has and always will be an outlet for me, whereas for the guys, they want it to be a career.

Right before we take the stage, I pull off my shirt and throw it with our stuff. These smaller venues get hot way faster than the bigger ones and I don't feel like playing in a soaked shirt tonight. One by one we take our places on the stage and right before it's my turn to walk out, I see her.

Olivia fucking Connoly.

You have got to me fucking shitting me. She looks as good as ever standing in the crowd. The lights reflect off her long strawberry blonde hair that flows behind her shoulders. She looks like a fucking goddess in the crowd. It's dark and I can't make out much, but I know her gray blue eyes are meeting mine.

As I play, there's not a doubt that I'm pushing myself harder, definitely showing off a little bit for her. We didn't hang around the same crowd or anything, we literally never have. I stuck with the guys and the party crowd, she did not. I did hang out with her best friend, Gracie and her twin, Daphne from time to time, but much to my disappointment, never Olivia.

She and I crossed paths in other ways, though. Sophomore year biology we got stuck being lab partners for half of the year. She was a freshman, quiet and shyer than Daphne, but the moment she walked into the room, it lit up with her presence. Aside from social media, I haven't seen her out and I *definitely* haven't seen her out at bars or clubs listening to our band.

The set ends without any issues. If anything, this was our best show yet. I'm dripping sweat so after we tear everything down, I go into the bathroom and rinse my face and shoulders, drying them off the best I can before I put my shirt back on. I head towards the bar to meet up with guys, not surprised when I see they're surrounded by people.

I *am* surprised, however, when I see Olivia standing with the group.

Derek is front and center, no shock there, and talking to everyone. Daphne is laughing at something Derek says while everyone else stands back and listens. By the way she's laughing and touching his arm, I can tell they are definitely hooking up.

I order my beer and join the group, lingering with Tieran. The hair on the back of my neck stands on end and I lift my eyes from the spot on the floor I've been staring at while listening to Derek talk.

At the edge of the circle, I find Olivia.

She's looking right at me.

I lift the corner of my mouth into a smirk and raise an eyebrow, as if to say *like what you see?* Even in the dark it's obvious when pink spreads across her cheeks. I motion my chin for her to come over to where I'm at. She lowers her gaze and bites her bottom lip slightly before walking over to me.

I turn around to the bartender. "Hey, Tavia. Can I get two shots of Patron?"

"You got it, Beck!" Octavia, the bartender, pours tequila into shot glasses and places them on the counter in front of me. "On the house. It was a great show."

"Thank you," I respond and grab the glasses from the countertop.

"Are one of those for me?" Olivia's voice is sweet and quiet, but I'm still able to hear her over the loud thumping of the music that's playing over the club's speakers.

"Depends. Do you like tequila?"

"I do."

"Then yes. This one is yours." I hold out the shot glass and hand it to her, bringing my own to cheers her. I throw it back and watch as she does the same. For someone who didn't party in high school, she takes it like a champ.

"Do you dance, Beckett Haven?"

Beckett. I haven't been called by my first name since high school.

"I do not dance, Olivia Connoly."

"Will you dance with me?" She sticks her bottom lip and pretends to pout.

"Not likely."

"I guess I'll find someone else to dance with then," she announces and turns on her heel towards the dance floor. I watch as she struts away, hoping the way her ass is shaking is a show just for me. Everyone on, and off, the dance floor's attention falls onto her as she sways to the music. I lean down and rest my elbow on the top of the counter, watching her as if there's not a care in the world.

Of course, some dickhead decides this is his shot and pushes his way through the crowd. He wraps his arm around the fort of her waist and pulls her into him. Olivia says something over her shoulder to him, which I can tell by the look on his face he didn't like. She tries to walk away from him but he pulls her against him, this time harder than the last. She fights against his hold as he attempts to sway her along with the music.

I'm starting to see red and before I realize it, I'm walking across the room towards them.

My fingers curl over forearm and I yank it off of her.

"Hey asshole, we're dancing here."

"Right, because it looks like she's having a great time," I say between gritted teeth.

He mutters something under his breath that sounds like *fuck this* and walks away only after throwing his hands in the air.

"You okay?" My hands glide gently across her slightly exposed stomach as I lean down to pull her closer so that I can whisper into her ear.

She shakes her head. "I guess I'm not dancing tonight."

The look on her face is nothing short of obvious disappointment. I tilt my head back and let out a throaty groan before offering to dance with her. Her eyes light up and the any traces of disappointment disappear.

She laces her fingers together and brings her hands to her chest. "Realllllyy?"

I nod in agreement and before I can respond, she wraps her arm around my neck and begins dancing. I'm standing there probably awkward as hell, but she takes my hands and one by one places them on her hips. She sways back and forth, and I can't help but become completely intoxicated by her. The hairs on the nape of my neck rise and I know people are staring at us, *her* for that matter.

A part of me, a *big* part of me, wants to show everyone that she's mine. Even if it's only for the night. I grip onto her hips and pull her closer to me. She lifts her chin and her eyes meet mine.

My hand travels up her side, riding the curve of her waist and full breasts. Her breath hitches as I bring my hand to her jaw. The lights from the room around us change color and direction, bouncing off her soft skin. Her lips part and I move my hand to intertwine into her hair.

At this moment, it's just her and I. Everyone else begins to fade as I lean down and place my mouth on hers.

Fuck. She tastes like vanilla frosting and sunshine. How is that even possible?

A small moan escapes her lips, vibrating against my own. I'm surprised when the tip of her tongue runs along my lower lip. I tilt her head back, relishing in yet another moan that escapes her.

She has me fighting every urge to take her right here.

"Do you—"

"Yes," she answers breathlessly and takes my hand into hers, guiding me towards the entrance. I look back at the group,

Derek sits fake clapping. Daphne and Gracie's mouths are wide open as if this is some kind of miracle.

The fall air bites me on the tip of my nose the moment we exit the club, and my ears are full of static from the lack of music pounding in them. Once we get away from the people trying to get in the door, she stops and looks at me.

"Where do you live?"

I raise an eyebrow and tower over her, slowly pushing her up against the brick wall of the building. I click my tongue. "You sure you want to do this, Freckles?"

"Yes, but if you call me that again I'll change my mind."

"I doubt that." I lean down to whisper against her ear, "You and I both know that your pussy is dripping for me. Isn't it, *Freckles?*" I take her earlobe in between my teeth and lightly nibble. A chill runs up her spine, confirming my suspicion. "I just live around the corner." She nods and I lace her fingers in mine, leading her down the street.

Every time I look over at her she's biting on her lower lip, so it's obvious she's kind of nervous. If I'm being honest, I'm kind of nervous too. High school me *never* thought I'd have a chance with a girl like Olivia, but here I am with my hand in hers taking her back to my place. I rub my thumb against the softness of her palm, in a failed attempt to calm her nerves. She looks up at me through her blonde hair and gives me a soft smile.

"We don't have to—"

"No. I *want* to. It's just been awhile and..." She pushes her hair behind her ears. "I don't normally just go home with someone like this."

Fuck. She's cute.

"First time for everything, Freckles." My voice drops. "I

promise not to bite." She blushes and drops her gaze to the floor.

Unless you ask me.

We walk up the short steps that lead to my front door. I notice the front porch lights are off, but the rest of the house is empty. I breathe a sigh of relief because that means Blaire isn't home.

Olivia releases my hand so I can pull the key out of my pocket to unlock the door. I jimmy the handle, gesturing for her to go in once I get the door open.

"Can I get you something to drink?" I turn on the floor lamp that stands by the couch.

"I think I'm okay." She plays with the hem of her shirt.

I stalk towards her. My cock twitches against my jeans and I move to close the space between us. She nibbles on the corner of her lip as I come closer to where she stands, practically backing her up against the wall. I step forward and press my body against hers. A small gasp leaves her soft lips as I take her face into my hands. Shock spreads through me when she wraps her arms around my neck and deepens the kiss, using her tongue to gain entrance. It takes every ounce of my self control not to rip her clothes off when I part my mouth and our tongues meet.

My lips don't leave hers as I direct her down the halfway towards my bedroom in a mess of teeth and hands. Regardless of my attempt to be smooth, we back up against my door jam. The LED lights that line the edge of my ceiling cast red across my otherwise monochrome black and gray room. I grip to the collar of my shirt and pull it over my head, throwing it across the room towards the laundry basket. Olivia runs her fingertips along my chest and arms, almost as if she's tracing the tattoos that cover them.

"Did they hurt?" Her voice is low and shaky. I move the straps of her shirt down her arms, pushing the fabric away at the same time. Her full breasts slowly fall out of the confines of her shirt as I guide to the floor.

"I've been through worse." I move her hair away from her neck and lower my mouth, leaving gentle kisses just below her jaw.

My palm slides down her back and towards the waistband of her jeans. Goosebumps pebble along her skin as I unbutton them, my lips never leaving her soft skin while I caress along her shoulders.

This isn't like me. Sex has always just been that...sex. It's always been meaningless and has zero emotional connection. I'm not one to savor the moment, but I find myself really wanting to take my time with Olivia.

I grip onto the top of her pants and panties, pulling them down together. *Fuck me. She is a literal fucking angel.* Slowly, I guide her towards the edge of the bed. Her hands grab onto my black comforter as I kneel before her and prop her feet up on my bed frame, leaving trails of kisses and nibbles up her leg before settling in between her thighs.

With one long, slow motion I like her pussy and suck her clit into my mouth. Her hand unclenches from the bedding and intertwines into my hair. She moans low and covers her mouth with her free hand.

"You better move that hand, Freckles. I want to hear you scream my name as you come." I throw her legs over my shoulders and bury my face deeper, feasting on her pussy lick it's my last meal.

My tongue circles over her throbbing clit and moans, *loud* moans, escape her lips. I slide my hand up her thigh and slide a finger into her entrance. Her hips roll in response, and she mews my name as her body shakes, pussy tightening around my fingers.

"Oh, Beck."

Fuck.

"Say it again."

She looks down at me through hooded eyes. "*Beck.*"

I stand and pull off my pants and underwear in one swift motion. My cock springs free and she lets out a soft gasp.

"Like what you see?"

he props herself up on her elbows and nods as she takes her bottom lip in between her teeth, something I noticed she does frequently. Her long hair is scattered on the bed behind her and her cheeks are flushed with a rosy glow. I open the drawer of my bedside table and pull out a condom.

The foil tears easily between my teeth and I roll the condom on myself. My palms guide her knees wide and line myself up to her entrance, slowly sliding into her tight pussy while holding her gaze.

Her eyes shut and she tilts her head back. I savor as her lips part while I find the right rhythm of my thrusts. I wrap my arm around her knee and bring her leg up above my shoulder, her hips moving to meet mine thrust for thrust. Olivia's pussy squeezes around me and I pull out just slightly so I don't come already. This is fucking *heaven* and I want to revel in every fucking second we have together.

I drop my forehead to hers and try to steady myself. "You okay?"

She's breathless.

I release her leg and move my hand to behind her head. In one movement, my lips are on hers and our tongues meet. I thrust into her, deep and hard. She moans against my lips as I pick up my speed, knowing at this point there's nothing I can do to stop my release.

"Fuck, baby. I'm going to come." My voice is strained as her pussy clenches around me. Heat radiates, working its way up my lower spine as my own release nears. My vision blurs and she shudders around me.

Olivia falls back onto the bed and gasps to catch her breath. I plop down beside to allow my own racing heart to still. Without a word she stands, wrapping herself in my sheets, and begins to look for her clothes. My stomach twists and before I can stop the word vomit, "stay the night" blurts from my mouth.

Her eyebrows furrow and she shrugs, pointing to the bathroom. "This way to the bathroom?"

I nod and pull on a pair of underwear and grabbing a shirt for Olivia to wear from my drawer before crawling into bed.

"Uhm. I put a shirt for you to wear on the bed."

"Thanks, Beckett."

I nod and adjust the comforter back onto the bed. I hadn't realized it got so tangled while we were having sex. She pulls the shirt on and I have to hide the grin that forms when I see her wearing one of my old band tees.

She slides into the bed next to me and I have to fight every urge to wrap her into my arms. I roll over and adjust to where I can still feel the warmth radiating off her body, but I'm not actually touching her. This isn't like me, *at all*. I don't kiss during sex and I definitely don't cuddle, but fuck I want to hold her.

5

High school me would be high fiving myself for waking up next to Beck.

Adult me? I'm crapping my pants.

Not only was he the best sex I've had, literally ever, but I find myself wanting to linger just a little bit longer this morning as he sleeps soundly beside me.

I hesitated when he asked me to stay the night. His place was dark when we came in and we headed straight into his bedroom, so I didn't get a chance to see how his apartment is decorated. He stirs, groaning slightly as he rolls over. I close my eyes so freaking fast, the weight of his torso crossing my stomach takes me by surprise. That's when I remember I'm wearing Beck's shirt. The same Beck that has his arm draped across my torso.

My phone starts to ring with an incoming call. On full blast, of course, because why would I put it on silent? Beck groans, rolling over and covering his head with his pillow. My stomach immediately misses the weight of his arm. I run across the room to my purse and fish around for my cell phone. **Daphne** flashes across the screen. The call ends, but immediately the phone lights up with another.

Me: I'll call you in a sec.

Daphne: I'm happy to know you're alive.

Me: Dramatic.

Daphne: I was worried, okay?

Daphne: Did you go home with Beck?

I turn from where I stand and look around the room for my clothes, finding them in a pile in the corner of the room. I'm surprised by the cleanliness of his space. The floor is obviously freshly vacuumed, the lines from the brush are still present on the gray carpet. His bed is in the center of two small windows, and it has dark gray sheets with a black comforter. Not that I expected any different, honestly. There are two bedside tables on either side, one with a lamp and the other with a photograph of him, another guy around our age, a girl who looks younger, and an older couple. I cross the room on my tip toes and lean down to get a closer look. My chest tightens at the light radiating from his smile.

I quickly get dressed, grab my shoes, and go to the door of his bedroom. I turn and take him in once more from over my shoulder, his back is exposed and I practically start drooling when I see the tattoos that span across his shoulder blades.

Get a grip, Olivia.

I'm very predictable, but *this,* being with Beck, isn't something I could have ever expected I'd do. A part of me wishes he'd wake up and ask me to stay, but I don't wake him as

I leave. I don't leave a note or my number. Truthfully, I don't ever expect to see him again.

I sneak out through the door of his bedroom, surprised as I walk through the wall way and find a very clean living room and kitchen. There's no overwhelming smell of dirty socks or nasty dishes in the sink, just...*him.* I unlock the door and slide out of the opening, making sure to lock it as I sneak out. My phone vibrates in my hand. There's no surprise it's my sister when I lift it up to check.

"Hello?"

"So did you finally get fucked?"

"Jesus, Daph, can you get any more vulgar?"

I have to lift it away from ear when she screams into the phone. I hit the button on the crosswalk and wait for my turn to walk across the street.

"It *was* Beck, wasn't it? God, you guys were practically eye fucking each other all night. And when you got on that dance floor...my god. You could practically smell your pheromones."

"That's gross," I whisper into the phone. I'm hoping the woman next to me can't hear our conversation.

"So. Was he good? He looks like he'd be *so* good."

Of course he was.

"I'm not talking about that with you, D."

"You're no fun. I *need* all the details, Liv."

"I'll be home soon. Love you."

I hang up the phone right after she says *I love you* back. The thoughts of my night with Beck fill my mind. There's no ignoring the ache that begins to form between my legs as I remember the tender way he kissed my skin.

The walk from his house to my apartment is surprisingly short, only after I stopped for a drink at Solid Grounds on the way home. I didn't realize how close he lives to me, but why would I know where his apartment was anyways?

I take a sip of my iced matcha latte and practically groan out loud. After my long night, and the day I know I'm going to have, I need it. My heels click on the sidewalk, mixing with the sound of morning traffic. This is my quiet before the storm because I know once I walk into my apartment, my sister will be insistent on me answering every question she has about my time with Beck.

I take a deep breath and walk through the rotating doors of my apartment building. I dig around in my small bag for my house keys, feeling relieved when I finally find them in the very bottom. For such a small bag it sure does hold a lot and the last thing I need is to have accidently left my key at Beckett's house.

There's no mistaking my sister's squeal as I open the door.

"Thank you, Mel. A million times thank you!" She hangs up the phone and runs up to me, wrapping her arms around my neck. "I got the job!"

"Congratulations, sis!" I respond, not fully sure which job it is exactly, since she has submitted headshots and audition tapes to basically everything.

"I leave for like a month next week!"

"Wow. That's great. I'm super proud of you!"

"I'm going to call mom."

And just like that...me getting laid is no longer going to be the topic of conversation and I am instantly relieved. I love my sister but compared to her, I am much more reserved. Especially when it comes to talking about my sex life.

I walk into my room and grab a pair of workout clothes. Even though I'm going to go to the gym right now, I still want to shower the night off me. Even if that means I shower twice today. After I'm done, I throw my hair into a low pony and grab my gym bag. I yell out to Daphne as I leave, but she's in her room squealing to someone on the phone so I'm not sure she hears me.

My phone chimes as I get into the elevator and I know it's one of two people.

> Gracie: Waiting for all the details.

> Me: Details to what?

The little bubbles pop up letting me know she's responding.

> Gracie: Don't act dumb, Olivia Connoly

> Gracie: You know exactly what I'm talking about.

> Me: It was…fine.

> Gracie: Fucking liar. You don't have sex with your high school crush and say it was fine.

> Me: What would you rather me say?

> Gracie: The truth.

> Gracie: It was absolutely mind blowing, wasn't it?

> Me: Yes.

Unlike my sister, she won't drop it until she finds out *most* of the details. I'm thankful because she won't ask for specifics since she knows I'm not comfortable talking about it in detail.

> Gracie: I fucking knew it.

I wave at the person working the front desk, Nikki I think is her name, and walk towards the lockers. After entering my combination, I grab my headphones and phone before throwing my bag into it and shutting it. I get on my preferred treadmill and start my work out. After a few minutes, when I'm at the best part of my playlist, I can feel that someone is standing behind me.

I bring the treadmill to a stop.

"Can I help?"

I take one of my headphones out, turn around, and immediately choke on my words. "You?" I swallow. Hard. His blonde hair is cut short, but not short enough for me to miss the natural curl. His eyes are a *stunning* deep green with speckles of brown and they remind me of a moody forest. I could get lost in them.

"Hi. I'm sorry. My name is Holt and I've been watching you for a while. Gosh, that sounds like I'm a stalker." He runs his hands down his face. "I don't mean it like it sounded. I just work out here, too and I see you from time to time."

I can't help but take a moment to consider him. Even through his thick stubble I can make out the squareness of his jaw.

"All creepiness aside, I'd like to know if you'd like to go on a date with me?"

"What did you have in mind?"

"Dinner, maybe?"

"I can do dinner."

"Great. Awesome." He smiles and man, it's absolutely beautiful. He waves and turns to walk away.

"Don't you need my number?"

"Yes! I do." Holt turns and pulls his phone out of the pocket of his gym shorts, handing it to me. "Also, probably your name."

"Olivia."

"*Olivia*," he repeats. I type my number into his phone, and return it to him. "Great. I'll text you soon."

I smile and put my headphones back in. My music pauses and alerts me to a text message.

> Unknown number: This is Holt. I'm really looking forward to dinner. How's tomorrow? Too soon?

That was fast.

> Me: Tomorrow sounds great. :)

I put my headphones back into my ear and start my workout while I'm still floating on cloud nine. I turn back on the treadmill and start the incline, slow and steady. As my heartbeat begins to rise, I can't fight the flashbacks of the night before that flit through my mind. Specifically, the sight of Beck's lips trailing up my inner thigh. Nobody had ever seemed to *enjoy* it as much as he did. *I want to hear you scream my name.* Heat travels from the pit of my stomach and up to my face. I look around and the redness of my cheeks deepen. Logically, I know that not a single person in here knows what I'm thinking about, but I decide to turn off my treadmill and go home anyways.

HOLT TEXTS me bright and early to figure out what I want for dinner. We go back and forth for a short amount of time before he recommends a steakhouse around the corner from the gym. He offered to pick me up, but I'm not sure I'm ready for him to know where I live. I check my phone to see what time it is and see a text from Gracie.

> Gracie: I'm on standby if you need me to call
> and pretend like there's an emergency.

> Me: I will keep that in mind.

> Gracie: Have fun!

I finish curling the last couple face-framing pieces of my hair and do one last check in the mirror before heading down to the lobby. Even though the restaurant is only a block and half away, I still call a ride share so that I don't have to worry about parking. It's been awhile since I've gone on a date, so my stomach is twisting and flipping in every direction as I walk through the front doors of my apartment building. Something about that night with Beck gave me a new sense of confidence, a sense of feeling *wanted*. After verifying the name of the driver and that his license plates match the app, I slide into the back of the sedan. I don't know if the driver can sense my anxiety, but he doesn't try to force any small talk.

I'm grateful for the music that's playing throughout the car. It's making the ride seem a little less awkward, especially as we sit at a red light for longer than the drive itself should have taken. He pulls up against the curb and turns to smile at me. "I hope you have a great night."

"Thank you," I unbuckle my seatbelt and open the door. "Stay safe."

I stand up and smooth out my floral babydoll dress. The doorman opens the door for me and gestures to walk in. I make my way towards the hostess and smile, but I hear my name from behind and turn turn to find Holt standing near the waiting area.

"You look gorgeous." He leans down, places his hand on my lower back, and kisses me gently on my cheek.

"Thank you so much."

"They said they wouldn't seat us until the whole party was here." His voice progressively gets louder as he continues. "Even though we had a reservation."

"Oh, am I late?"

"What? No. I was just a little early."

"It's not a big deal. I'm sure they'll seat us soon."

"I'm going to go back and talk to the hostess again."

The flipping my stomach was doing turns into wrenching. I'm not sure what to do except stand where he left me. The hostesses face shifts and by the way Holt is standing, I feel like he's not being the nicest. He turns to walk back over to me, his face red, but he smiles.

"We're going to be seated right now."

"Mr. Pierce, we can seat you now."

He places his hand back on my lower back and guides me towards the hostess. I keep Gracie in the back of my mind as we are placed at our table. I make sure to say thank you and pick up the menu.

"Your waiter, Kyren, will be with you in a moment to take

your drink order." She turns and it's like she can't get away from the table fast enough.

The menu itself looks decent enough, but then I see the price tag and my stomach drops. *Sixty-five dollars for a steak? Holy heck.* My face must have given me away because Holt clears his throat, "I asked you on the date, so order whatever you want. Don't worry about the price."

I look up from my menu and he winks.

Kyren arrives and takes our drink order. A sweetened black tea for me and whiskey and coke for Holt. I have to hide the grimace on my face because I *hate* the smell of whiskey. It doesn't take long for me to settle on the chicken marsala. I've had it before at other restaurants, so I know I'll like it. Everything else on the menu is...different.

"So." Holt closes his menu and sets it on the table. "Tell me about yourself, Olivia."

"What do you want to know?"

"Everything. What do you do for work?" He folds his hands and places them on the table. Something about this feels more like an interview than a date.

"Well, I'm a teacher. I teach high school art. What about you?"

"I'm a criminal defense attorney."

"That sounds...interesting?"

It opens the floodgate and he spends the next fifteen minutes explaining what he does on a daily basis. By the time our food arrives, I can tell you everything he does during his work week, down to what he has for lunch. I can't help but feel annoyed that so much of this conversation has been about him.

My chicken marsala is cooked to perfection and the green

beans look, and smell, absolutely divine. I begin bringing the fork to my mouth when he sighs and looks down at his plate.

"Is something wrong with your food?"

"No, but I have to apologize for my behavior tonight."

"What do you mean?" I play ignorant to his actions, just to play devil's advocate here.

"I was really nervous to go out with you. I've been hurt pretty bad before and I feel like I wasn't myself in order to guard my heart." I put my fork down and give him my undivided attention as he continues. "My ex-fiance and I were together for almost five years. We had plans to get married two *months* before she left. It wasn't until a couple months after she was gone that I discovered she had been cheating on me."

"Oh, Holt. I'm so sorry." My heart aches for him and what he's experienced.

"I'm not normally like this, so on edge, I mean. I'm just so scared of getting hurt again. She crushed my heart into a million pieces, and it took me a while to feel ready to give love a chance again. I just hope I didn't ruin my chances at a second date."

"This one's not done yet, is it?" I offer.

He smiles and returns his attention to his meal.

Hurt is something I understand all too well. So, knowing that he's been hurt and is just guarding himself makes me feel more understanding. We chit chat in between bites where we share our likes, dislikes, and things we are passionate about. I learn that Holt enjoys nice meals, travel, and things being clean and organized. He learns that I enjoy yoga, baking, and being with family and friends. I told him all about Gracie, my mom, and my sisters. Including that it was just Mattie's birthday, but leaving out the fact that I went home with Beck.

As the date wraps up, I feel like I see a different side of Holt than I did at the beginning of our date. He's kind to the waitress and even leaves a tip that's *definitely* more than twenty percent of the total. He hands the valet his ticket and we wait for his car to be brought around.

"Can I take you back to your place? I won't come up or anything. I'd just like to know that you get home safe."

"That's fine with me."

"I had a really nice time with you tonight." He smiles and takes a step to close the distance between us. I know in the pit of my stomach he's going to kiss me. A part of me *really* wants him to, while the other part of me still feels hesitant. But relief comes in a wave when the valet arrives and hands him the keys to his Audi.

Holt opens the door, waiting for me to slide in before shutting it, and walks around to the driver's side where he joins me in the tight space. His car smells like leather and a strong cologne.

I give him the directions to my apartment building, but other than that we are silent during the short car ride. Butterflies dance in my belly as he pulls against the sidewalk. I unbuckle in my seat and turn to face him.

He rests his elbow on the center divider and smiles. "I hope I can see you again."

"We can definitely make that happen." I open the door. "Goodnight."

He doesn't try to kiss me or stop me as I get out of his car and out on the sidewalk.

"Goodnight, Olivia," he responds.

When I'm inside the building, the sound of his car speeding

off echoes into the lobby. I can't decide if I'm disappointed or happy that he didn't try to kiss me, but I know it'll be something I think about for the next couple of days.

6

I've never found myself wanting *more* from someone, but I haven't been able to stop thinking about Olivia since she left. I've tried hard to keep myself busy for the last couple of weeks, Derek has us practicing basically every free moment and work at my dad's shop has picked up, so it hasn't been too hard to distract myself. It's not until I'm home alone that thoughts of her linger.

My phone rings with a phone call and I don't even have to look at it to know it's Derek. I groan and roll my eyes before hitting the answer key. His voice immediately fills my ears through the speaker of my headphones.

"Finally, you answer." Girls are giggling in the background.

"This is the first time you called me."

"But I've texted you like five times."

"Well, now you sound like you're my jealous boyfriend." Granted, he's probably worse. He wants to know where I'm at all the time now. Especially since our demo has been getting some traction online.

"Whatever, prick. When are you coming? We can't practice without our drummer."

"I'm working, Derek. I only have a few more days to finish this—"

"Yeah, yeah. The table you're working on or *whatever*."

The way he discounts my job pisses me off. Not all of us can live off our parents forever. Derek's parents are one of the three founding families of Dryer Hill, and believe me, he will not let anyone forget it.

"Yeah, the table *and* chairs, asshole. Some of us have to work for a living, Derek."

"Well, practice starts in an hour. So, be here or we'll have to replace you."

I hang up the call and wait for the sound of my music to turn back on. This long term client of ours ordered a table in solid parota wood with a bench and four chairs to match. It's stunning, but finicky to work with. Tieran handled the steel structure beneath all of the wood, for support, and I am responsible for the rest of it. Dad will come in and do the upholstery on the chairs and bench when I'm done.

Music has always been my outlet, especially as an idiot who wanted to do nothing but drink and fuck. It kept me out of trouble. It brought me a sense of *self*. When I became an adult though, Dad showed me the art of carpentry and well...I found something music never gave me.

I found control and a way to express myself that was entirely different. There's a freedom with carpentry that I don't experience anywhere else. I can put on my headphones and just build. I love music, absolutely, the guys are great, and the rush I get from shows is unmatched. There's just something about a quiet life that's been calling me for years.

I turn up the volume on my headphones and finish sanding the top of the table. Tomorrow, I'll stain and varnish it then begin working on the bench. The smell of freshly cut wood fills the air as I drag, push, and pull the orbital sander along the grain.

When my phone starts to vibrate in my pocket, I realize I've probably lost track of time. My music is paused, and Derek's incoming phone call is announced again. I turn off my sander and answer.

I lower my mask. "I'm on my way, D."

"It's time to practice so hurry up."

"I said I was on my way." I hang up and shove my phone back into my pocket. I grab my rag and dust off the particles of wood to the best of my ability. With my music back on, I clean up my workspace, making sure everything goes back into its home. Dad's really laid back with everything *except* shop cleanliness.

The moon is already high in the sky by the time I finally leave the shop. I hop into the truck and hook my phone up to play something as I start the drive. It's not long until I'm cruising up the gravel road towards practice. Everyone's cars are in the small parking lot, and I can see light coming from inside of the building. I park and turn off my car, preparing myself for the fight that will most likely happen when I walk in.

I run my hand through my hair as I walk in and my breath catches in my throat when I meet eyes that are identical to Olivia's, but it takes me only a second to recognize it's Daphne.

"Hey Beck." She smiles.

"Hey Daph." I wave. "D." I tilt my chin down. I can tell by the look on his face, he's definitely pissed that I'm so late. He won't act like a *complete* prick with Daphne here.

I fist bump Tieran and Hayes before taking my spot at the drums. Michelle and the other groupies are sitting across the room on the couches that Derek brought into the space when we first started practicing. They used to be a light gray, but from all the people who've sat, and done who knows what else on them, they're honestly just gross. Derek slaps Daphne's ass and points her towards the direction of the couches, but she takes one look at Michelle and sits at the small high-top table we have opposite them.

Derek takes his place at the microphone and turns to face us, listing the songs we are practicing in order. He wants to start with *Time Away*, move into *Lunar Secrets*, and end with *Final Stranger*. There's a few other originals that we like to sing for shows and at least one or two covers we throw in there too, for the people who may not know our stuff yet.

Lunar Secrets is the only song I wrote myself and it's one of the most vulnerable things I've ever done. I was shocked when Derek loved it enough to include it in our set list. It all started with just a few lines:

Darkness falls and we're alive.
A spark ignites, we're taking flight.
Lunar secrets lead the way.
There's a truth hidden faraway,
In the moon as it decays.
Lunar secrets set us free.

"Again."

"D, we've practiced it at least six times. We sounded *great*," Tieran pleads.

"Not signing worthy, though."

Everyone but Derek groans and the music starts back up. I know that Ti and I are in agreement that the seventh round is unnecessary. The song comes to an end and by the look on Derek's face, it's evident he's not happy with that take either.

"If you guys—"

"We aren't doing it again, Derek." I rise to my feet and put my sticks on the chair behind me. "I've been at the shop since six-thirty this morning and it's..." I pull my phone out of my back pocket. "Almost fucking one. I'm going home."

"Even the girls went home like five songs ago dude," Tieran chimes in.

"If you don't get serious about Skarred, I *will* replace you." Derek jabs his fingers against my chest.

"Do it then, D. I love making music, but you're taking all of the joy out of it." My blood boils. The anger in his face falters for a split second. He rolls his eyes and bends down to pick up his beer can. "What the fuck ever. Go home and be back here tomorrow at the same time."

My teeth gnash as I stalk out of the building, heading straight for my truck.

"Beck!" Tieran yells, jogging up to catch up to me. "You good? It looked like you wanted to take Derek out."

I run my hand down my face. "I'm just so sick of his shit. I love Skarred, too, but I have a job. Not everyone has rich parents to fall back on."

"He's getting worse the closer he thinks we are to getting a deal."

"Don't get me wrong, it'd be cool as hell if we ever got signed. Like that's the goal...right? To get signed?" I look down at my feet and kick pebbles around in the dirt. "I don't know, man."

"You don't want to get signed?"

"It's not that. I just don't know that the rockstar life is the kind of lifestyle I want. It's hard enough when Derek brings around random chicks, take into consideration all of the drugs and alcohol. It'll get worse if we get big. I've spent the last ten years trying to *not* be like my dad. I don't know that I'm strong enough to not give in if I'm around it all of the time."

"I get it, Beck. My fear is that I won't love it anymore. You're right though, Derek is taking all of the fun and love out of it for sure." He looks over his shoulder, back towards the warehouse. "Between us, I'm actually going to step out of the band soon. I'm not that hard to replace. I got offered a new position and I'm going to accept it."

"That's amazing, Ti. You deserve it!"

"Derek will see it as a betrayal."

"Derek can come talk to me then. We both know he's been looking for an excuse to try and kick my ass for years."

"Thanks, man. Alright, I'll let you go. Give Blaire my love." He turns and heads over to his car. "Oh, before I forget. Are we still going to watch that one band?"

"Yeah, for sure. They buy the photos I take of them."

My love for photography started six years ago, by complete accident, and with every show it grows. I'm not half bad and Wrecked Youth is one of like two bands who actually pay me for my photos.

"Okay, cool. See you tomorrow at practice."

"Bye, Ti." I get into my car and make my way home.

The lights are off when I pull up to the house. With it being so late, I'm not surprised that Blaire is already sleeping. There's a slight chill in the air as I walk up to the front door. As soon as I'm inside, I head to the shower, desperate to wash the day off of me. I welcome the warmth of the water as it covers my skin, but as most nights, thoughts of Olivia find their way into my mind. Tonight, it's the memory of the sweet sounds she made as I buried myself into her. My dick instantly hardens at the thought.

I move my hand over my cock and circle my head before sliding it back down my shaft. A low groan escapes my throat as I tighten the grip I have on myself. My strokes become faster and tighter as I think about her pussy tightening around my cock. I put my free hand up against the shower wall, bracing myself as the sensation builds. Cum finally spills out over my hand and onto the floor of the shower.

Fuck. I need to taste her again.

I sigh and finish my shower, the onset of exhaustion hits me like a ton of bricks. After I dry off, I go into my room and put on a pair of shorts, throwing my towel into my dirty clothes hamper. I toss myself onto the bed and immediately, the loneliness I've felt for the past few weeks creeps in.

Being single has always been easy, simple even. But since that *one* night with Olivia, I've found myself wanting more.

I love Daphne, but the last couple weeks have been so quiet and I love the quiet.

Coming home after working with teenagers every day to a silent apartment has been really nice.

And, well, Holt not getting interrogated every time he's here has been nice, too. I haven't had to worry about her *friends* being in the house when I come home, but I'd be lying if I said I wasn't excited for her to come home soon.

Holt has been hanging out here once or twice a week since our first date. We've taken turns ordering in or going out and it's a welcome distraction from my day to day. He's decided he wants to take our relationship slow, *really* get to know one another before we have sex, so we haven't slept together yet. We've had a couple of heavy make out sessions, but he stops before we take it too far.

That doesn't stop me from thinking about my night with Beck.

Often.

Especially when it's late at night and my vibrator is calling my name. But, to be honest, I need something that Beck can't give: emotional attachment and romance. Both of which, Holt does amazingly. He's always bringing me flowers and little gifts and wanting to take me to nice restaurants.

Today, I woke up feeling so physically drained that I decided to forego the gym today. It's cold in my apartment, but I know I need to pull myself out of bed. Do I want to? Absolutely not. My bed is insanely comfortable, and my down comforter is working some kind of magic.

I groan and stretch my back. There's a dull ache on my tailbone that tells me I probably slept wrong, so I stand and try to unkink my back. It's so sore.

I grab my tumbler from the bedside table and drag myself into the kitchen to pour some sweet tea, which I bought a jug of from my favorite restaurant.

My phone dings with an alert, but I know it's either Gracie or Holt, so I ignore it and unload the dishwasher. The porcelain dishes clink as I put them away in the cabinets. My sister and I don't agree on much, but we quickly agreed on the white porcelain bowl and plate sets from Costco when we moved into the apartment.

I slept in later than normal, so my body knows it's past time for breakfast and my stomach twists in anger. I rummage through the pantry, quickly realizing that I have nothing that sounds good. I open our fridge to find, again, nothing worth eating. The stove reads 8:25, and I decide maybe I'll just go get breakfast instead.

My phone dings again, alerting me to my unread text.

> Holt: Good morning, sexy. Wanna get together later?

> Me: Want to play hooky from the gym, get breakfast?

I feel hopeful that he'll say yes, but if not, I'll just go by myself. I would *kill* for something with salsa and avocado right now. My stomach squeezes in confirmation that it, too, would like that.

> Holt: Don't have to ask me twice. Meet you in the lobby of your apartment?

I practically jump for joy and head back to my room to get ready.

> Me: See you in ten!

After grabbing jeans, a shirt, and throwing on a sweatshirt, I change and brush out my hair. I don't have time to curl or straighten it, so I decide to just dutch braid it. The bags under my eyes are dark, so I add a touch of concealer, curl my lashes, throw on some mascara, and add a little bit of tinted lip gloss before sliding on my ankle boots and grabbing my bag.

I lock the door behind me and head towards the elevator. It jolts as it begins moving, causing my stomach to flip and some slight nausea to set in. When it gets to the main floor and the doors open, Holt is standing there with his back to the elevator.

"Hey, you." He spins s the doors slide open and hands me a flower.

"Hi." I take the rose from his outstretched hand and bring it to my nose, inhaling its deep scent. "It's beautiful, thank you."

"Ready to go?"

"Yes. I'm starving."

Holt and I exit the revolving doors and my breath gets stuck in my throat when the cold air hits me. I always forget how cold Dryer Hill gets in the fall. We join the crowd of everyone else walking on the street and begin our trek to breakfast.

"Where do you want to go?" Holt asks as he takes his hand in mine.

"I was thinking Solid Grounds. They make a really good breakfast scramble."

"Oh, I didn't realize we'd just be going to a coffee shop for a meal. I guess if that's *really* where you want to go." His tone takes me by surprise and for some reason I feel kind of embarrassed.

"I mean, I'm open to wherever."

"You aren't really dressed for the bistro, but I guess there's somewhere in the middle we can go."

I tug on the hem of my sweater, suddenly feeling like I chose the wrong outfit to wear for, what I thought was, a casual breakfast.

He directs me to cross the street, and I follow his lead, very aware of the firm hand pressed up against my back. After a short distance down the street, in silence, we arrive at a restaurant. The outside of the building is urban and still seems very upscale. Holt said I wasn't dressed appropriately for the bistro he wanted to go to, but I guess I'm still not dressed correctly.

He opens the door and guides me inside, where my assumptions are proven correct. Everyone looks like they are wearing their Sunday best, while I'm wearing a Dryer Hill University pull over and oversized ripped jeans.

"For two please." Holt holds up two fingers at the hostess. She smiles, showing her sparkling white teeth at him.

"Of course, right this way sir." She purrs and looks me up and down, her smile twisting into a scowl.

She sits us at a round table with two chairs across from each other. The table is set with a white tablecloth, two porcelain plates, silverware, and a linen napkin. *A freaking linen napkin?! I'm definitely not dressed right.*

"Your server will be Natalia. She'll be right with you." The hostess places her hand on his forearm and drags her long acrylic nails towards the top of his hand. I swear she winks at him as she walks away. Holt doesn't even *try* to hide the fact that he's watching her.

I clear my throat and open the menu, frustrated at how rude the whole interaction was. Tears sting my eyes as I try to hide my disappointment when I find that this is definitely fancier than I was craving.

"I know *exactly* what I'm going to have," Holt announces and closes his menu, placing it on the edge of the table. "Did you have a chance to look at the menu?"

"I didn't want something fancy," I mutter under my breath.

"So, what? Now you're mad that I took you to a *nice* restaurant?"

"I'm not mad, Holt. It's just not what I was in the mood for."

"You sound very ungrateful. You're getting a free meal, *Olivia*." The way he says my name sounds like an insult.

I stare in shock and confusion, caught off guard.

"I didn't mean to sound ungrateful, I'm sorry."

The waitress comes to our table, and I try my best to avoid looking at her, especially when I hear the flirty tone she uses to talk to Holt.

He orders our drinks and moves on to our meals, "I'll have the salmon and arugula frittata, and she'll have the spinach brunch salad. Thank you."

I look up from the menu and at the moment our eyes meet, he takes the menu from my grip and hands it to the waitress. She smiles and walks away, definitely shaking her hips more than necessary. I can feel myself shrinking in the chair as I listen to Holt ramble on and on about the gym and how hectic work has been for him at the law firm, especially since he's on track to become a partner in the next six months.

"Are you even listening?" His brows furrow.

"Yeah, I am. I'm sorry. I'm just so hungry."

"They should be here any minute. You're going to love the salad, it's a favorite of mine."

Then you should have gotten it.

I force a smile and nod, leaning forward to pretend like I care about what he's saying as he complains about a court case he has this week. Heat washes over my chest. My stomach tightens and I can feel the bile rise in my throat.

I'm going to be sick. I jump up as Holt is mid-sentence and rush as fast as I can towards the bathroom.

As I barge in, a stall becomes available, and I practically push the older woman out of the way in my frenzy. Vomit spills out of my mouth and into the toilet. I'm just grateful I didn't make a mess.

After a minute, I'm just dry heaving and my muscle tremble with weakness. Finally, I'm able to compose myself and breathe through the nausea. I flush the toilet and wash my hands, swishing some water around in my mouth to get rid of the acidic taste that lingers.

On the walk back to our table, people stare and my cheeks heat.

"Are you okay?" Holt asks as I sit back down.

"I'm so sorry. I don't know where that came from." I take a small drink from my water.

The waitress returns with two plates, placing them in front of the both of us. I raise my hand to say something to her, but she walks away.

"I can't eat this." I push the plate away.

"Why not?"

"It has nuts." He looks at me like I've suddenly grown horns. "I'm allergic to nuts." I tilt my head, confused because I *swear* we've had this conversation.

"Why didn't you tell them when they took our order?"

"You ordered for me? I didn't know what was even on it."

"So, now it's my fault?"

"That's not what I'm saying. Why are you being this way today?"

"You're right." He takes a deep breath and sets his fork down. "I'm just under so much stress at work. I didn't mean to take it out on you. Forgive me?"

"Of course. I just wish you would communicate that with me instead of being mean." I slump in my chair.

He raises his hand. "Excuse me?"

Our waitress practically runs over to our table, her blouse suddenly has the two buttons undone. "What can I do to help you, *sir?*" She practically moans that last word. I have to breathe through the bile that rises in my throat once more.

"My girlfriend is severely allergic to nuts; can I please have this remade with no nuts?"

Girlfriend?

"Of course. I'm so sorry about that." Her tone is dryer than it was before and the look of disappointment is prominent on her face. She looks at me and smirks. I am definitely too scared to try and eat my salad now.

"Are you sure you're okay? You look kind of green."

"I'm not sure, I think I might be sick again."

"Do you think you ate something that upset your stomach?"

I shrug, trying to recall the last thing I ate or drank. Aside from some water and sweet tea from this morning, I have *yet* to put anything in my stomach.

"I haven't eaten anything today."

"Do you think you should go to the doctor?"

My stomach twists again and I can feel the heat begin to form in my chest; I nod in confirmation and get up to go back to the bathroom.

THE WAIT TIME for urgent care isn't very long, but I hate the waiting in the lobby. I've never been a big fan of doctors to begin with. Daphne and I were born prematurely, so Mom was afraid of every single germ that existed. If we even got a sniffle, we were at the doctor's office.

Holt sits beside me, scrolling aimlessly through videos on his phone. The nausea has finally subsided, but I refused to eat my salad. On the way here, I rummage around in my purse for a protein bar and ate that instead.

"I probably picked up a stomach bug from one of my

students," I whisper to Holt. He makes a *hmph* noise and keeps scrolling.

"Olivia Connoly?" The nurse calls. Holt looks up at me and I gesture for him to come.

They take my vitals and ask the typical questions, including when my last cycle was.

I can't remember, so I pull out my period tracking app and realize I'm late.

Like *late,* late.

The nurse hands me a cup and points me in the direction of the bathroom. I lock the door behind me and do as I'm told. Once I'm done, I place it in the little metal cabinet in the wall and wash my hands.

I can't be pregnant. I know I can't.

I haven't even had...oh, my god.

Oh.

My.

God.

I pull my phone out of my purse with shaking fingers.

> Me: SOS

> Gracie: What's wrong?

> Daph: ???

> Me: I'm late.

> Daph: Late?

> Gracie: Late to what?

> Gracie: Oh shit. You mean LATE late?!

> Daph: WHAT!?

Me: At urgent care now.

Me: WITH HOLT.

Gracie: NO, YOU ARE NOT!

Daph: I'm trying not to laugh because I understand this is a serious situation. But you're at UC with your current boyfriend, while possibly carrying your high school crushes baby?

Me: Not my boyfriend.

Gracie: Let me know when you're home and I'll come over.

Daph: This would happen when I'm across the country.

I walk out of the bathroom and force a smile, when really, I'm crapping myself. They bring Holt and I into a room and I try to steady my breath.

"Okay. So, there is something I have to tell you," I start, fidgeting with a tear in my jeans.

"Okay..." He raises a brow.

"I did have a one night stand, but it was right before I met you. We used a condom *and* I'm on birth control."

"Then what's the problem?"

"I'm like *really* late and I'm never late. Which I know that's something women say, but like I'm serious." I'm rambling. I know I am, but I'm so scared.

"Okay."

"Okay?"

"Well, I mean you have options if you are. We will discuss them."

We? Is there actually a we?

There's a knock on the door and a doctor strides into the room. I think I could cut the air with a knife.

"Can you confirm your name and date of birth for me?"

I do.

"Well, Miss Connoly...according to your test results, you're pregnant. According to your last menstrual cycle, I'd say about five weeks."

I'm pregnant.

BECK

8

"This band is good!" Tieran shouts into my ear. I lift the viewfinder back up to my eye and snap a photo of the lead singer, Lance, singing into the mic and throwing up his other hand in the air. The atmosphere is absolutely stellar here as they play.

I move onto taking photos of the guitarist, Amara, as she makes her way over to interact with the singer. As I go to step to the side, I accidentally bump into someone.

"Shit. My bad." I move the camera down and away from my face.

"You can bump into me anytime." A patron looks me up and down before sauntering away. I watch her with absolutely no shame. She flips her long dark hair over her shoulder and turns to look at me. She's cute, like *really* cute. Her hair has peaks of crimson red peeking out of the dark base. This girl is exactly my type, right down to the fishnet stockings and combat boots.

"Damn, dude. She's hot, and by the way she's checking you out, she thinks you are, too."

"That obvious?"

"Hell yeah, you should introduce yourself."

I shrug and return to snapping photos of the band, focusing my attention on the drummer, Weston, during his solo. I can feel the girl's eyes on me as I do. The way she keeps looking at me, I know I could easily get her to agree to come back to my place. But I'm not sure if I want to or not.

The band finishes their set and the crowd begs for more. The whole room chants their name in hopes they'll come back on stage.

Since I've photographed them before, Tieran and I are given backstage privileges. We show our wristbands to the security guard, and he lets us down the hallway. Skarred has played here a couple of times, so we know our way around easily enough. I knock on the door at the end of the hall and wait for a response.

"Come in," Lance calls.

I open the door and Tieran and I walk through the threshold. "Hey guys, great show! This is my friend and teammate, Tieran."

"Hey Tieran!" Lance greets. "I know Beck knows everyone, but I'm Lance, Weston is on the drums, Amara is our guitarist, and my brother, Link plays bass. Our new manager slash social media content manager should be coming in any minute. You haven't met her yet, Beck." As if summoned, the door swings open. "Speak of the devil. Tieran, Beck, this is our manager, Sage."

"Hey again." It's the woman from the crowd. She smirks and props out her hip.

"You guys already know each other?" Link motions back and forth between us.

"He bumped into me in the crowd, not that I'm complaining."

"Jeez, Sage. Come on strong, much?" Weston shakes his head, tutting.

"Do you *really* want me to respond to that?" Everyone in the band shouts "no!' in unison and laughs. From this interaction, I get the feeling that she's a total flirt and everyone knows it. "So, Beck, what do you got for us?"

I turn on my camera and scroll to the gallery, handing it to Lance. Everyone in the band, including Sage, huddles around the small screen. My anxiety always spikes when people look at the photographs I've taken. You never know if someone is going to hate something you feel so confident in, and that vulnerability makes me uneasy.

"These are fucking sick!" Amara exclaims. I release a sigh of relief, and the tightness in my chest disappears.

"I just need to edit them and then I'll send them to the same email as last time."

"Sounds great, man. Once we get paid for this job, we'll send you some cash." Lance looks towards Sage and clears his throat.

"We also want to offer you the official band photographer title. So like promos, concerts that you are able to attend, etc."

"Oh. Wow. Really?" I don't think I could hide the shock on my face even if I tried.

"Yeah. The band was recently offered a contract with Rising Phoenix Records and that was one the stipulations in their terms, that you were their band photographer, as long as you wanted it." Sage reaches into a bag and pulls out a stack of paper. "This is your contract with the band. You'd be an independent contractor. It lays out all of your responsibilities and compensation, if you accept. But we'd need promo material as soon as possible for their signing party."

"Which you'd be invited to," Lance interjects.

"Lance has mentioned this may be important for you, so we'd like you to also know that as a whole, the band and record company have a no drug use clause, so no drugs will be present at parties or anything. But please review the contract first. My contact information is on the back page."

"Thanks, guys. This is amazing. I'll definitely think about it and let you know." Thinking about it would be easy. I mean, how fucking cool would it be to combine my passions for both music and photography into an actual paying job? Sure, Skarred could go far. I have no doubt that we could. I just don't know that I want to be included in that *we* anymore.

Tieran and I say our goodbyes and leave the venue, finding ourselves at the bar a few doors down. We sit at one of the high tables and wait for the waitress to come around. We both order a beer and I add on an order of wings. Photography can be hungry work.

"So." Tieran adjusts in his seat. "Are you thinking about taking that offer?"

"I'd be lying if I said it wasn't fucking tempting."

"Do you think Derek would be mad?"

"Oh, I'm sure he will be. I just don't know that I really care." The bartender comes over and drops off our beers, followed shortly by our wings. I pick one up and bring it to my mouth. "I love Skarred, but I'm *so* sick of it being Derek's show."

Tieran agrees and fills me in on the new electrical apprenticeship he has been offered. He tells me how much work and time is going to go into it. If any of us won't have time for Skarred, it'll be Tieran.

I feel like I'm in my own world as I move on to my second beer. I can't seem to get my mind off of this new job opportunity, but I know if I were to take it, I wouldn't be able to balance Skarred, the shop, and photography. I won't give up working with my family because I have too much love for carpentry. Something about using my hands helps me turn off the noises in my head. And well, photography helps me escape through art, so I'm not willing to quit that either.

"Fancy meeting you here," a quiet female voice pulls me from my thoughts. I look up from the bubbles floating to the top of my beer to see Sage sliding into one of the chairs at our table. She flags down the bartender, who comes over and takes her order of the same beer that Tieran and I are drinking. "Do you guys come to this bar often?"

I shrug. Tieran understands me, and my silence well enough to answer so that things don't get uncomfortable. "Sometimes after we play, we go to whatever bar is close."

"Nice. So, do you guys play in several venues around Dryer Hill?"

Tieran casts an *are you going to respond at all or am I going to be doing all of the talking* look my way before responding. "We've played mainly in Dryer, but out of town once or twice."

"Your band is Skarred, right?"

"Yeah. That's us." Tieran stands up from the barstool and announces that he's going to the bathroom and will be right back, leaving Sage and I alone.

I tap my finger against the glass and pretend to be interested in whatever is playing on the T.V. on the wall.

"So, do you have a girlfriend or...?" she drawls.

"I don't *do* the girlfriend thing."

"Oh." Sage arches an eyebrow. "That's good because neither do I. If you want to get out of here...?"

Not moving my eyes away from the television, I respond, "I don't think that's a good idea."

"If it's because of the job you were offered with the band, there's nothing in the contract that prohibits it. Plus, nothing is signed yet."

"I'm sure you're great, Sage, but I just don't think it's a good idea."

"Okay, I get it. I know I definitely come off too strong. I'm sorry if I'm doing anything to make you uncomfortable."

I let out a sigh and finally look at her. "You didn't do anything to make me uncomfortable. I'm just...not looking for *anything* right now."

As we sit in silence, I gaze over my shoulder back towards the bathroom to see where the fuck Tieran is. The bartender brings us over another round, and I ask for the table's tab because I'm ready to go home and fucking crash.

"Can I ask one question?" she starts with a small smile. I nod in approval, curious as to what she's going to say. "What's her name? The one who ruined every other girl for you?"

Without hesitation I answer, "Olivia. Her name is Olivia."

Olivia has ruined absolutely anyone else for me.

It's her or no one.

"That's a pretty name. She's lucky to have someone who wants her that bad. Does she know how you feel?"

"She doesn't and probably never will. I wasn't joking earlier when I said that I don't do relationships, and a girl like her deserves someone who wants that future." I shake my head.

"What's stopping you?"

"From?"

"Wanting a future?"

I shrug, knowing the answer. "This is a deep conversation to have with someone who's a stranger."

"But the perfect bar conversation." She holds up her beer with a grin.

"I guess it's just easier that way, to be single."

"Because nobody gets hurt."

"Exactly."

"I understand that all too well, emo boy. But imagine what kind of life you're missing out on when you don't give something a chance because you're scared of getting hurt."

"Emo boy?"

"Yes. Emo boy."

"I suppose I've been called worse."

She belts out a laugh and takes the last drink of her beer. "It was good chatting with you, Beck. Let me know about the contract, yeah?"

"I'll do that."

She stands and waves to the bartender, then to me, and leaves the bar. I sit there for the next few minutes wondering where Tieran is, so finally I text him.

> Me: Where the fuck did you go?

> Tieran: I called a rideshare so that you could go home with Sage.

> Me: Well, she just left.

> Me: I wasn't going to sleep with her.

> Tieran: She was literally you if you were a woman dude.

> Tieran: Like it was kind of freaking me out.

> Me: Well, maybe that's why I wasn't interested.

Maybe I want something different.

Her words are on repeat in my mind and I wonder how right she is.

Olivia

9

Seven Weeks Pregnant

I know I need to tell Beck, but I'm avoiding that at all costs until I know for sure what I'm going to do. The urgent care doctor was able to give me information for a clinic that would do an ultrasound and go over my options. Holt tried to have a conversation with me about what *he* thinks I should do, but I dissociated pretty quickly and didn't hear a word he said.

Daphne is due to come home soon and honestly all I want to do is hug my sister.

Gracie hasn't left my side in the last two weeks, even going as far as trying to go to work with me. That was where I drew the line, especially since she has her own job to go to.

I sit on my couch, bouncing my leg, while waiting for her to get here to go with me to the clinic. I'm stifling the urge to bite the skin around my fingernails when my phone vibrates with an alert.

Gracie: I'm downstairs. Want me to come up?

Me: No. I'm coming down.

I grab my purse and lock the door behind me, practically running to the elevator. The moment the doors ding open, I head straight to the revolving exit door. I brace myself for the downpour of rain as I rush towards Gracie's Honda Civic that's parked along the front sidewalk.

"Hey. I grabbed you a coffee." She hands me a small, iced coffee when I buckled my seatbelt.

"Thank you. I don't know if my nerves can handle the caffeine, though."

"I got you decaf." She winks.

I inhale and smile, sinking deeper into her passenger seat as she pulls into traffic. She reaches over the center console and places her hand on my forearm, squeezing slightly. As if to just let me know *I'm here for you* and right now, her just being with me is all I need. The car ride is quiet, the sound of her driving playlist keeps it from being completely silent.

Before long, she's pulling off the road and into the parking lot of the clinic.

My chest instantly tightens as she puts the car in park. Gracie turns the car off, but makes no move to get out.

"I'm ready, I think," I murmur.

"What do you need from me, babe? Do you want me to go in with you? Or do you want me to stay out here?"

I sit and consider her questions. What *do* I need from her?

"Come with me, please. They're just going to do an ultrasound. I haven't made up my mind yet."

"Okay." She adjusts herself in the seat to face me. "I hope

you know that I love and support you *whatever* you decide to do."

I nod, fighting to swallow the knot in my throat, and unbuckle my seat belt.

My feet are heavy, like I'm practically dragging them through quick sand, as we walk to the entrance of the building. Gracie goes in front of me and opens the door, dramatically bowing like I'm a queen entering her castle. She's always been good at lightening the mood and I know she's just trying to make me laugh. The waiting room is fairly empty, besides me there's a heavily pregnant woman and a couple sitting in the corner. I check in and sit next to Gracie near the wall.

It's quiet. No one speaks and I pull out my e-reader, desperate for some kind of relief from reality. It only takes a few minutes before they call me back. Gracie stays seated, but I motion for her to come with me.

The nurse doesn't say much while she takes my vitals and directs us to room number three, instructing me to undress from the waist down.

Everything about the dim lighted room feels cold. The paper on the bedding rustles as I sit down, scooting to the edge to make it easier when I have to put my feet in the stirrups.

"I don't think I wore the right socks," I whisper.

"Your socks are definitely sexy enough for the gyno, babe."

We both laugh and for the first time in weeks, I feel *okay*.

There's a knock on the door and it swings open. The technician smiles at me and introduces herself. She has me verify my information and goes down a list of questions, including making sure we can speak freely in front of Gracie.

"We're going to have to do the ultrasound vaginally. It will only be uncomfortable for a second. Now, go ahead and lie back, scoot as close to the edge as possible for me." She instructs. "This might be cold." She puts gel on the tip of the transducer and inserts it.

I adjust myself to see the screen and that's when I catch sight of it.

My little bean.

My baby.

Its little heart flickers on the screen and in that moment, I know I'm having the baby. I look over to where Gracie is sitting and the light reflects off the tears filling her eyes. She prints out two copies of the sonograms, hands them both to me, and says she'll give me a second to get dressed.

Gracie says nothing as I get dressed. I don't think either of us really knows what to say, but I can tell that the air in the room has shifted. I return to my spot on the edge of the bed and turn towards my best friend.

"So, I guess I'm having a baby?"

"*We're* having a baby." She gets up and stands in front of me, taking my hands in her own. "You are absolutely *not* doing this alone." I don't even realize that tears are streaming down my face until she wipes them off of my cheeks. The doctor knocks on the door again and peeks in through a crack. She and the nurse from earlier come into the room and stand along the counter.

"According to your last menstrual, your due date is July twenty-third, so right now, we're looking at around seven weeks. You do have options if you'd like to discuss those. Would you need anyone to go over them with you?"

"No, thank you. I'll be keeping the baby." Gracie squeezes my arm in reassurance.

"Okay," She clasps her hands together. "We will put

together a folder with resources, a list of doctors in the area, and anything else you may need. Everyone at the clinic is also here for whatever you need." She smiles and for the first time I get a chance to really look at her. She has kind eyes and lines around her eyes and mouth, making it obvious that she spends a good amount of time smiling.

"Thank you."

She nods and slides out of the door, leaving Gracie and I in the room alone.

"How do I tell Beck? I don't even know how to get a hold of him."

"I know you well enough to know that you're one hundred percent sure it's his, so I won't ask about that. I think you just have to rip the bandaid off babe."

My shoulders sag, and I know she's right. He *absolutely* needs to know and sooner rather than later, but I need to get the courage to do it first.

I WAS STARVING after my appointment, so we stopped by one of those build-your-own-burrito-bowl places. The moment we walk, in I'm head over heels for whoever's cooking because it smells absolutely *delish*. Gracie and I stand in line behind a few other people when my phone starts to vibrate repeatedly. I pull it out of my bag and see **Daphne** on the screen.

"Hey, what's up?" I asked, phone to my ear.

"I just got back to the apartment. I'll send you my burrito order."

Gracie looks at me with furrowed brows and mouths *who is that?* I show her the screen and she nods in immediate understanding.

"How do you know where I am?"

"Find Your Friends, duh." The phone lie dies, and I can't help but laugh. Leave it to my sister to demand me buy her food the moment she gets back into town.

A text comes through by the time we get up to the front of the line and I recite her order to the employee, which is not much different than mine. The main difference is that I get a bowl, where she gets a burrito, and I get extra guac while she gets none.

I do decide to go with light chicken this time because the thought of meat...barf.

Gracie orders sweet tea for the three of us and pays for all three meals, much to my disapproval. We find a spot in the corner of the restaurant and sit down to dig in. I'm about halfway through my bowl when the burning sensation of heartburn begins to fill my chest. I could honestly cry right now.

It doesn't help that the door swings open and my sister comes practically running towards me. Before I can even realize that I actually *am* crying, my cheeks are drenched in salty tears. Her arms wrap around me, and she runs her fingers through my hair as I sob into her chest. I'm sure everyone in this restaurant thinks we are wackadoos, but I don't care.

"Are you okay?" she asks. I manage to mumble something that sounds like *hmm* in between choking on sobs. She moves against me and releases a deep breath. "So, we're gonna have a baby?"

I nod, understanding that she and Gracie must have been having a silent conversation while I sobbed into her chest.

"Have you talked to mom?"

I can only shake my head. I suck in a deep breath, pulling away from my twin and sitting back in my chair to return to my burrito bowl. Heartburn or not, I'm going to keep eating. After I stick a bite into my mouth, I rummage around in my purse and pull out the sonogram to show Daphne. She takes it from me and examines it for a second. Her hand goes up to her mouth, tears filling her eyes.

She points to the image and asks, "Is this the baby? *Your* baby?"

"That's my little nugget," I shrug.

I stare at my identical twin, and I think it finally hits me, and I mean like *really* hits me. My mind starts to make mental lists of everything I need to do and buy, but the panic chases it and I can feel my chest constrict.

"Hey. Don't do that." Gracie touches my hand gently.

"We're here for you, babe." My sister reaches over the table and brushes my other hand. "You won't have to do anything alone, ever."

Tears sting my eyes and my vision blurs.

I've always wanted to be a mom, but I had an order in which I wanted things to happen.

Of course, nothing goes to plan. I rest my hand on my lower stomach and close my eyes to steady my breathing.

Everything is going to be okay.

Everything is going to be okay.

This may not have happened in the order I wanted things to happen. You know the one? Meet the love of your life, date, move in together, get engaged, the big wedding, etc. Despite this deviance, I won't regret my choice to keep my baby.

But now that I decided to keep him, or her, I need to let Beck know.

10

’m basically dragging my feet to the warehouse for practice because I do *not* want to be here tonight.

After working almost nonstop the last two days, the only place I want to be is my bed. If Derek has us do more than two takes of one song, I might lose my shit. Doing six or seven takes is unnecessary, especially when they’re songs we could play in our sleep.

“There he is!” Derek yells from the couch as I step through the already open door. His voice has a hint of a slur and by the color of the drink in his cup, it’s obvious he skipped straight to the hard liquor tonight. I make eye contact with Tieran and he gives a subtle head shake, as if to tell me *don’t say anything.* I roll my eyes and sit on the stool behind my drums.

Derek takes a moment to kiss on the newest groupie's neck and stumbles his way towards his mic. Earlier this afternoon, he sent us the song order we were practicing tonight, so I already know we’re opening with *Ghost of Fate*. Derek may be a lot of things, but one thing I will give him is that this fucker is talented.

One of the girls sitting on the couch motions for him to come over. He stops, mid fucking song, to walk over to where the three of them are sitting. The one who waved him down, Darcy if I remember correctly, pulls a small bag from her bra and wiggles it in the air with a sheepish smile.

Derek pulls her into a heated kiss like we aren't in the middle of something.

"What the fuck." Tieran whips around to meet my gaze. I shrug, but my stomach sinks when the girl lines some of the white powder from the bag onto the coffee table.

"Woah." Hayes lifts the strap of his guitar up and over his head. "I don't fuck with that. I'm leaving." Without another word he puts his guitar in its stand and walks out of the building.

"Where the fuck do you think—" Derek is cut off by the sound of the door slamming.

"He can leave, baby. The other guys will party with us." Michelle looks at me and winks.

"Do you ever fucking go home?" I ask as I stand from my drums. "And no, the other guys will absolutely not fucking party with you. Now get the fuck out before I call the cops."

Derek laughs and somehow pulls himself to his feet. He obviously has issues balancing because he sways back and forth a couple of times before straightening himself out. "You wouldn't call the cops on me, Becky boy."

"The fuck?"

Tieran looks pissed *and* scared at the same time. My blood was already hot before I got here, but seeing the look on Tieran's face makes it boil.

"Go home, D. We can try again in a couple of days. But you guys." I wave my finger back and forth between the three girls. "Don't fucking come back. You're no longer welcome here. Especially you." I point at Michelle. Her face reddens and she looks like I just kicked her dog or something, but she kind of just pisses me off more than the rest.

"They're here for *me*, asshole." Derek wobbles over to where I'm standing and gets toe to toe with me.

"So, you go with them. For someone who is so desperate for this band to get signed, you sure are drinking, and apparently snorting, our chances away."

"I'm just letting loose, man. You should try it sometime." He turns and picks up the little bag and wiggles in front of my face. I slap that shit out of his hand and watch him as it falls to the floor.

"Why the fuck did you do that?"

"Let's just go, Beck." Tieran pleads behind me and lightly places his hand on my shoulder. I know he can see that both Derek and I are getting pissed.

"Yeah, Beck. Better go listen to your bestie." The girls giggle behind Derek.

"There's no lie about that and Tieran is triple the friend you've ever been." I turn to motion for Tieran to walk in front of me, but instead I'm met with Tieran's face dropping as Derek's fist hits my temple. It was a cheap shot, and one Derek is going to regret.

The ringing echoes throughout my head and I have to make a conscious effort to not stumble. I crack my neck and glare at Derek. "Are you fucking serious, D?"

He shrugs and puts his fists up, bracing himself for a fight. I want to punch him back so fucking bad, but I motion for Tieran to walk out.

"Come on. Fight me, Beck."

"I'm not going to fight you. But you just seriously fucked up." I shake my head in disappointment and look back at the girls, who are now huddled together on the couch. "I'm not joking. Don't fucking come back here." Derek makes sure to stay out of my way as I walk past him, keeping his fists raised in case I decide to change my mind.

Tieran is already halfway to the cars by the time I walk out of the door. Not that I blame him, he's always avoided confrontation. He looks back and relief washes over his face when he sees it's me.

"I'm surprised you didn't punch him back."

"I wanted to, but what good would that have done?"

He shrugs and unlocks his car. "I'll text you later."

I nod and watch as he gets into his car. As I unlock my truck and slide into the driver's seat, the sound of footsteps on the pebble walkway echo in the dark. I glance across the truck bed and spy the three girls walking towards one of their cars. Michelle looks up at me and quickly back down, crossing her arms and hurrying back into the vehicle. I can't even feel bad for the way I spoke to her, or to anyone else in the room for that matter.

I was grateful when I woke up without a huge headache. Even though he was drunk, and probably high, Derek hit me pretty good. Thankfully, I still have a few more weeks to work on my current custom piece, a pine loft bed. Today, all I'm going to be able to do is get the wood cut into the correct lengths.

Using my circular saw, I cut the pine to size. One by one, I cut the legs, the inner slat rail, the lower frame, top rail, and all of the spacer blocks. I lay the pieces up against the wall, making sure to label each to keep them together so that tomorrow I can work on sanding them before assembling the puzzle into something usable.

After what feels like hours of cutting, I clean up my station so that I can leave for the night. My dad's office door closes and his voice carries with to the two other carpenters' in the shop before he finally makes his way to me.

He smiles and stops at my little corner of the big room. "Hey, kiddo."

"Hey, dad."

"You did great work with that table. The bed looks like it's going to be good, too. You really have a natural talent, son."

Son.

Even after all of these years, that still pulls at something in my chest.

"Thanks." I continue wiping off my table.

"You got a concert this weekend?"

"A show, yeah." I shrug, not sure if it's actually going to happen or not. Not after last night. "Well, I mean maybe. I don't know."

"You don't know? Did something happen with your friends?" He leans up against the work table.

"You can say that."

"Do you want to talk about it?"

"Derek just made stupid choices, and I didn't want to be caught in the middle of it."

He walks around to the opposite side of the table and stands beside me. His hand raises up and rests on my shoulder. Despite the years I've had with this family, I stiffen. Physical affection has always been something I struggle with. Dad pulls his hand away slowly and lets it rest by his side. Both of my parents have always been really good about my boundaries.

"I'm proud of you, then. I don't know what the stupid choices were, but I'm proud of you for standing your ground."

"Derek had drugs and I—" I take a deep breath, "I don't want that shit around me."

"I know your history with drugs and I don't blame you." He nods his head in understanding because of all the people in my life, he and Mom would know best. "You've come far, Beckett. You really stepped up and got your life together. Mom and I are proud of the man you've become."

"I wouldn't have been able to do it without you guys."

He smiles and nods, just a slight movement of his chin, and we say our goodbyes.

I finish cleaning my work area when my phone vibrates in my back pocket. I'm only half surprised when I pull it out to see the group chat blowing up.

Derek: Look, guys. I'm sorry about yesterday.

Tieran: I think you could do better than that.

Hayes: Seriously, D. That was bullshit.

Derek: I fucked up. I know.

Derek: What can I do?

Hayes: No more chicks.

Tieran: No more hard alcohol.

I chime in.

Me: And no more fucking drugs.

Derek: Done.

I'm not stupid enough to actually trust him, so I'm fully prepared to keep him at arm's length. If the band wasn't set to play a couple of shows, I would've told him to fuck right off.

TIERAN and I decide to ride to the gig together. Derek and Hayes are already in the back room by the time we got there. The room is thick with discomfort and I can practically see the relief Hayes feels when Tieran and I walk into the room. Ti lifts his hand up and gives everyone in the room a small wave.

"I know I said it earlier, but I *am* sorry." Derek lifts his arm and rubs the back of his neck.

"We know." Ti gives him a tight lipped smile.

I cross my arms and lean back against the wall. I don't have anything to say right now, not anything nice anyway. The stage manager knocks on the door to let us know it's time to take the stage. Derek stands and shakes his hands, leading us as we take turns filing out of the room, one by one, and onto the stage.

The lights in the building go low and spotlights shine onto the stage. I take a deep breath and count us in.

Our set list starts with Ghosts of Fate.

I'm chasing the shadows of what used to be,
But your love is a ghost and I need to be free.
We danced in the fire but the flames burned too bright,
You slipped through my fingers like ashes in the night.

The lyrics pull at something I've tried to bury deep. I lift my eyes, depending on muscle memory while I search the crowd. I don't even question who I'm looking for because I *know* I'm looking for Olivia in the sea of people. There's little to no chance she's actually out there, so I just dissociate in the music.

We go through three more songs and close out with *Flowing Tides*. I'm relieved when we finish our set. I grab a small towel and wipe off the sweat from my brow, before heading to the bar. It's there I take a seat on one of the barstools at the countertop and ask the bartender for an IPA.

As I wait, I run my hand through my sweat soaked hair and release a long exhale.

"Long day?" a familiar voice asks. I look over and see Gracie getting comfortable in the barstool beside me.

"Hey, Gracie." The bartender sets my beer on the counter, dripping condensation.

"You guys gave a good show tonight."

"Thanks." I take a drink from my beer. "So, you here alone?" I look around for a familiar head of blonde hair.

"Olivia's not here."

"Ah. Okay."

"You thinkin' about her or somethin'?"

"Yeah. I guess. A bit. She doing okay?"

Gracie shrugs and takes a sip from whatever fruity drink she has. "She's been seeing someone for a little bit."

"You don't seem too excited about that."

"I don't know him, but something seems off." She shrugs again. "You should try and talk to her soon though."

"Oh yeah? Wh-"

I'm cut off when Hayes and Tieran walk over to us. "Hey, baby."

She spins the barstool around at Hayes's smirk. He moves to stand in between her legs and grips a handful of her hair at the nape of her neck, pulling her in for a kiss. It doesn't take an idiot to see that they're going home together. I reach for Gracie's arm, to ask her *why* I should talk to Olivia, but Haye's is already pulling her away.

What the hell is going on and why do I hope Gracie said that because Olivia is thinking about me?

Olivia

11

Ten Weeks Pregnant

My sister offered to come with me to talk to our mom, but I knew it was something I needed to do on my own. I stand in front of the black iron fence that lines the boundary of my mom's house, my childhood home. My stomach is swirling with anxiety and nausea. After Dad left and Mom was stuck with three girls to raise, she couldn't afford much. Her car is in the carport, which is good since I didn't give her a heads up that I was coming. I've had three weeks to wrap my head around becoming a mom, but it took me that long to mentally prepare to tell my own mother.

She always wanted more for us, a better life for us than she was forced to have as a single parent. My stomach tightens as I make my way up the red bricked stairs and knock on the front door. The door swings open and Mom's short, brown curly hair bobs from the movement.

"Livy, baby. Why didn't you just walk in?"

"Oh." I shrug. "I don't know."

She opens the door and gestures for me to come in. "What a nice surprise. I made sweet tea and fresh cookies, do you want some?"

I nod, my mouth instantly waters when I think of my mom's chocolate chip cookies.

The living room is the same as it was when I was a kid, clean and free of clutter but still very cozy. I sit on the dark brown pleather sectional in my favorite spot—up against the arm of the couch. Mom comes in, sets the drinks and plate of cookies on the coffee table, and settles in the arm chair across from where I'm sitting.

I grab a cookie and sit back against the couch, bringing my legs beneath me.

"So, what's up, sweet girl?" She smiles softly, her mother's intuition no doubt signaling her there's a reason for my visit today.

I take another bite of the cookie, my absolute favorite, if not to just give myself another moment of silence before I drop this bomb on her. Her green eyes stare back at me, and I can see the concern while she searches my face for any kind of hint.

"Well." I swallow the last bit of the cookie and continue. "I had to go to the doctor a few weeks ago for what I thought was a case of food poisoning or the flu."

"Okay..." She tilts her head to the side and I can tell by the look on her face she knows exactly what I'm about to say next.

"The doctor informed me it wasn't either, that I was actually pregnant. I know you're so disappointed and I'm sorry. I don't know what else to say except I'm sorry," I say everything so quickly that I have to gasp for breath at the end. A lump sits in my throat and I bite my bottom lip to try and stop the tears that I know are going to start falling.

"I could *never* be disappointed in you, Liv, and if I didn't do a good enough job trying to prove that to you when you were little, then *I'm sorry*. I'm assuming you wanted to tell me because you decided to continue the pregnancy?" I nod. "Okay. So, I'm going to be a grandma. This is exciting news!" I don't know if my confusion is written on my face or what, but she laughs and continues, "Did you *want* me to be mad at you, baby?"

"Not necessarily. I just know you don't want this kind of life for us."

"And what kind of life is that?"

"Single parenthood."

"Oh." She gets up from the chair and comes to sit next to me on the couch. "Of course I didn't want any of you guys to become single parents, ever. But you have something I didn't have, baby. You have a village of people, myself included, that will be there for you every step of the way." Mom wraps her arm around me and pulls me into a hug, every flood gate that was stopping my tears from falling breaks and the tears begin pouring.

She rubs my back softly as I choke out sobs. I thought I was all cried out, but it seems like crying and eating are all I do, as long as I'm not feeling sick. Finally, I pull myself together, wipe my eyes, and pull out of her embrace.

"Is it the guy you've been seeing? Holt, right?"

"No."

"Oh, okay." Her eyes are full of questions, but I know she won't ask them, so I take a deep breath.

"Do you remember Beckett Haven, *Beck*, Daphne and I went to school with him?"

"The guy that was like a grade above you? You had a crush on him for quite some time."

"Anyways." I roll my eyes and shake my head. Was I *that* obvious? "He played at the club we took Mattie to for her birthday. We ended up dancing and one thing led to another and a few weeks later, I'm pregnant. Despite being on birth control *and* using a condom. I really don't understand how this happened."

My mom shrugs. "Typically, yes, two forms of birth control are ideal, but sometimes things like this just happen. Does he know yet?"

I shake my head. "Not yet. He's next on my list, but I wanted to tell you first. I think telling you is scarier."

"You think I'm scary?" She fakes a dramatic sigh and places her hand on her heart.

I laugh and come to stand, desperate to go and tell Beck to just get it over with before I lose my nerve. "I better go to Beck's before I chicken out."

"Okay baby." She rises to her feet in front of me and holds onto my arms. "No matter what happens, you are *not* alone."

I nod and bite my bottom lip. My mom pulls me in for one more hug, squeezing me before she lets go. She stands at the door watching me as I get into my car.

"I'm just a phone call away, love you!" she hollers. I blow her kiss and get into my car where I let out a long breath and the weight in my chest is gone. Telling my mom was one of the things that's been causing me more stress than I thought it would.

Now I need to pull off the Band-Aid and let Beck know.

THE DRIVE to Beck's place is short. I stare up at the house from where I stand on the sidewalk, remembering when I snuck out of here all those weeks ago. Granted, I didn't know then that I was bringing home a keepsake, but I'm honestly a little surprised that I even remembered where the house is to begin with. This is *definitely* it.

I take the small flight of stairs and knock on the door. The butterflies in my stomach are swarming around like a tsunami in my stomach and if I didn't know any better, I'd say I'm about to be sick. I hold down the nausea as I wait for someone to open the door. There's a rattle with the sound of the chain lock, then the deadbolt.

A young girl, probably around Mattie's age, opens the door and smiles.

"Can I help you?" Her voice is soft, but deep. It only takes one look into her dark brown eyes to know that she's definitely related to Beck.

"Hi. I'm sorry to bug you, but I'm looking for Beck?"

"Did he hit your car or run over your dog?"

"What? No. Neither." I don't know if the look on my face is shocked, horrified, or a combination of the two, but the girl starts to giggle.

"I'm just kidding. Come on in." She opens the door the rest of the way, inviting me inside.

I'm timid as I enter. She disappears down the short hallway and knocks on his bedroom door. It creaks open and she whispers something before the door shuts and she comes back down the hallway with a smile.

"He'll be out in a second. Can I get you some water or something?"

"I'm okay, thank you…" I give her a questioning look.

"Oh, duh." She facepalms her forehead and extends the same hand out to me. "I'm his sister, Blaire, sorry."

"Olivia." I shake her hand and smile.

"I've heard that name before." She walks away and continues talking, this time I think it's to herself. "Where have I heard that name before?"

The bedroom door opens and shuts, and Beck soon joins me. Of course, shirtless. *Does he own a shirt?*

The reality of this moment hits me like a semi-truck and I realize I have no idea how I'm going to tell him.

"Hey, Freckles. Miss me?" He glides his hand through his tousled hair.

"Hi. Can we talk?" I look towards where Blaire sits on the couch, lip between my teeth.

"Beat it, Squirt." He gestures to the hallway. She sticks her tongue out, but looks over to me.

"It was nice to meet you, Olivia. You're *really* pretty."

I smile and tell her thanks. When she's gone, Beck takes a seat on the couch and motions for me to sit across from him. When I do, he expands his arms and drapes them across the frame of the couch, placing one ankle on the opposite knee. The butterflies swarm around in my stomach and I'm absolutely going to puke, but I take a deep breath and begin saying what I came here to say.

"I'm sorry for dropping by unannounced, but I wasn't sure how to get a hold of you."

"Yeah, it would've been nice for you to leave me a number or something."

"I didn't have any intention of seeing you again, so I didn't think it was necessary."

"But you came back for seconds." He lifts his eyebrow and smirks a cocky grin.

"Not exactly..." He raises his brow. "Well, I had to go to the doctor."

"I'm clean. If you got something, it's not from me."

I scoff, a little irritated with his tone. I take a deep breath and calm myself before I speak. "I mean I didn't *get* something, but I did *leave* with something." I reach into my bag and pull out the copy of the sonogram and hand it to him. "I'm pregnant."

BECK

12

I'm pregnant.

The room spins, but stays still at the same time. How is that possible? I swear if I wasn't sitting down, the ground would be shaking where I stood. She's pregnant? But we wore a condom *and* I'm pretty sure she said she was on birth control.

"Beckett? Are you okay?"

My hands shake as I go to take the sonogram from her. I've never seen one of these before, but it doesn't take much for me to be able to understand what I'm looking at.

"I, uhm, give me a second."

"Of course." She sits back on the couch and leans forward. "I just want you to know I don't expect anything from you. I was raised by a single mother, so I know how things go. I just wanted you to know about him or her, that's all." *She's cute as fuck when she rambles.*

"Why wouldn't I want to be involved?" I look at her and then back to the sonogram, this is my kid.

98

Our kid.

I'm going to be a fucking dad.

"I...I didn't think you would want to. I just wanted you to know that you had the option. I made the choice to keep them without you, and I just want you to know you also have the choice."

"I'd love to be as involved as you want me to be."

"Okay." She looks down at her hands and smiles.

"How pregnant are you?"

Olivia laughs, and not like a forced laugh, like a *real* laugh.

"What?"

She wipes away a tear that escaped during her short laughing episode. "It's how *far along* am I? I'm eleven, almost twelve, weeks. So almost into my second trimester."

"I don't know much about pregnancy."

"That's okay. I can answer whatever questions you have."

"I have a ton, but I won't bombard you right now. Can I keep this?" I hold up the sonogram and kind of wiggle it.

"Yeah, I asked the technician for a second copy. That one's yours to keep."

"When do you go to the doctor next?"

"My standing appointments are the first Tuesdays of the month at four. I can give you the information to my doctor. You're more than welcome to come to my appointments with me."

"I'd like that, but there's something we should do first."

"Hm?"

"We should exchange numbers." I raise my eyebrow and hand her my locked phone. "The codes 1313."

"I don't feel comfortable entering, or *knowing*, your phone passcode."

"Well, now you do and I'm not changing it."

She rolls her eyes and hands me her own phone. "Mine doesn't have a code." After a moment, we hand one another back our phones and she laughs when she looks at what I put myself down as in her contacts. "Really? *My Hot Baby Daddy?*"

"What did you put yours under?" I shrug.

"Olivia Connoly. My name?"

"I'll change it." I open my phone and go to my contacts, finding her immediately.

"To what?"

"Freckles."

"You don't think it's weird that you gave me a nickname?"

"Not even a little bit. That's just who you are to me, Freckles."

She smiles, glancing down as she does. The reason she got this nickname is because of the cluster of the cutest freckles covering the bridge of her nose and expanding onto her cheeks. They grow darker as the blush creeps over her fair skin.

"I better get going." She stands and smooths out her shirt.

"Can I text you? Is that allowed?"

"You can text me anytime." Olivia smiles softly. The kind of smile that threatens to melt my heart of ice. "I have my *do not disturb* on during school hours, but just while I'm at work."

"You're a teacher?"

"I'm an art teacher. High school. I guess we don't know much about each other, huh?"

"We have like, what? Thirty weeks or something to learn it all?"

"We do." She makes her way to the front door and opens it, glancing back at me one last time. "Bye, Beckett. I'll text you the information for my doctor's appointment and office."

"See ya, Freckles."

I watch through the window as she walks to her car. I'm not sure how she expected me to react, but my heart did something weird when she said I didn't have be involved. I know what it's like to have a piece of shit for a parent and I promised myself a long time ago that I'd never do that if I ever had kids.

"She's really pretty, Becks." Blaire says as she comes up beside me. "Definitely different from the normal riff-raff you have here."

"She's pregnant."

"Why did she come and—" she gasps and hits my arm, "you're gonna be a fucking *dad?!*"

"I'm going to be a fucking dad."

The words seem to barely register as I say them out loud. I feel like it's going to take me a long time to be able to come to terms with what exactly that means. Not just for me, but for my future and for the band. Derek's probably going to lose his shit, especially now that he's working so much harder to get us signed.

"When you gonna tell mom and dad?"

"I'll have to tell them soon, I guess. You know they'll want to meet her."

"I'm gonna be a fucking aunt, dude," Blaire looks at me and squeals. I pat her on the shoulder and head toward my room. "You know that you're going to be a great dad, right?" I shrug and keep walking.

I check my phone and see that I have three unread texts. Two from the group chat and one from Olivia.

Derek: Practice at 2.

Tieran: No girls this time, D.

I'm so sick of the groupies that hang around all of the time, so I thumbs up Tieran's message and go to open Olivia's. It's a screenshot and address to her doctor's office. I save the information in my phone's calendar.

> Me: Thanks for the information. I wouldn't miss it.

> Freckles: 😊

I check the time and put my phone down on the bed. There's only about two hours before I have to be at practice, so I grab clothes and jump in the shower.

THE TRUCK JERKS as I put it in park outside my parents' house. Still holding onto the steering wheel, I take a deep breath and prepare myself. I have to be at practice in less than an hour, so I know I don't have time to fuck around.

I'm relieved to see both Mom and Dad's cars are in the car port. I'm not sure what I'm expecting, but my stomach squeezes in anticipation. The walk through their wooden fence and up the stone walkway is short. The stairs are only a step and I'm at the front door. I knock twice as I open the door and try to hide the shaking in my voice. "Ma? Pop? You here?"

"Becks, is that you?" Mom calls from the kitchen before she peaks her head around the wall. "Hey sweetheart! I didn't expect to see you! Grant, come inside!"

"Huh? What?" Dad calls from the backyard where he's weeding the garden, like he does every weekend.

"I said *come inside!* Beck's here!" she yells through the cracked window. "Do you want some tea? It's fresh."

"*Erm.* Sure, Ma."

She nods, grabs a glass, and starts to pour me some tea. Dad joins us as she hands me the glass, a smudge of dirt on his cheek. I motion to the table and they both sit across from me.

"So, what's going on? You look like you've seen a ghost." Dad's eyebrows furrow.

I take another drink of my tea to buy myself some time. They are the last people I want to disappoint and it's not like Olivia and I are *together* or anything.

I clear my throat. "I slept with someone a couple months ago and just found out she's pregnant."

My mom sucks in a breath but doesn't say anything as I continue.

"She's decided to keep it, and I told her I'd like to be as involved as possible." I reach into my pocket and pull out the sonogram, sliding it across the table to my parents. My stomach twists as they sit there, each of them holding one side of the paper. I could honestly vomit while my parents contemplate in silence, but I clear my throat again. "I won't be like *him.* I'm going to quit drinking and partying. I won't continue the cycle I was born into." My throat burns as the words finish coming out of my mouth.

"Beck, I *never* thought you'd be like him." Dad reaches over the table and grabs my trembling hand. "I was only silent because I was wondering what my grandpa name would be. I'm kind of gunning for Poppop."

"Ooh! I'd love Mema."

"Wait. You guys aren't mad?"

"Why would we be mad, sweetheart?" Mom tilts her head slightly to the side.

"I don't know. I assumed...I just expected you guys would be disappointed."

"Well, you know what assuming does. Don't ya? We love babies and the fact that it's *yours* makes it all the more special." Something in my heart tightens.

"When can we meet her?"

"We don't know that it's a girl yet since Olivia is only–"

"Not the baby, goof. The mom, Olivia, you said her name is? That's beautiful."

"Tell us about her, son," Dad encourages.

"Well, yes. Her name is Olivia, and she has a twin sister, Daphne. We all went to school together." Then it hits me...I don't really know shit about her.

"I can tell you realized you need to get to know her. Luckily there's like seven more months for you guys to get to know one another," Mom says as she stands and gets back to the dishes she was washing in the sink.

"Invite her for dinner soon. I'd like to meet her." Dad rises and pushes his chair in. He walks over to where Mom stands at the sink and kisses her on the temple. "I'm sure Mom would, too. I gotta get back to the grass before I lose daylight. Love you, son."

Just like that, Dad walks out of the house and back into the backyard. As if I didn't just give him life altering news. That's Dad for you, though. His response isn't surprising, but I know he and Mom will talk about it in length tonight.

"I agree with Dad, you know. I think you should invite her

over so that we can meet her. She's going to be in our life forever now, so it's important that we form a relationship."

Forever.

For some reason, up until this moment I didn't really realize how permanent this would be. The baby will be in my life as long as I'm around. But my brain hasn't had a moment to process that Olivia would be, too.

Me: Hi.

Me: My parents want you over for dinner soon.

Freckles: I would love to! How soon is soon?

I look up from my phone and ask Mom, "When do you want to do this? She asked *how soon is soon?*"

The smile on my mom's face lights up. "How about family dinner tomorrow? She can get to know your sister, too."

Me: Is tomorrow too early?

Freckles: Tomorrow is great!

Me: Cool. See you then, Freckles.

Freckles: Have a good night, Beckett!

I text her the address and kiss my mom on the cheek before I leave to go to practice, suddenly feeling nervous for family dinner tomorrow.

BLAIRE HELPS Mom set the table while I pace the living room. I've never, and I really mean *never,* brought a girl home to meet my parents. So, this entire experience is new to me, especially since this woman is carrying a whole ass child that's mine.

"You're going to put a hole in my floor doin' all that pacin', Beck." Mom calls from the dining room. Immediately I stop, but the urge to continue gnaws at my gut.

I open my mouth to respond, but a knock on the door causes me to shut it with a snap. My hands shake as I reach for the doorknob. I swing the door open and forget how to breathe. Olivia stands there with a small bag of something and a bouquet of sunflowers with some white filler flowers, her mouth is opened in a huge smile.

"Hey!" she exclaims, raising her eyebrows in question when I don't respond.

"Ignore my son's lack of manners, please come in!" My mom and Olivia walk past me, and the smell of her sweet vanilla perfume fills my nostrils. "I'm Celeste and you know Blaire already." My mother looks back at me with an *are you serious* look. I shrug my shoulders and shut the door as she walks Olivia to the kitchen.

"It's so nice to meet you. Hi again, Blaire!" She waves to my sister who is standing against the countertop. "These are for you. I hope you like chocolate chip, they're my specialty."

"Oh, you are just the sweetest! Grant will be so excited." As if hearing his name summons him, my dad walks into the kitchen from the yard.

"I'll be what now?" He extends his hand to Olivia and grins. "I'm Grant, but everyone calls me Pop."

"Olivia was so nice and baked some chocolate chip

cookies." Mom holds up the bag and shakes it for effect. "I don't know that I'll be sharing though. They smell divine."

"I know everyone says their chocolate chip cookies are the best, but mine really are." Olivia glows with pride. *Fuck.* She's absolutely stunning. Her long hair is curled and pinned back so that it's out of her face. The light blue dress she's wearing somehow hugs every single one of her curves while still flowing loosely. It doesn't help that I know what's under that dress.

"Son?" My mom looks at me with a raised brow.

"Huh?"

"You checked out there for a second, maybe it's time to eat."

"*Erm.* Yeah maybe."

What I'm craving isn't on tonight's menu.

My dad leads us to the dining room where burgers and all the fixings are laid out family style. Mom must have been cooking all day because there's pasta, macaroni, *and* potato salad scattered across the table. We all get seated and make our plates. I listen while Blaire and Olivia somehow get on some topic of a reality dating show where the people get married without seeing each other, but they are *professionally* matched.

Whatever the hell that means.

"So, Olivia. Beck mentioned you have a twin sister. Do you have any other siblings?" My dad catches her mid bite, so she quickly finishes and responds.

"Yes, I have an identical twin, Daphne, and our younger sister Mattie. Then my best friend, Gracie, who's basically adopted by my mom."

"It's just your mom and sisters, then?"

"Yeah. My dad left shortly after Mattie was born. So, it's been the four of us for as long as I can remember."

"Your mom must be one hell of a woman."

"Oh, yeah. She's absolutely amazing."

"Were you a cute baby?" my sister asks.

"I think so. My mom has hundreds of photos everywhere." She puts some food on her fork. "What about Beckett?" She slides the fork in her mouth and begins chewing on her bite. A quick glimpse of sadness washes across my mom's face.

"Unfortunately, we don't know. Their biological parents didn't take any photos."

"Oh. I'm so sorry. I didn't realize." Blush deepens the already pink on Olivia's cheeks to red.

"Of course not sweetheart. Don't apologize." Mom smiles and reaches for Olivia's hand. "Beck and Blaire don't talk about their childhood much, if at all really."

Olivia nods and takes a sip of her sweet tea.

There's no way she'd have any idea about my childhood. By the time we had met, I was so deeply embarrassed of my "parents" and home life that I never spoke about it. The only person who ever knew anything was Tieran and that's because I'd show up to his house bloody and bruised frequently enough that he had to know what was going on.

Blaire, sensing everyone's awkwardness, perks up and turns to Olivia. "So, what do you do for work?"

I've never felt so thankful that my sister was nosey as we all welcome the change of subject.

"I teach high school art. I absolutely love it, especially my advanced class. They're literally so great."

Mom grins and I know exactly what she's thinking. "I taught for twenty years, myself. It's so rewarding." She continues to explain what she taught over the years and her and Olivia talk for the remainder of dinner. I just sit back and watch Olivia light up as she tells us about her kids.

Dinner comes to an end, and we begin to clear off the table. I find my sister standing at the fridge while everyone else disperses into the living room. Mom put the sonogram up on the refrigerator door, front and center. I walk up next to her and bump her shoulder with mine. As we stand there, the only sound is the faint conversation between my parents and Olivia in the next room.

"I know I've already said it, but I'm going to say it again. You're gonna be a great dad."

"I'll try and do the best I can."

Blaire sighs and turns her body to face me. "You took care of me my whole life. You protected me, loved me, and made sure I was always safe. I know you're going to be a great dad because you were my parent when all you needed was a parent yourself."

I open my mouth to respond but close it just as fast. I don't know what to say. I've never been one to talk about my feelings with anyone, not even my sister.

"Beck, come walk Olivia to her car!" Mom yells from the other room.

I can hear Olivia refusing, but I head towards the front door and gesture for her to step outside anyways. She says goodbye to my parents and sister and smiles at me as she walks through the doorway. Neither of us speak as we make our way down the walkway to the driver's side door of her car, but once we get there she stops and turns to me.

"Your family is amazing. Thank you so much for inviting me." I nod and put my hands in the pockets of my jeans. "I'll see you at my appointment?"

"I'll be there."

"Great." She's all sunshine as she opens her car door. "I'll see you then."

"Bye, Freckles." I grab onto the frame of her car and wait for her to slide in. I shut the door and watch as she backs out of the driveway, honking twice as she drives away. Her lights disappear in the distance.

My phone vibrates in my back pocket. I half expect it to be a text from Derek, but I'm surprised when I see it's a text from Olivia.

> Freckles: I really did have a great time. I hope we can become good friends. ♥

My stomach sinks when I read that word.

Friends.

I don't want to just be friends.

I want her to be *mine.*

Olivia

13

Eleven Weeks Pregnant

It's hard to hide the smile on my face when I leave Beck's house. The whole interaction with him felt so...natural. I get into my car and grab my phone. It was vibrating while I was talking to Beck, but I ignored it so he and I could talk.

> Holt: Dinner tonight?

Two minutes later.

> Holt: Is that a no?

> Holt: Hello?

> Holt: Olivia?

Five minutes later.

> Holt: I made dinner reservations at 6:30 at the bistro.

Ten minutes later.

> Holt: Where are you?

I connect phone to the car via Bluetooth and call Holt. I realize it's after eight and I know he must be frantic. I can't imagine how worried he must be about me.

I shouldn't have ignored my phone.

"Olivia?" he answers.

"Hey! I'm so sorry I didn't get your texts. I had dinner plans, remember?"

"Where were you?" He lets out a loud sigh. "I was *worried.*"

"I know. I'm sorry. I had that dinner with Beck and his family. Then Beck and I talked and I didn't have my phone readily available."

It goes silent and I have to check to make sure that the call didn't drop. When I see it's still in progress, I ask, "Holt? Are you there?"

"Beck?"

"Yeah, I told you about the dinner with his family."

"I see. You didn't think it was important to *remind* me?"

"Honestly? I didn't even think about it. I'm so sorry, honey. I'll do better to remind you next time."

"Next time?"

"Well, they want to get to know me. As I'm sure Beck does."

"You mean he wants to *fuck* you. Again"

I'm stunned by not only the choice of words, but his tone.

"Excuse me?"

"You heard me, Olivia."

"I...I don't think that's the truth at all, Holt."

The phone beeps, signaling the end of the phone call. He hung up on me.

I try to call him back and after two rings, it's forwarded to voicemail. My stomach twists and turns with an overwhelming sense of anxiety.

It's not until I autopilot into my parking garage that I realize I've driven the rest of the way home in complete silence. I pull into my spot, put the car in park and turn it off, and grab my purse. I check my phone one more time to see if Holt tried to return my phone calls but can't say I'm surprised to see that he hasn't.

It's occurring to me now that it's normal for him to give me somewhat of a silent treatment when I do something to upset him.

Me: I'm sorry that I didn't remind you.

Me: Please call me back.

I head into my apartment and fully expect to go to the bathroom to shower, but I'm surprised to find my sisters and mom all sitting on the couch in the living room. By the vibe throughout the house, I can tell something's not right. My mom smiles with tightly closed lips, but it's Daphne's face that gives it away.

"What's wrong?"

"Hi sweetheart, come sit with us." Mom pats on the couch cushion.

"I just got home. I really just want to shower and—"

"Seriously, Liv. Just sit down." Daphne stands and I know if

I don't sit on the couch, she'll drag me over there. I take my shoes off and set my bag down on the counter. I look between the three of them before sitting down closest to Mattie and setting my hands on my knees. I can feel my frustration rising the longer I sit here in the center of their gazes.

"So?" I snap. My stomach squeezes in anticipation while I wait for someone to speak.

Mom casts a weary glance at my sisters and back at me. "Some concerns have been brought to my attention, and I want to speak with you about them. If that's okay?" I nod and fight the urge to give Daphne a dirty look. I know she's said something to our mom, I just don't know what. "This new guy you're seeing, Holt. Things are okay?"

"Things are great. I don't know why you're asking about him."

"Because he's basically fucking stalking you, Liv. He wants to know your location and who you're with twenty four seven and—" Mom raises her hand to quiet Daphne

"What your sister means to say is that there are some things happening that appear toxic."

"He just likes to know that I'm safe. That's all." My throat tightens and burns as the onset of tears sting my eyes.

"We're frightened it's more than that, love."

"What else would it be?"

"Fucking abuse, Liv. He gets mad when you even hang out with *us.* He only wants you to go to the gym with *him.* You guys have only been seeing each other for a little bit and he's around literally all the time. If he gets mad, he gives you the silent treatment. That's not normal. That's control."

"He is *not* abusing me. He just cares about me." I take a deep breath to combat the instinct to lash out to protect myself.

I roll my eyes and sit back on the couch, checking my phone to see if he's responded to any of my texts.

Me: Babe?

Me: Are you there?

Me: Please stop ignoring me.

Me: I'm sorry.

"I think what Daph is trying to say." Mattie clears her throat, so I put my phone down. "Is that certain behavior seems like red flags from the outside. We love you and as your sisters, we are just worried about you. You're constantly checking your phone and you're anxious. It's just not like you, Liv."

I uncross my legs and move to my feet. My gut fills with desperation to be out of the conversation. I leave my sisters and mother in the living room and go into my bedroom to get my pajamas. I am so physically *and* mentally exhausted that I just want to curl into bed and sleep for the next two days. Instead, I force myself to get into the shower. Maybe, hopefully, I'll feel better after showering.

I don't look towards the living room when I cross the hall into the bathroom. I'm fully aware that my mom and sisters are still there talking and I'm not interested in anything they have to say. I check my phone again before I turn the sound on and put it face up on the counter.

But what if my mother and sisters are right? I start the shower and let it warm up. *No. Holt cares about me. I just don't think sometimes, and I do things that make him mad.* I take off my clothes and throw them in the hamper. *Like I should have reminded him about dinner with Beck's family.* I test the water to make sure it's not too hot before getting into the spray. *He has every right to be upset with me.* I put body wash onto my loofah and lather it up. *He'll talk to me when he's ready.* I wash the soap off of my body and stand beneath the water. My stomach clenches and I don't know if it's because of dinner or my anxiety.

I turn off the shower and grab my towel to dry off. The screen of my phone lights up with an incoming phone call. I rush over to it, almost tripping on the bathroom rug, to see it's finally Holt. I take a deep breath and shake off any of the anxiety. He doesn't like it when I sound upset.

"Hey!"

"I'm downstairs. Where are you?" I open my mouth to respond but bite my lip because I'm so scared to make him mad again.

"Erm. I thought we weren't having dinner."

"We aren't, but I'd still like to see my girlfriend." *Girlfriend.* Every time he calls me that, I want to remind him that he has, in fact, never asked me to be his girlfriend.

"I just got out of the shower, so give me like two minutes!"

"Pack a bag. You're staying the night."

"At your house?" *I've never slept over at his house.*

"No, Olivia, in my car." He lets out a frustrated sigh. "Yes, at my house."

"Okay! I'll see you in a couple minutes."

For the first time in the last few hours, I feel like I can breathe.

It's after eleven and exhaustion is hitting me *hard.* I rush to my room and throw on a dress, forgoing my comfortable lounge set because Holt thinks wearing loungewear outside of the house is tacky. I throw a couple of pairs of pajamas and work clothes in my duffle bag before going back to the bathroom to get my toiletries. I zip up the bag and take a deep breath before walking out of my room. My mom and both my sister's turn to face me.

"I'm staying at Holt's for a couple of days. I'll see you guys soon." I stop at the door and look back to where they sit on the couch. "I promise everything is fine. I love you, guys."

I let the door shut behind me and start the walk towards the elevator. For whatever reason, the hallway seems to be extra long tonight. The elevator opens the moment I press the down arrow and it step in. My finger sinks into the button for the base floor and I wait patiently for the elevator to arrive at my destination. My lower back is hurting, so I shift my weight back and forth between my hips to alleviate some of the pain. That's one part of pregnancy I don't think I was truly ready for, the hip and back pain. It makes it even worse that I'm not even in my second trimester yet, so I know this is just the tip of the iceberg.

Holt's car is sitting on the edge of the street. I can see the light from his phone shining on his face as I get closer to the passenger side door. I swing open the backseat and throw my duffle bag into it before climbing into the front.

"Hey," I mumble as I buckle my seatbelt. He puts his phone down and smiles, leaning over to kiss me. His tongue invades my mouth almost instantly and I have to stifle the urge to gag when the faint taste of whiskey and tobacco hits me.

"I missed you." He practically purrs against my lip.

"Me, too." I scrunch my shoulders in hopes he gets the hint and moves his hand away from my face. Instead, he pulls me in for another kiss. Once again, his tongue is in my mouth and I'm holding back the gag that's fighting to come up to the surface.

He pulls back and sits back in his seat, looking back at me with a smile. We still haven't slept together, and I doubt we will now that I'm starting to show a little bit. It's mainly just bloat right now, but I know Holt isn't crazy about the idea of me gaining weight.

"Are you ready to go?"

"Yeah, but before we go, I just need to say sorry for earlier. I didn't mean to make you upset."

"No. That was all me. Sometimes I just get so *jealous*. You're so beautiful and I know you can have any guy you want."

"But I want *you,* babe." Holt reaches over and puts his hand on my knee.

"I like this dress. Is it new?" He puts the car into drive and pulls out onto the road, making sure to look over his shoulder before merging.

"No. I've had it for a while. There's just not a lot of things that fit me right now." I fluff the bottom of the dress out and smooth out the fabric.

"Once you're not pregnant anymore, we can get you back into the gym and back to your pre-pregnancy weight." He winks.

"Sounds good." Suddenly, I feel little. I sink back into my seat.

"But we will have to be strict with your diet and work out regime."

"We have quite some time before that."

"I just want you to be the best you that you can be." He squeezes my knee tightly and holds it for a minute before letting go of the grip. "Oh, before I forget. I'm pretty private about my information, so if you could stop sharing your location to anyone, I'd appreciate it."

"Oh, uhm..."

"It's just because my ex would show up to my last house and

cause a lot of problems. If you don't want to, that's fine. We can just go back to your place."

I dig through my small crossbody and pull out my phone. "It's no problem. I understand. Your privacy is important."

As much as I understand, I can't help but feel torn about removing my families access to my location. Things seem to be so on edge between Holt and I right now, that I don't want to give him anymore reason to be upset.

"Thanks for understanding, babe. You're amazing." He gives one more squeeze on my knee before pulling his hand away and putting it on the steering wheel. I lean my head back on the seat and look out the window, watching the buildings pass as we drive through Dryer Hill.

I MUST HAVE DOZED off because I jolt awake when we come to a stop. It takes a minute for my eyes to adjust to the lack of light. I wipe away some drool that pooled at the edge of my mouth with the back of my hand. I must have been asleep for some time.

"You're finally awake! I'm glad because I definitely wouldn't have been able to carry you inside. We're here."

"Where is here? I feel like I was asleep for hours."

"Port Green. I just needed to get something, but we're going to go back to Dryer Hill now."

"Isn't Port Green like an hour and a half outside of Dryer?"

"It is. Now, lock the doors and don't open them until I come back."

My gut twists in warning as he opens the door. The second it closes behind him, I click the lock. Twice. I watch him as he walks up a flight of stairs and knocks on door to a broken down house. At least I *think* it's a house. I can't really make out where we are because there's literally not a single light on.

In the distance, Holt disappears from view into the mouth of the building. Panic rises in my chest, and I pull out my phone, immediately sharing my location back to my mom, sisters, and Gracie. My phone vibrates almost instantly.

> Gracie: Why did it just notify me that you shared your location? When did you stop?

> Daphne: Seriously. Me too. What the fuck?

> Gracie: Did he tell you to stop sharing your location?

I roll my eyes.

> Daphne: You have to see how dangerous that is?

> Gracie: Liv? Please say something.

> Me: Can't talk now.

I faintly hear a door shut and can barely make out Holt walking back to the car.

> Daphne: You can't be fucking serious, Olivia.

> Gracie: Seriously?

I turn off my phone screen and shove my phone back into my bag. I don't unlock the door until I can see it's Holt and he's standing at the driver's side door. Without saying anything he opens the glove compartment and throws something into it, closing it before I get a chance to see.

"Why are we here, Holt?" He puts the car into drive and speeds out of there so fast, that my head slams into the seat. "What is going on? I'm scared and you're not saying anything?"

He hits his fists onto the steering wheel and scrunches his face. "Why are you asking so many fucking questions, Olivia?"

I shrug and sink myself even deeper into my seat. My hand finds its way to my lower belly, and I cradle the bottom of my stomach, almost to remind myself that I'm not alone. If I wasn't already anxious, the way he's driving would sure do it. Holt is weaving in and out of traffic, definitely driving over the speed limit.

"I'm... 'm sorry, Holt. I won't ask any more questions." I swallow and try to steady my voice. "Please, slow down." A lump builds up in my throat and I choke back a sob.

He looks over at me. His brows are furrowed in anger but his features quickly soften. The car slows down and he reaches across the center divider, gently running his finger up my face. It takes me a moment to notice he wiped away a tear that was streaming down my cheek.

"I didn't mean to scare you. It overwhelms me when you question me like that." I nod and give him a small smile. "Now, what can I do to cheer my girl up?"

"I don't mean to be a party pooper, but I'm actually exhausted. I'd really love to just go back to your place and sleep."

"Your wish is my command, baby." He reaches down and puts his hand on my leg. I cross my arms in front of my chest and watch as the trees eventually turn into buildings. I stay silent for the next hour and listen while he plays his music on shuffle.

We pull into a driveway in a neighborhood I've never been in before and he puts the car into park. I'm beyond relieved when he tells me that this is his house. I get out of the car and pull my duffle bag from the backseat, cautiously following him up the steps and in the front door.

Holt's house is cold and empty. There's no decoration or color literally anywhere. His couch is leather and black, and a love seat sits in front of a huge television.

We trek down a long hallway and he points to each of the three doors at the end. "This is the bathroom, my bedroom, and the guest room." He walks into the room he pointed out as his. There's literally only a bed and dresser in the room. The entire house seems empty, and it makes me want to go back home, but I'm so exhausted I could sleep anywhere.

I rustle through my duffle bag and pull out a pair of my pajamas. In the bathroom, I shut and lock the door before pulling my phone from my bag. I'm *not* surprised when I see all the missed texts.

Gracie: What the fuck is going on?

Daphne: If I don't hear from you in like an hour I'm calling the cops.

Mattie: Jeez. What did I miss?

Daphne: I don't even know.

Me: I'm fine. I'm at Holt's house. I'll have to fill you guys in later. I'm safe.

Daphne: I'm half tempted to come and get you.

> Me: Don't. I'll be home in a couple of days.

> Me: I have my doctor's appointment Tuesday and then I'll come home.

Holt knocks on the door. "Everything okay in there?" I almost drop my phone in the sink but end up catching it before it hits.

"Yeah, just changing. Be out in a second!"

> Me: I'll text you guys later. Love you

I slide my phone back into my bag and hurriedly switch into my pajamas. I open the door, practically crashing into Holt when I step out of the door.

"Oh, sorry."

"Ready for bed?"

"Yes. I'm exhausted." He escorts me back to his room where I put everything in my duffle bag and zip it up. I turn around and meet Holt's gaze. He pats the bed next to him, inviting me to come lay down. I smile and crawl beneath the covers. His arm wraps around my waist, pulling me close.

"I'm sorry I yelled at you earlier, baby." He nuzzles into my neck.

"It's okay," I whisper into the empty room.

"It's not. I shouldn't have. It won't happen again."

I nod, knowing he can't see it but can feel the movement. I don't know how to respond. This isn't the first time he's yelled at me and something deep inside of me knows it won't be the last either.

BECK

14

*T*oday is Olivia's sixteen week doctor's appointment. This will be the first time in a month that I've seen or talked to her, really. We've texted here and there, but it seems to only be right before school starts and during her lunch break. I've seen Daphne at shows here and there and spoken to her, but she says Olivia has been staying off and on at her boyfriend's house.

Apparently, nobody trusts him.

I'm getting close to wrapping up my bunk bed commission. Since I need to leave early, I chose today to paint the wood. It's going to be in light pink because it's going in their daughter's room. I start with the primer and put a coat of the pink on. There were over a dozen pieces of wood, so I'll just have to finish tomorrow. My phone alarm goes off, alerting me that it's time to start cleaning up so I can go to the doctor's appointment.

My dad's office door shuts, signaling his daily walk through.

He stops at everyone's work area before coming to mine. "Today is Olivia's big ultrasound?"

"Yeah. The doctor said since she's almost sixteen weeks, we should be able to see what the baby is."

My dad pats me on the shoulder and smiles. "I sure am excited. Mom's been bursting at the seams to start buying stuff."

"Me, too. I decided that I'm going to buy a house." I pause and take a deep breath. "But don't worry about Blaire. I already talked to my landlord and since we have been good tenants, he's going to transfer the rental agreement to her."

"I think that's a great idea, son. I'm proud of you. When are you going to start looking?"

"I've already started, actually. I saw a few houses, but I'm seeing one tonight after the appointment that I have a *really* good feeling about."

"Good. Good. I can't wait to hear all about it. Is it close by?"

"I focused on the area closest to Olivia's school, so that it was easier for her to do pick up or drop offs when the baby gets old enough. Or even stay if she needs to."

My dad's eyes grow in shock, but he smirks and dips his chin. "Alright. Well, I gotta get back. Let us know how the appointment goes."

"Will do."

My phone chimes with an alert, Olivia's specific ringtone, so I pull it out to check.

Freckles: Is there any way you can pick me up from work?

Freckles: My car isn't here.

Me: Sure. Be there soon.

Freckles: Thank you so much 😊

I have a few questions, but my main one is, why doesn't she have her car? I bite my tongue, for now, and decide it's best to wait to talk to her about it. Our *friendship* is still fairly new, and I don't want to push her past her comfort zone. I grab a trash bag and walk out to my truck. It's literally only me ever in it, so I never clean the damn thing. I grab all of the food wrappers, empty soda cans, and whatever random articles of trash I can find and toss it all in the bag. For someone who keeps their house pretty clean, I sure don't take care of my truck.

Her school is about fifteen minutes down the road and another ten from the doctor's office. I put my key in the ignition and turn it, listening to the roar of my engine.

On the main road, music flows from my speakers and fills the cab with the sounds of my favorite metal band. One of the plus sides of living in Dryer Hill is the lack of traffic.

It's not long before I'm in front of Olivia's school. The door to the office swings open and there's a chance that I'm hallucinating because time slows as she steals every ounce of light the sun produces. Her long blonde hair swings behind her as she waves to the people in the office. She's wearing a floral, flowy short-sleeve dress that accentuates her small baby bump.

"Hey! Thanks so much for picking me up." She pulls open the passenger door and slides in.

"It's not a problem." This is as good of a time as any, so I jump in with the question. "What happened to your car?" I pull out onto the street.

"Oh, *erm.* Holt's car didn't have gas, and he had to run some errands."

So, he leaves her carless? I suck in a deep breath.

"Holt's your boyfriend?"

"*Boyfriend* is a loose term. He hasn't actually asked me. I guess it's just kind of implied." She shrugs and chews on her bottom lip. I can tell by the way she moves her hand to her arm, she's uncomfortable so I decide to change the subject.

"Are you excited about your appointment?"

"I am! Daphne and Gracie want to throw us a gender reveal party. Your family is obviously invited." *Us.*

"What is that?"

"It's a party where the baby's gender is revealed in some way. They want a cake!" She covers her face with her hands, "Oh shoot!"

"What's wrong?"

"I'm supposed to take the envelope from the doctor's office to the bakery. I totally forgot when I let Holt have my car."

"I can take it. Which bakery?"

"Are you sure?"

"Yeah. I wouldn't offer it if I wasn't."

"Crumbs and Cakes. Off of Main St." I nod. "You're absolutely the best." She reaches over and pats my thigh.

I pull into the parking lot of the hospital, where the doctor's office is, and find a parking spot as close as I can that will fit the truck.

We walk through the parking lot towards the front door of the hospital, turning right to go down the hallway that leads to the offices. My finger lightly brushes against the top of Olivia's hand and I literally *ache* with the desire to lace her fingers in mine. I open the door to the office for her and walk in behind. She goes and checks in with the receptionist while I find a seat. There're only a few other people in the waiting room, so there's plenty of seating available. Olivia turns from the front desk and looks around for a moment. She smiles at everyone in the room before her eyes land on me and she joins me.

"Clara said it shouldn't take very long, but we have to see the ultrasound technician first."

"Clara?"

"The receptionist. I try really hard to remember everyone's know that works here. The nurse I see every appointment is Eden. Which reminds me, I need to ask her about the book she was reading last month. Then there's three ultrasound techs: Tilly, Harper, and Beau. I think I'm seeing Harper today. Which is great because she's also pregnant and should have found out what she was having last week."

A small chuckle escapes and I shake my head.

"What?" She tilts hers.

"You are just one of the only people I've ever met who takes the time to actually learn everyone's name and about their life." Her face falls. "It's not a bad thing. I like it."

"You don't think I'm too...nosey." She looks down and starts picking at her cuticles.

"What? No. Not at all. I think you care about people very deeply. That's not a bad quality, Freckles."

She glances up at me with gratitude in her eyes. I want to reach out and touch her, but more than anything I want to kick the ass of anyone who's ever made her question anything about herself. I open my mouth to respond, to let her know she's not too much of *anything*, but her name is called, and she turns to raise her hand. Olivia stands and walks to the door, mindlessly I follow. *I'd follow her anywhere.* The nurse takes her weight and blood pressure. Olivia is anxiously waiting to discuss Eden's most recent read with her. The moment the cuff is off, she can't ask fast enough.

"So, how was the book?"

"It was *so* good! The husband was a contract killer, but it was *very* Sweet Home Alabama-esque. I would absolutely have to recommend it."

"I will definitely check it out!"

Eden takes us down the hall and into exam room four, letting us know that the ultrasound tech will be in first. Olivia goes into the room alone so that she can change into the gown whileI stand outside with my back against the wall and my arms crossed across my chest. I ignore the looks and smirks by all the nurses who are walking past me. Most of them we went to school with, and I've probably slept with at least one or two, maybe more. I've been to every one of Olivia's doctor's appointments since she told me about the baby, but this is the first ultrasound she's had since the initial one. The door creaks open and Olivia's head pops out, but I see her hair first.

"Hey, you can come in now."

I slide in through the door and sit on one of the two chairs that line the wall. The paper crinkles beneath Olivia as she slides onto the examination table. She looks at me and lifts her shoulders up.

"I am so nervous!"

"I am too, kind of," I confess.

"Do you have a preference?"

"On what the baby is?" She nods. "Not really. I just want a healthy baby."

"Me, too, but I think I'd love to have a boy." There's a knock on the door and the ultrasound technician walks in. I can tell by the excitement on Olivia's face, this must be Harper.

"Hey, Olivia. Can you confirm your date of birth for me?" Olivia confirms, and I make a mental note to remember that her birthday is the thirteenth of July. "Perfect, lay back for me." Olivia does as she's told and adjusts herself until she's comfortable. "This might be a little cold." Harper squeezes some gel onto Olivia's stomach and runs the ultrasound wand onto it.

Obviously, I haven't seen Olivia's stomach since our one night together. It's a little round below her belly button, but I think it's the cutest fucking thing I've ever seen. Especially knowing it's *my* baby.

"How are you feeling? Did you find out what you're having?"

"I'm okay. Exhausted. We found out it's a boy!"

Olivia squeals and Harper looks away from the computer screen for a moment before turning to look back.

"Alright and here is your baby." She turns the screen to where we can both look at it. I'm not a super emotional guy, but I have to choke back a sob when I see the baby, *our baby*, swimming around on the screen. "I know we are doing a gender reveal party so when I get to that point, I'll turn the screen and give it to you in a sealed envelope."

Olivia turns to me and smiles.

THE REST of her appointment went smoothly. The doctor was satisfied with the baby's growth and development and had little to be concerned with. I could physically see the relief of that news lift off of Olivia's shoulders. Afterwards, she asks me to take her back to her apartment. I've never been there, so I have to type it into my GPS. I pull up against the sidewalk and put the truck in park.

"Thank you again for taking me, Beckett."

"I'm here anytime you need anything."

"I appreciate that." She reaches for the door and clicks her tongue. "Please don't forget to take the envelope to the bakery."

"I wouldn't dream of disappointing you, Freckles."

"See you Saturday?"

"I'll be there."

She jumps down out of the truck and turns to me one last time before she shuts the door. "Daph and Gracie said that we are supposed to wear whatever color we want the baby to be, pink for girl and blue for boy."

"I literally don't own anything except black and gray."

"I guess you get to go shopping then." She teases and shuts the door. I watch until she disappears into the front of her apartment building before driving two blocks over to the bakery.

I pull up to the line of buildings on Maine Street and into one of the designated parking spots labeled **Ten Minute Parking ONLY.** The door to this place is fucking yellow. Not a light pastel yellow either. Like an *in your face* canary yellow. When I step inside, the door doesn't *ding* like most businesses. No, instead it sounds like wind chimes in the summer wind.

"Hello! I'll be right there!" a voice sings from the back. I look around at the different cookies, cakes and cupcakes that are in the refrigerators while I wait. Whoever this baker is, they sure are talented.

The bakery has white and soft pink striped walls with hot pink and gold accents around the room. There's a couple of small white tables along the window lined wall, but other than that the decoration is minimal. Except for the wall that is completely covered in pink, white, and yellow artificial flowers.

"Hi! What sweet treat can I interest you in today?" She must have snuck up behind me while I was looking at the walls. Her long dark hair is pulled back into a loose braid. She smiles big and looks at me with questions in her ice blue eyes.

"I'm here to drop off an envelope."

"Oh! You must be friends of Daphne."

"Uhm, sure. I'm the father of the baby, Beckett."

"Hi! I'm Elizabeth." She sticks her hand out and I shake it. "Congratulations on your baby. I'm a mom myself. It's amazing."

"Thanks. Here's you are." I hand over the envelope.

"Great. Thank you *so* much! I'm so excited to make this cake. It'll be ready for pick up Saturday at ten."

"I think Daphne or Gracie are picking it up. I don't know."

"Not a problem." She smiles.

"Alright, well, Thanks." I turn and walk towards the door. "Shit. I'm sure it's already in some notes, but Olivia has a nut allergy."

"Yes! That's actually my specialty. We are an allergy friendly bakery. But thank you *so* much for reminding me."

I throw a thumbs up and walk out of the door. *Why did I just thumbs up the baker? Idiot.*

Me: Envelope is delivered.

Freckles: You're seriously the best! Thank you!

Me: Anytime.

Freckles:

I start the engine and look out onto the street before I put the car in drive. Across the street, I see a car that looks suspiciously familiar with a person who is even *more* familiar. Michelle is standing in an alleyway with some random man. She looks around in the most obvious way I've *ever* seen before pulling cash out of her bag and handing it to this dude. I can only see the back of his head, but since he has Olivia's car, I think it's safe to say this is the boyfriend.

He slides something into her clenched hand, which she throws in her purse, before hurriedly jumping into the car and speeding off down Maine Street.

What. The. Fuck.

Olivia

15

Sixteen Weeks Pregnant

Since the girls requested us to wear whatever color we had hope for, I ordered a long sleeve blue maxi dress. It's tight enough that it hugs my little belly, but not too tight that I'm uncomfortable. My mom and sisters are all wearing different shades of pink, but Gracie is also "team boy". Mattie helped me with my hair by loosely curling it and twisting half of it back into a braid.

I don't think I have ever seen so much pink and blue before. Ever. Daphne and Gracie did such a wonderful job decorating our apartment. There's an adorable craft paper banner across the top of the island that reads "He or she, what will baby be?" beneath a blue and pink bow that scales the top of the banner.

The cake they ordered from Crumbs and Cakes is literally the cutest thing I've ever seen in my life. It's a layered heart shaped cake decorated with vintage edges and delicate little pink and blue flowers.

But my favorite decoration *has* to be the garland of blue and pink bows strung across the walls.

We decided to hold the gender reveal here because I want it to be intimate. The only people invited are Beck, both our families, and our friends. I'm excited to see how everyone interacts with one another, but I'd be lying if I said I wasn't nervous to see how Holt is with everyone. Especially since he has already voiced how he feels about Beck.

"When's everyone coming?" I ask from where I was banished, the couch.

"The invite said two."

"I am *so* anxious, I might burst." I check the time on my phone and let out a groan. It's *almost* two.

"Are you sure you don't just have to pee again?" Gracie jokes and pours herself a mimosa.

"I *always* have to pee."

There's a knock at the front door and I practically leap off the couch. I recognize the guys from the band when they walk through the front door, but I'm surprised to see all of them except for Tieran in bright pink.

"Yes! More team girl!" Daphne says and throws her hands around Derek's neck.

I walk by them and give Tieran a high five. He laughs and follows me to the couch. "There seems to be little people who are hoping for a boy," he whispers.

"Right? I was thinking the same thing."

Another knock.

This time, Derek opens the door and Holt walks in. He looks Derek up and down, like he's sizing him up or something. My stomach does a flip and I really hope they don't start fighting. Holt looks around the room, stopping when he finds me. I can recognize the look on his face almost immediately when he sees me sitting with Tieran. I'm so focused on the look in his eye that I don't notice he was wearing a gray shirt until Gracie asks, "Where's your pink or blue?"

"Yeah, I wasn't doing that."

Gracie holds herself back from saying what I know she wants to say and looks at me. Her eyebrow raises and she is *visibly* biting her lip. I shrug a little and meet Holt.

"I'm glad you came."

"Is that Beck?" He points to Tieran.

"No, that's Tieran, one of his friends from his band. He's really nice. You guys might get along."

Holt wraps his arms around my waist and bends down. I can smell the whiskey before he even opens his mouth to whisper, "Did you spread your legs for him, too?" I hold back the tears that are burning my eyes and shake my head no. He lets out a *hmph* and makes a beeline over to the snacks.

Everyone's staring at me, I know it, but I can't meet their faces. Instead, I scramble to the bathroom.

My stomach sinks the moment I hear another knock on the door. I know it's Beck, but I don't trust that Holt won't make things uncomfortable. I really hoped he'd be friendly with everyone, especially because of the baby, but I guess I was wrong.

Did you spread your legs for him, too?

I finish washing my hands and open the door, making sure I'm smiling. No matter how fake it is. Celeste, Grant, and Blaire are all dressed in blue. "I see you guys are also team boy!"

"Not me." I turn around to Beck dressed in pink, holding a bouquet of sunflowers. "I had to search several stores for this shade of pink, ya know."

"It's a really good shade. What is that? Salmon?"

"I think it's more of a flamingo pink, don't you?" He raises a brow and for a second, I can't tell if he's joking or if he's serious. It only takes the slight movement of the corner of his mouth to make me bust out in laughter. Holt's arm slides around my waist, and I snap my lips shut.

"These are for you." Beck hands me a bouquet of flowers. I inhale the scent of them deeply, especially the white roses. Even though sunflowers are my absolute favorite flower, roses are my favorite to smell.

"I'll take those!" Mattie exclaims and walks with them towards the sink.

Beck looks up from me, towards Holt, and his lips lose any hint of a smile.

"You must be the boyfriend." His voice is dry.

"I am." Holt puffs out his chest and squeezes me tighter. I swear if he could, he would pee on me to mark his territory. I don't know if everyone else in here can feel the tension, but suddenly all of the guys in Skarred stand behind Beck. Even Tieran crosses his arm in a way that says *don't start something you can't finish*.

"Okay so, let's get this party going," my mom announces. Celeste sings her agreement. I can tell they're both trying to lower the raging testosterone.

I wiggle my way out of Holt's grip and walk closer to Beck, who has not broken the stare down with Holt. I lightly touch his arm and smile. "Are you ready to find out what the baby is?"

"I would love to find out what *our* baby is," he responds, not breaking eye contact with Holt until he finishes his sentence. His eyes soften when they meet mine and I fight the urge to lace my fingers with his.

Daphne directs us to the cake with two champagne glasses. "Okay, so I saw this in a video, and I thought it was so freaking cute. You guys push the mouth of the glasses into the cake and pull it out, then we will see what the baby is!"

"Sounds easy enough." Beck takes the glasses from my sister and hands one to me. We turn to face the cake, both putting the glasses on the top. "Look at me." My stomach swirls with butterflies at his command. I smile and fight the urge to look at Holt. I know he is probably fuming right now. I look into Beck's eyes and the room around us seems to disappear. We push the top of the glasses down through the layers of cake and frosting. "Ready?" I nod and pull the glass away from the cake.

Together, we look down. Everyone around us erupts in cheers and *whoops* when the color pink is revealed. I can't help but feel disappointed that it's not blue. I for sure thought it was going to be a boy. I had everything, down to his name, picked out.

"Hey," Beck whispers. "It's okay to be disappointed. I know you wanted a boy."

I shake my head and smile, trying to fight back the onset of tears. "I feel stupid."

"For what?"

"Not feeling as excited as I should."

"You can feel disappointed and still be happy about something. Don't feel stupid, Freckles." He puts his cake filled glass onto the counter and pulls me into a hug. I close my eyes and breathe him in deep.

We turn to our family and friends, who are either still cheering or in my mother's and Celeste's case, sobbing. Except Holt. Who is standing there with his arms crossed and his brows furrowed. I'm definitely going to hear what he has to say later.

Beck walks through the crowd right towards his family. Blaire wraps her arms around him and buries her face into his shoulder. His arms tighten around her and for a second, just a second, I see a different version of Beck. The walls he has built up to protect himself are down and his entire demeanor softens.

Daphne and Mattie come beside me, placing their heads on my shoulders.

"You guys ready for a niece?" I ask.

"Are *you* ready for us to have a niece?" Daphne counters.

"She's going to be so freaking spoiled." Mattie sniffles.

Mom walks to the couch and calls me over. I kiss both of my sisters on the top of their heads and walk through the crowd to sit beside my mom. She pats me on the knee and pulls a bag off of the floor. It's a gift bag that is light gray with a sun and the lyrics to *you are my sunshine* are written across rain clouds.

"What's this?"

"It's just a little something I made." Mom smiles and puts the bag onto my lap. I pull out the white tissue paper and pull out a folded up blanket. It's a beautifully crocheted baby blanket with stripes of white, cream, and two different shades of yellow. Mom runs her hand across it and smiles. "I wanted to be the first one to give you something for the baby. I started making it right after you told me."

I pick it up and lift it to my chest, squeezing it tightly as I choke back the sob that's building in my throat. "I...I love it."

"I'm glad, sweet girl. You're gonna make a great mama." Mom wraps her arms around me and pulls me into a hug.

AFTER TWO MORE HOURS OF hugs, tears, and laughter...I am tapped out. Daphne and Gracie spent the last hour cleaning up the aftermath of the party, refusing me every time I tried to help. Daphne ended up going home with Derek and I don't know where Gracie went, but she and Hayes seem to be getting a little friendly. Beck and Tieran hang back later than everyone else and at one point, it was just the three of us and Holt.

Now, it's the two of us.

I have already showered and changed into a matching short and cami set. The atmosphere around Holt is tense. I know something is bothering him, I just have to find the right way to break the ice.

"How did you like everyone?" I test the waters. Holt shrugs and changes through the channels on the TV in the living room. "Are you okay?"

He turns off the TV and faces me, slamming down the remote on the coffee table. "No, I'm actually *not* okay."

I rear back. "What's wrong?"

"Do you realize how fucking stupid it makes me look when you practically *throw* yourself at every other man here?"

"Who was I throwing myself at?" I grab one of the pillows off the couch and place it against my torso, desperate for some type of comfort.

"Literally everyone. Especially Beck."

"I am carrying Beck's child, Holt. It's important that he and I have a friendship. Which is all we are, *friends.*"

"Friends? You don't practically fuck your friends in front of everyone."

"What are you even talking about?"

"That little hug after the cake cutting? You looked like you were enjoying it a little too much."

"I don't know how you got that out of a hug."

"You really are *that* stupid, Olivia." The way he says my name sends a chill down my spine. I don't know if I should stand or if I should move to a different spot on the couch, but something in my gut says I'm in danger. "You were flirting with everything that had a dick."

"I'm…I'm sorry, Holt. I didn't realize I was flirting."

"You're *my* girlfriend!" he shouts. I want to correct him. I want to tell him I'm *not* his girlfriend because he hasn't asked me, but instead I stay quiet. "You're my fucking girlfriend and you were acting like a slut."

"I'm sorry." It's all I can say.

"You're *sorry*? Sorry!?" In one fluid motion he moves his hands under the coffee table and next thing I know it's up in the air. The remote goes flying and hits the television, causing a spider web crack to form from the top left corner. I tighten my grip on the pillow, pushing it against my belly. He walks over to the side table where the vase of sunflowers is sitting. "He brought you fucking flowers, Olivia." I open my mouth to respond, but before I have a chance, the vase is flying across the room and right towards me.

It crashes into my shoulder and water spills out all over me and the pillow. I look up to meet his eyes. Eyes that were full of anger and now hold an apology. "Olivia…I. I just get so mad." He starts to walk towards me.

"Don't come any closer." I jump up and off the couch.

"Olivia."

I grab my phone off the counter, open the door, and run down the hallway. My heartbeat echoes in my ears, drowning out the sound of my own breathing as I take the stairs down to the main lobby. I pick up my phone to call the only person I know who would be here without question.

The phone rings twice and when I hear his voice, I feel like I can breathe again.

"Beck. I need you."

BECK

16

didn't know it was possible for my heart to beat as fast as it is, but there's a chance it's going to rip out of my chest. I jump up from where I was sitting on my couch and yank on my shoes.

"Olivia? What's wrong." I ask, phone between my head and shoulder.

"I...can you come and get me, please?"

God, this can't be good. My vision blurs fuzzy with rage and I can't keep my thoughts straight. I'm out the front door without a second thought.

"Are you at your apartment?"

"I'm in the lobby."

"Okay. I'll be there in five."

"St—stay on the phone with me please." The fear in her voice makes me physically ill. I can *hear* that she's shaking, and I know it has something to do with that piece of shit, Holt. I should have told her I saw him and Michelle dealing.

"Whatever you need."

I hop into the truck and speed off down the road, practically peeling out as I pull onto the street. I know I need to calm down, at least a little bit, so that she doesn't feel more anxious than she already is.

"Are you almost here?" she quavers.

"I'm pulling up now."

"Okay."

"Are you okay?"

"Not right now, but I will be."

I pull up against the sidewalk, accidentally running over the curb some. I throw it in park, get out and run into her apartment complex. She is pacing back and forth in the main lobby. Her hair and shirt are completely drenched and she isn't wearing any shoes. Without thinking, I take her face in my hands. It's obvious she's been crying because her eyes are red and blotchy. I scan her face and then my eyes look over the rest of her exposed flesh.

That's when I see it.

The dark red, practically purple, bruise on her arm.

"What the fuck is that? Who did that to you?" I'm vibrating with violence.

She looks away, tearing her face from my hands. Her cheeks redden with embarrassment.

"Olivia. Did that fucking asshole do this to you?" She nods, refusing to meet my eyes. I try to steady my shaking hands and give her my keys. "Go sit in my car."

"But Beck…"

"Freckles. Please." I don't want her to be in the apartment, in the building even, when I come face to face with Holt. I kiss her forehead and usher her towards the door. She casts an unsure glance over her shoulder, tears glistening on her cheek.

I was already mad, but now I'm livid. I don't wait for the elevator, opting instead to use the stairs. Each step fuels the fire that's raging through my veins.

When I get to the door, I take a deep breath and throw it open.

"Olivia, baby, is that you?" His stupid ass gets up from the couch and makes for the door.

"No. It's not Olivia."

"Beck?" His eyes flare wide.

"Tonight, I'm your worst fucking nightmare. How dare you touch her. How dare you make her fucking cry." We're toe to toe in the living room and the air crackles with fury.

"Look. It was a misunderstanding." He raises his hand.

"No. You look, asshole. Stay the fuck away from my girl."

"Your girl?"

"Yes. *My* fucking girl."

"Last I checked, she's my girl." The longer I look at his face the madder I get, so I punch him.

His nose cracks under the pressure of my fist and the noise riles me further.

Dazed, he falls back onto the floor, hand clutching at his face. I hover above him, holding his shirt in one hand as I continue to wail him with the other.

My vision bleeds red and I can feel myself fading into the nothingness of pure hatred. Blood is pouring from his nose and his right eye is swollen shut. I might kill this piece of shit with my bare hands.

"B...Beck?" A shaky voice says my name. *Olivia.* I cock my elbow back, ready to hit him again as my chest heaves with anger. "Please stop," she sobs. I look away from the trash in my hand and turn to look over my shoulder. She lifts her palm and runs it lightly over her stomach.

"Why didn't you stay in the car?" I sigh, releasing the grip I have on Holt's shirt. He lands with a small *thud* and rolls over onto his side, groaning as he curls into the fetal position.

"I didn't want you to do something crazy, but I see I was too late."

"Get some of your things. You're staying at my house."

"Just," she takes a deep breath, "don't kill him."

"I won't."

While she gets her stuff, I go into the kitchen and wipe the blood off my hands. My knuckles are red and cracked, they will definitely be bruised tomorrow. In the living room, I flip over the coffee table and try to pick up some of the things that were scattered during his hissy fit. Olivia comes out of her room with a small duffle bag. Her eyes are redder than they were before, so I know she hasn't stopped crying.

"I'll meet you downstairs," I say.

Holt mutters something under his breath, but I can't make it out. Once the door shuts behind her, I hover over him again, taking his shirt in my hand.

"If you so much as contact her, I'll do one of two things: I'll either kill you or turn you in for dealing." The eye that's *not* swollen shut widens. "Yeah, I saw you dealing to Michelle. She'd definitely turn you in if it meant getting on my good side. Don't fucking push me. Be gone by the morning. Got it?"

He nods and I let him fall again. I stomp out of the apartment and over to the elevator.

While I wait for it to get to the floor, I send Derek a text.

> Me: If Daphne is still with you, don't let her go home.

> Me: I'll explain tomorrow.

> Derek: You okay?

The elevator arrives at the floor and the doors open. I get inside and hit the button for the lobby.

> Me: Yeah.

I'm aware of the looks I'm getting as I walk through the people

coming and going. There's blood spray on my arms and shirt, but I don't care. He probably would have been dead if Olivia hadn't come up to make sure he wasn't. I hop in my truck where Olivia sniffles and frantically wipes away at the tears that are falling from her eyes.

"I'm sorry," I whisper.

"For what?"

"That you had to see that." *I promise I'm not a monster.* Olivia shrugs. I put the truck into park and pulled out onto the street. "Do you wanna tell me what happened?"

"He accused me of flirting and sleeping with all the guys in your band."

"What?"

"He said I was too *friendly* with everyone, and it just escalated from there. I just made him mad."

"I'm going to stop you there. *You* did absolutely nothing wrong, Freckles. That guy is a piece of shit. If he got mad, that was on him. *Not you.*"

"Okay."

"No. I want you to repeat it. Say *it wasn't my fault.*"

"It wasn't my fault," she whispers, her breath shaky.

"If he calls or texts, I want you to tell me. Okay?" She nods. "Listen to me, Olivia, and I mean *really* listen. This won't be the last time."

"I know." She wipes tears away from her face and lifts her legs up, bringing her knees to her chest.

"I am sorry that you had to go through that. I'm so sorry."

"You didn't do anything wrong. Everyone warned me. My mom and sisters, they knew. I'm sure Gracie did. I just ignored all the signs."

I'm sorry I didn't do more to protect you.

We pull up to my house and I grab her duffle bag before sliding out of the cab of my truck. I follow her up to the front door and unlock it, motioning for her to go in before me.

"Do you need to shower or anything?"

"I should, but I'm so tired."

"Well, you know where it is if you decide you want to. You can take my bed, and I'll sleep on the couch."

"No. Please don't let me put you out."

"You're not putting me out. You're carrying my child, Freckles. I won't let you sleep on the couch."

She gives me a slight smile and walks down the hallway. I follow into my room so that I can grab a change of clothes. She pulls the comforter back and sits on the edge of the bed. I lift up the shirt and throw it in my clothes hamper and do the same thing to my jeans, pulling on my pajama pants.

"Beckett? Will you sleep with me? I don't want to be alone."

"Whatever you need." I walk around to the opposite side of the bed and get under the blankets. I'm kind of relieved I'm not sleeping on the couch. I'd do whatever she needs, but that couch really does suck.

"Thank you. For coming to save me."

"I want to say *anytime*, but let's not make it a habit". She laughs, and not a courtesy laugh, a real one.

"Good night." She nestles into the pillow and I find it hard to resist not pulling her into me.

"Night." I lay on my back and watch the fan spin around. There's a conflicting emotion swirling inside of me. I *should* feel bad about beating Holt up, but I don't. And if he even comes near Olivia again, I won't stop myself.

OLIVIA IS STILL SOUND asleep when I creep out of my room. I don't want to wake her after the night she had, so I make sure I shut the door quietly. When I turn around, I almost run into my sister.

"Is that Olivia?"

"Yes."

"Did she sleep over?" She raises a brow.

"*Mmhmm*, but nothing happened. Her piece of shit boyfriend-not-really-her-boyfriend hurt her."

"Did you kill him?"

"I would have if she hadn't stopped me." I scoot past her and towards the kitchen, where I grab my mug and start up my coffee maker. "I need to go back to her apartment and handle the mess. Can you stay here so that she's not alone when she wakes up?" My sister nods and looks at me with concerned filled eyes. "I just want to make sure he's out."

"She's that girl you had a crush on in high school, huh?" I turn and lean up against the counter, nodding in confirmation. "Shit. I knew her name sounded familiar. Does she know?"

"No." I shake my head. "It will complicate things."

"But it's *so* obvious that you love her."

"It's complicated, Squirt."

"So, you *doooo* love her," she teases. I shrug because I'm honestly unsure what I feel for Olivia. I've had a soft spot for her since the day we got paired together in class. There was a constant dark cloud above my head, but she became the sunlight that broke through.

"I have to go. I'll be back."

Blaire waves dramatically and I roll my eyes and pull out my phone to send a text to Olivia so she at least knows where I am.

> Me: I didn't want to wake you. I have a couple of errands to run. Be back soon.

> Me: My sister is home though, so you're not alone.

I slide my phone back into my pocket and head to my truck. I grip the steering wheel a little too tight driving to her apartment building. If that motherfucker is still there, what am I supposed to do? He'll end up dead and I'll end up in jail, which won't be good for anyone.

I pull into the parking garage, which my truck is almost too tall for, next to Olivia's car. My heart rate quickens as I walk into the open elevator. I try to prepare myself for what's going to happen next. The door to her apartment is unlocked, so I open it. I look behind every door and in every room, pleased to find that piece of shit is gone. He cleaned up the apartment, for the most part, but the TV in their living room is still shattered.

I check around the sectional, just to be safe.

There's a small puddle of dried blood on the tile. I can't leave that for Daphne or Olivia to be forced to clean up. In the kitchen, I let the water heat up and search for a rag and cleaning supplies. I look in the hall closet and find the floor cleaning supplies next to a mop and bucket. After grabbing the floor cleaner and the bucket, I go into the bathroom to look for a rag. I feel weird looking through Olivia's things, so I'm relieved when I open the cabinet under the sink and find a stack of rags. I grab one and go back to my task.

I only fill the bucket up a quarter of the way and add a small amount of the cleaning liquid into the water. In front of the blood stain, I get onto my knees, grab the rag out of the water and ring it out, ignoring the way my hands burn from the extreme temperature.

The rag hits the floor with a *splat* and I start to scrub off the dried blood.

It takes ages but finally, the blood is off of the floor. In the bathroom, I dump the rusty colored water down the drain. My phone starts to vibrate in my pocket, so I dry my hands off on my shirt, half expecting to see Derek or Blaire calling. I don't recognize the number, so I push accept and lift it to my ear.

"Hello?"

"Hi, is this Beckett Haven?" My stomach sinks. *Fuck, did Holt end up dying? Is this a cop or something?*

"Yes." I hold my breath.

"This is Raquel with Always Home Realty."

"Oh, sure. What can I do for you?" I close my eyes and

pinch the bridge of my nose. I'm able to take a deep breath now, but fuck I thought I killed Holt.

"I wanted to call and let you know that we had two homes become available this week in the Dryer Hill District, but only one fits the qualifications you needed. It's a short sale, so it would be pretty cut and dry."

"Great. I'm interested."

"Can you meet me there in say," she goes quiet, "thirty minutes?"

"I can do that."

"Great. See you soon! I'll send the address to this number."

WHEN I FOUND out Olivia was pregnant, it was important for me that the baby have stability. So, I knew I needed to buy a house. I just had no idea that it would be so hard to find one close to the high school she worked at. I didn't want her to have to worry about commuting too far with the baby, but I also wanted her to have space there if she wanted.

That's why I'm here, sitting in front of a three bedroom, two bathroom house waiting for a real estate agent.

According to the information I found on the internet, it's newly renovated and the deck has been recently redone, too. A black BMW pulls up behind me through my rearview mirror and assuming it's the agent, I get out of my truck.

"Mr. Haven?" she asks, stepping out of her car and closing the door.

"Beck is fine."

"Ready to go see the house?" I nod and follow her up the stairs that get up to the front door.

We walk into the open concept main room. The living room is front and center, with the breakfast nook and kitchen off to the left. There's plenty of windows allowing for natural lighting and I'm happy enough with the amount of cabinet space. The walls of the house are a bright white, which will *have* to change.

"As you can see, the natural lighting is amazing. The hardwood floor has been recently redone." I look down at the light wooden floors as I follow her toward the hallway. She points to the kitchen. "All the appliances are brand new and come with the house." There're three doors on the right side and two on the left. I open the first door on the left and find a linen closet. "Here's the first of the bedrooms with the first bathroom between them."

In the first bedroom, I immediately imagine Olivia using it as a studio. I can see her easel in the corner, paint scattered everywhere. Before I get too far ahead of myself, I head into the next room. *This* room will be the baby's room. Just like the room before, I let myself envision the baby's crib up against the wall, her toys scattered over the floor.

"Then here's the master bedroom with an attached, private bathroom."

I walk around the master and into the bathroom. "I like it."

"Are you interested in me writing up an offer?"

"Sure. Yeah. Let's do it."

"I'll go back to my office and get started. Keep a lookout in your email so that you can e-sign some documents for me."

I follow her out of the house and back to the cars where we say our goodbyes and get into our cars. I pull my phone out and see a missed call from Derek, so I call him back.

"So, are you going to finally fill me in?"

"Yeah, sorry." I let everything flow out of me. I tell him about watching shithead deal to Michelle, Olivia calling after the party, and me beating the shit out of him.

"Fuck, man. Are you okay?"

"Yeah. I cleaned up the mess, so tell Daph she's good to go back home."

"Thanks. I'll let her know when she gets out of the shower. You going home?"

"Yeah."

"Alright. See you later for practice?" I let my head fall back onto the headrest.

"I can't do it tonight, man."

He lets out a deep sigh and I know he's irritated, but I just don't want to leave Olivia for longer than I have to. "Alright, I get it."

"Thanks, D." We say our goodbyes and hang up the call.

I'm barely able to sit my phone down in the cup holder before it vibrates with an alert.

> Lance: Hey, man. Sage said she hasn't heard from you, and I just wanted to check in.

Fuck.

> Me: Sorry, man. Shit has just gotten crazy. I'll email her about the contract soon.

> Lance: You still have time. Just wanted to check in.

As if I wasn't starting to sink already, now I have to find a way to tell Derek I'm done with Skarred.

Olivia

17

Sixteen Weeks Pregnant

It took me two hours after waking up to finally crawl out of bed. I don't want to dig through my bag right now, so I go to Beck's closet and grab whatever shirt I can find. If I'm being honest, I don't even remember what I packed. My adrenaline was so high that I think I blacked out or something and just threw in random stuff. I decide on an old band t-shirt and pull it on over my head before rereading Beck's text message again, *be back soon.*

When I step out of Beck's bedroom, the scent of pancakes hits me in the face and I practically float towards the kitchen.

"That smells *so* good."

"Oh! Good morning." Blaire spins around with the spatula in her hand and smiles.

"Can I help with anything?"

"They're just about done but thank you. Just sit right there." She points at the table with the spatula.

"Are you sure there's not something I can do?"

"Positive!"

I raise my hands and go to sit down at the table, basically twiddling my thumbs while I

wait. "Do you know when Beck will be back? I must have been asleep so hard I didn't even notice that he left."

"He should be back soon. He just said he had some stuff to take care of."

Did he mean Holt when he said that?

"Oh. Okay."

She walks around the small island and puts a plate in front of me with two of

the most perfect pancakes I've ever seen in my life.

"These look and smell amazing."

"I don't know how to cook much, but I make a mean pancake. It's one of the couple of

things we almost always had the ingredients for as a kid, so I was practically making pancakes as a toddler." She gives me a cup of orange juice and sits down across from me with her own plate.

"Thank you." I take a drink from the glass, realizing that I have obviously not been

drinking the right OJ because this is *amazing*. We both start to cut up and eat our pancakes, which are absolutely delicious.

"Have you guys thought of a name for the baby yet?"

I shake my head and finish chewing my bite of food. "Now that we know she's a girl, I'm going to start making lists."

"I'm so excited to have a niece."

"I'm glad." I smile and take another bite of my pancake.

Blaire goes on to tell me about how much fun her new job is and how much she likes her bosses, but especially Charlie. I listen to her talk about how she wants to eventually get to the point where she can edit, but she likes being an assistant, and how she wants to go back to college. Which I absolutely encourage her to do.

My phone starts to vibrate with alert.

After alert, after alert.

"I'm so sorry," I whisper as I lift my phone screen up to see what's going on.

"You're totally fine. Are you done?" I nod and she takes my plate to the kitchen.

Daphne: What the fuck is going on?

Daphne: Derek just said something happened with Holt?

Gracie: Wait what happened with that asshole?

Daphne: Liv?

Gracie: I'm about to drive over to your fucking apartment.

Me: Well, I'm not there.

Daphne: Where the hell are you?

Me: Beck's.

Gracie: We'll come back to that.

Daphne: Seriously. We aren't letting that go.

Daphne: But what happened with Holt?

Me: He got really mad, broke our TV, and threw a vase and it hit me.

Daphne: IT HIT YOU

Daphne: ARE YOU OKAY

Me: Calm down with the caps.

Me: Beck came and got me, which is why I'm at his place.

Gracie: But are you okay?

Me: I have a bruise on my shoulder, but Beck…took care of Holt.

Gracie: …What do you mean?

Me: I don't think we will be seeing Holt ever again.

Daphne: Okay, but like…that's kind of hot?

I physically laugh out loud and look towards the kitchen to Blaire, who's doing dishes and oblivious to my conversation. I will *not* admit to my sister that it was in fact kind of hot.

Me: I think that I'll be back at the apartment tonight.

Gracie: Dinner soon?

Me: Sure.

Daphne: Are you sure you're okay?

Me: Yeah. I'm okay.

To be honest, I don't think I'm lying. I *am* okay, but I feel stupid. How did I not notice every little red flag? How did I let this happen? I let out a sigh and stand up from the chair.

"Can I at least help clean up?"

"I'm basically already done." Blaire smiles. I don't know

how I didn't notice it before, but she's basically a mini Beck. Just without the tattoos. She has the same dark colored hair, but hers is long and she wears it straight. Even their eye shape is similar.

"Do you like cookies?"

"Uhm, absolutely."

"Let me bake for you then? I make a mean chocolate chip."

"You don't have to ask me twice! I'll get out of your way."

I walk around the island and rummage through their refrigerator and pantry, getting all of the supplies and ingredients I need to make the cookies. She sits on a barstool on the opposite end of the island and watches me as I combine all of the ingredients. Besides painting, this is when my mind goes quiet. I don't have to *think* when I'm baking or painting. My hands can do all of the work for me while my mind just... hushes.

After I'm done combining the dry and wet ingredients, I fold in the chocolate chips. I grab the spoon off the counter and scoop up some of the dough. I roll it in between the palms of my hand to form a ball before placing it on a baking sheet lined with parchment paper. Once I put it in the preheated oven, I set a timer on my phone.

"You did that so effortlessly."

"I've always loved baking. It was really important to my mom that we all learn how to cook and bake. Now, it's my comfort activity." I shrug and begin to wash my hands. Blaire and I talk about my job as a teacher and my sisters until the cookies are done baking.

I pull them out of the oven. The smell of fresh cookies flows through the air in the kitchen. I hear the front door open, and Blaire says, "You're just in time. Olivia made cookies." I peek around the corner and see Beck walking into the living room, taking his boots off by the front door.

"Cookies?" He raises a brow.

"The *best* cookies." The corner of his lip curves in a slight smile and he walks through the kitchen, heading straight for the tray. He lifts one up and moves it to his mouth.

"Careful the just came of the—" He takes a bite and opens his mouth, making small breathing noises to alleviate the heat. "Oven."

I can't help but laugh. And I mean *really* laugh. Like a full, hold on to my belly, snorting kind of laugh.

Beck stalks towards me, his eyes full of fire. "You think that's funny, Freckles?"

I back up out of the kitchen, still laughing, and run towards the living room. Beck follows behind and wraps his arms around my waist, gently placing me on the couch where he proceeds to tickle me.

Freaking tickle me! His fingers push and wiggle into my sides and hips. I buck beneath him as he hovers over me. He ensures not to put any actual weight on me, even though I think I'd welcome it.

"I think I'm going to pee," I cry between laughs. He releases his hold and helps me to my feet. I run down the hall and into the bathroom.

Did I really have to pee? Yes. I have to pee literally every other minute of the day. But I needed to get a grip on myself. I haven't slept with anyone since the night I got pregnant, and nobody warned me that I'd get so...excited all the time.

Eighteen Weeks Pregnant

BETWEEN WORK and going back and forth between mine and Beck's place the last couple of weeks, I'm exhausted. I don't know what Holt did to my car, but it's not running right so poor Beck has had to take me to and from everywhere while it's in the shop. He hasn't complained a single time, but it has given us plenty of time to get to know each other. I've even gone to watch his band practice a couple of times. Which is where we're supposed to go tonight, then back to my place.

I just had my eighteen week checkup last week. Beck thought it was important that we disclose to my OB the short, but *eventful* relationship I had with Holt. She recommended I seek out a therapist and even compiled a list of good therapists for me to consider.

I had my first session this week and I think it went okay. She was great, the therapist, and made me feel comfortable to open up about Holt. The plan is to be seen every other week, for now.

I finish picking up the projects from my last period and turn off all my electronics in the class, before heading out for the day. Butterflies swarm around in my stomach as I head across campus. I can see Beck's truck parked in the same place it is every day. I've allowed myself to enjoy the stability that has become my new routine with him. I say my goodbyes to the office staff and try to reel back the excitement building in my gut as I get closer to the passenger door.

"Hey." I'm breathless as I crawl into the truck seat.

"Hi, Freckles, how was your day?" He waits for me to put my seatbelt on and puts the truck into drive.

"Good. We're working on final projects since it's almost the end of the year."

"Lookin' forward to seeing them. Hungry?"

"Always."

"I want to show you something first."

"Okay..."

"Then we'll get you your burrito bowl."

We talk about my class projects, and he tells me about something he's working on at his dad's shop. After a short drive, we stop in front of a cute little house. I'm confused as to why we've stopped here because I've never seen it before.

"Is this what you wanted to show me?" He nods and runs his hand down his face.

"I just got the call that my offer was accepted."

"You bought a house?"

"I did."

"It's so close to my school."

"It is."

"You did that on purpose?" He nods and the butterflies in my stomach seem to multiply and form a swarm.

"I wanted it to be easy to transition the baby back and forth, but of course you're welcome literally anytime. I want it to be a house where we can be a family. I know we might not look like a normal family, but normal is overrated anyways."

Family. He wants us to be a family.

"It's beautiful." A lump forms in my throat.

"I'm glad you like it. Now let's go get your bowl."

I smile softly and turn to look at the house as he drives off. My eyes burn with the onset of tears at the thought of it, of us being a family.

"I know you prefer Taco Me Up, but there's another place around the corner that looks promising."

"As long as they have good guac, I'm sold."

He pulls the truck into a small parking lot. Honestly, I wasn't sure it would even fit because of how small the spots are. We both slide out and walk to the entrance. There's a small line, so I have hope I won't be disappointed.

As we stand in line, he tells me about the house. How many bedrooms and bathrooms it has, how it's recently been remodeled, and how he really just needs to paint. The excitement on his face is infectious. I don't think I've *ever* seen him this excited about something. It's nice.

We get up to the place where we order and I let Beck go before me. "Hi, before I place my order can I ask what kind of oil your tortilla chips are cooked in?"

"They're cooked in vegetable oil."

"Do you guys use peanut oil or anything that could be contaminated with tree nuts?"

"No."

"Perfect," he continues on to order. But when it's my turn I'm honestly so surprised that I didn't even hear the guy trying to take my order. "Freckles, you okay?"

"Huh?" I'm dazed.

He looks at me with a furrowed brow, concern covering every part of his face.

"Oh yeah. I'll have a burrito bowl, please. White rice, no

beans, *light* chicken, lettuce, medium salsa, and extra guac. Thank you." I walk down to the register to meet Beck.

"You sure you're okay?"

"How did you know I was allergic to peanuts?"

"Oh." He lets out a small chuckle. "Remember when we did in that one experiment in class? The one about nuts and the energy they produce or something? I can't really remember it all, but I do remember that you're allergic to nuts."

I look at him, completely shocked that he remembered something from that long ago and he only smiles and takes our tray over to a table by the window. As I follow him, I feel like I'm walking on a cloud.

That's when it hits me.

I think I'm falling for Beckett Haven.

18

fter two weeks of her refusal, I finally got Olivia to say yes to me replacing her TV. We went to the store after our early dinner to look at them and somehow, she convinced me to go to the baby clothes section. She picked out some of the frilliest outfits for the baby. They had more ruffles than I thought would be possible. The outfits weren't necessarily ones I'd pick, but the smile on her face is worth every minute of it.

One hour, and a few hundred dollars, later we finally leave the store with a new TV and two bags of baby clothes. I slide the box in the bed of the truck while she crawls into the passenger seat. After I've secured the TV, I slide into my driver's side.

"You know we still don't have a name for the baby," she pouts.

"We have time, Freckles."

"I *know* but Daphne and Gracie want to order custom decorations with her name for the shower. So, can we at talk about it? I have a list."

"Of course, you do. Got for it."

Olivia practically bursts with excitement and pulls her phone out of her bag.

She scrolls through her notes app and clears her throat. "Daisy?"

"No."

"You're no fun."

"Next."

"Luna?"

"Like from Harry Potter?" She nods excitedly. "Tempting, but no."

"What about Maisie? That's different." We come to a red light, and I turn to look at her. I have no words. I just stare at her with a blank expression. "So that's a no then." I nod and she rolls her eyes.

After a short drive, we get to her apartment building, and I pull into the parking spot in the garage. The TV isn't heavy, so I'm able to get it into the elevator and into the apartment with no problem. I have already removed the old one and taken it to the county dump, so it's an easy switch. The less time she has to spend with a broken TV as a reminder of what Holt did to her, the better. After I'm done installing the new one, I sit next to her on the couch. I throw my arm over the edge and she scoots closer, practically crawling into my side.

I scroll through the different apps before deciding on one and trying to find something to watch. I let my arm fall from atop the couch and wrap around her, pulling her into me. As if that was possible. She looks up through her full lashes and the atmosphere between us shifts.

Her lips part a little and the tip of her tongue runs along her bottom lip.

Fuck.

Her body shifts and she rises to her knees, swinging her leg across my lap so that she straddles me. She runs her hand through her long blonde hair and tosses it over her shoulder. Her face hovers just above mine. I release a sigh and let my head fall onto the back of the couch. *This is finally happening, but I'm blowing it.*

"I'm mortified." She covers her face. "I totally misread the last couple of weeks, didn't I?" Her face flushes red and her hands move from my shoulders to my chest and she pushes off in an attempt to get off my lap. I grip onto her hips, keeping her in place. *She's not going anywhere.*

"I want you." I tighten my hold on her hips. "*God,* I want you so bad. But I need to know you're sure. Once you kiss me, there will never be anyone else."

"I've never been so sure about anything before."

Her mouth meets mine in a soft and gentle kiss, but I want more. I *need* more. My hand travels up her back and I weave it through strands of her hair. I tighten my hold lightly, pushing her lips harder against mine. She moves her hips and grinds against my hardened cock that's begging to escape the confinement of my pants. Her lips open and her tongue glides along my bottom lip. I part my mouth and our tongues meet. I take her bottom lip in between my teeth and grip her hair tighter.

She whimpers and I think there's a really good chance I'm going to cum in my pants if she keeps grinding against me like this.

We're so wrapped up in our own world, we don't know we have an audience until Daphne coughs.

"Wel,l well, well." Olivia jumps off of me and sinks into the couch. I adjust my pants and glare between Daphne and Derek.

"Hey, guys."

"The TV looks nice," Daphne says with an amused smile, looking back and forth between Olivia and I on the couch. Olivia's face is crimson with embarrassment.

"I'm glad you like it." I try to send *can you go the fuck away* with my eyes.

"Well...we're going to go to my room." Daphne points towards the door near the couch and starts walking.

"See you guys at practice later?" Derek asks and mouths *sorry* before following Daphne into her room and shutting the door behind him.

"I'm sorry." Olivia wraps her arms around herself and nibbles her bottom lip.

"For?"

"I don't actually know."

"Then why apologize?"

"It felt like the right thing to do, I think."

"You have nothing to be sorry for, Freckles." I run my fingers through her hair and bring them behind her ear. Olivia jumps and smiles, grabbing my hand and pulling it towards her stomach.

"Wait for it!" She holds eye contact, never losing her grin. I can tell she's really excited about something, I just don't know what.

Until I feel it.

A slight little nudge beneath my palm. Just for long enough that I know it happened, but then it's gone. Olivia's hand pulls mine to the other side of her stomach and it happens again.

"Is that...?"

"Yes! That's our baby."

"That's amazing. When did that start?"

"I started to feel like it like a week or two ago. At first, I thought it was just gas, but then I realized it was her! I'm just excited you finally got to feel it, too." She smiles and releases my hand from her grip. Together we sit back against the couch and finally decide on a movie. We don't even make it past the opening credits before Olivia passes out.

I PULL up to the address that Sage gave me and put my truck into park. I'm supposed to be meeting the band here for their promotional photos, but really it feels like she's lured me here to my death. It took me way too long to get back to her, and the band, about the photography job. I know I dropped the ball, but I was so excited when they told me they still wanted me.

Cautiously, I get out of the car and head around to the door. I jiggle the handle and enter. There's at least a dozen people walking around the room. Sage and the band stand front and center.

"Look who showed up." Sage cocks her hip and crosses her arms.

"I seriously thought you were bringing me here to murder me."

I gaze around the room at the set up. I've never photographed in a setting like this, but I'm looking forward to how they'll turn out. I adjust the step ladder where I want it and then do the same to the lighting. The band gets into place and moves at my command. They arrange in a staggered line where I put Lance in the middle and adjust the other members of the band on his sides, placing Amara to his direct right. Weston is to his left and Link stands next to Amara. I get up on the step ladder and snap some pictures, both close and from the waist up.

I get down and move everyone again. This time, just spacing them out so that I can get full body shots from a lower angle. Everyone photographs so easily, that it's cake for me to get great photos with little issue. I won't know how good these photos really are until I'm able to upload them to my computer and edit them.

"I think those are going to be rad as hell," Sage comes behind me as I'm putting away my camera equipment.

"I think so, too."

She crosses her arms and raises her brow. "You ready to sign that contract?"

"Yeah. There's just one big thing."

"What's that?"

"I don't need an exclusivity clause. I can't travel too far, at least for the first year."

"What's too far?"

"Like a few hours away from Dryer."

"So definitely no out-of-states."

I know that Olivia wouldn't care if I traveled, but I'd care. I don't want there to be a chance of missing out on anything or being too far if an emergency happens.

"Oh yeah, absolutely not. I'd love to do it, but I can't travel far."

"I can make that adjustment to the contract."

"That would be awesome."

"If I email it over, will you actually sign it or get back to me quickly?"

"For sure. It's just been a crazy couple of months."

I don't give any more information than that.

"No problem. I'll send it over tomorrow."

I nod and finish putting my camera in its bag. I still have to find the right time to talk to Derek about Skarred. The band has been such a big piece of who I've been for a long time that I know it'll hurt everyone, but I have to do what's best for me and my family.

I talk to the members of Wrecked Youth for a minute, congratulating them again on their contract and upcoming tour. They tell me all about the different cities and venues they're going to be going to.

Two years ago I would have been drooling at the opportunity to have the experience they're going to be having, but now? Now, all I can think about is getting home and watching a movie with my pregnant...friend? I have no idea where we stand, not really. I told her that if she kissed me, I would be done for, but I don't know if she understood what I was really saying. I say goodbye to everyone and walk out to my truck.

Driving back to Olivia's apartment takes me right through the main streets of the city, so I pull over at the florist. I look around at all of the floral arrangements and loose bundles around the store. When it's finally my turn, I choose a green and yellow bouquet. I don't know shit about flowers, but the l florist say they're sunflowers, white spray roses, and green mini hydrangeas.

After I pay and the flowers are wrapped up, I head onto the sidewalk. The spring air is warm with a balmy breeze. A familiar laugh flows through the evening from across the street.

Anger boils when I catch sight of that fucker Holt with no one else but Michelle.

I can't say I'm surprised. She has always gone where she thinks she can get something, and it's obvious what she's getting from him. He opens the passenger side door to a car, I'm assuming hers, and his head lifts up.

He looks directly at me. You would have thought I threatened him with the way his face drains of all color. Well, not all color. There are deep brown and green blotches from where his bruises have faded over the last couple weeks.

I stare at him, void of all emotion, and he rushes to the driver's side door.

Good fucking riddance.

Olivia

19

My therapist and I spoke at length over the last two sessions about me not going to the gym. It was something that used to bring me joy, peace even. Especially after a long workday. But since everything happened with Holt, I haven't been able to go back. I don't know if it's fear that I'll see him or what exactly. My therapist recommended that I seek out a new gym or maybe a class.

So, I think that's what I'm doing before work.

Beck had to leave early to go work on some mysterious project at the shop. So, for the first time in weeks, I wake up in my bed alone. Nothing has happened between us since the day on the couch but I think he's just being patient and waiting for me to make the move.

After mindlessly scrolling through my phone for a few minutes, I toss the blankets off and force myself to crawl out of bed. I rummage through my dresser to piece together a workout set. It's only after pulling up my bottoms do I realize I will probably need to buy a few pairs of maternity shorts soon. I throw my hair up into a ponytail and brush my teeth, foregoing make-up until I'm done with class.

The gym I used to go to is just down the street, but there's another one on the street behind my apartment that I feel better about. I go into the kitchen and fill up a tumbler with ice and water before grabbing my bag and locking the door behind me as I leave.

The mid-April air is warm, but the wind brings a slight chill. I welcome the silence that the city has this early, before the sun has risen. There's hardly anyone on the street as I turn the corner onto the street of the gym. As I near the entrance, I see four or five other women entering through the front door. My stomach flips with excitement, but also anxiety, at the idea of meeting new people.

The gym, *sorry*, the studio is incredibly clean. The walls are a smokey gray and covered with shelves that have assorted live plants and crystals. The shelves and cubbies where we put our stuff are painted white. We walk across the light hardwood floor into the room at the end of the hall. There are dark green yoga mats scattered meticulously across the floor.

"Good morning, everyone. Welcome. Please, pick a space and introduce yourself to your neighbor," the instructor encourages us. She stands in the front of the room and smiles at us. I turn and smile to the woman next to me, who introduces herself as Estelle. She's due four weeks before I am with a little boy. I don't know if it's because it's too early in the morning, but I don't get the vibe that she was interested in talking more than that. My stomach tightens as I move onto the yoga mat. I look over my shoulder.

Yoga is safe. There's no way that Holt could be here.

The instructor has us start in easy pose. We all sit cross-legged with our palms face up, the back of our hands resting on our thighs. For a minute we close our eyes and take long, deep breaths in and out through our noses. Then we move into side bends, holding each for three breaths.

Progressively the poses get more difficult and after the pregnancy variation of the monkey god pose, my muscles are screaming. I almost hugged the instructor when she said we were going into guided meditation for the next five minutes to cool down before the end of class.

I've done yoga before, sure, but yoga while you're pregnant is definitely different. It feels really good to get my body up and moving again. I make sure to sign up for next week's class on my way out. The sun is finally rising when I step out of the *studio* and start my walk back to my apartment.

I can't explain why, but the hair on the back of my neck stands up and I have the eeriest feeling that I'm being watched. My stomach sinks and I turn to look over my shoulder, but nobody's there. I start to walk faster, panic building in my chest as I round the corner to my street. I practically crash through the revolving door of my building.

My thoughts are racing. I think I'm going to be sick.

"Miss Connoly?" The doorman slowly starts to walk over to me with palms up. "Are you okay?"

I nod and look over my shoulder into the street, but there's no one there. He directs me to sit on one of the couches in the lobby of the building. It feels like a weight is on my chest and I can't breathe. *Why can't I breathe?* I think I'm hyperventilating, but I can't form words to tell him what's going on.

"I'm going to call an ambulance," he says with wide eyes. I shake my head and hands, telling him not to.

I don't need to go to the hospital.

"Liv?" a familiar voice calls. It sounds like my head is under water, the sound of the voice is distorted. I turn and see my sister. I can't hold back the tears that begin to overflow. "Hey. Breath in." She takes her own deep breath. "Good. One, two, three. Okay. Hold. Perfect. Now out. One, two, three. Good."

I'm trying so hard to focus on what she's saying.

My racing heart begins to beat normally again.

"Keep breathing like that."

The lightness in my head leaves.

I do as she says and continue breathing while she turns to talk to the doorman. I can't hear what they're saying, but I think she's telling him that I'm okay. *Am I okay?* My breathing returns to normal and the weight on my chest slowly disappears. Daphne grabs onto my elbow and my lower back to help me to my feet. She links her arm with mine and guides me to the elevator. Her hand rubs circles on my back while we wait to get to our floor. We walk to our apartment in silence. It's inside where she brings me to the bathroom and starts the shower.

"I'll get you a comfy lounge set."

"I have work." I choke back a sob.

I can't imagine going to work after whatever *that* was.

"Call in sick. You need to rest."

I nod because she's right. I *do* need to rest. My energy level plummeted and I wish I could do nothing but sleep for days. Before I get into the shower, I have to text Beck so he doesn't leave work to come pick me up.

> Me: I'm not going to work today.

I expect a text back, but instead my phone rings with an incoming call. *Beck.*

"Hello?"

"What's wrong?"

Something about the concern that fills his voice makes the lump that's been sitting in my throat grow bigger. "Nothing." I somehow choke out.

"I'll come home right now." *Home.*

"No. Stay at work. I'm fine."

"You don't sound fine."

"I just had like a little *thing*. Daph is here."

"What kind of little *thing?* Is the baby okay?"

I nod, forgetting that he can't see me.

"We are both okay. I don't know what happened. My chest just started to feel tight, my heart started beating really fast, and I felt like someone was following me. I don't know. It was weird."

"Freckles, you need to call your therapist and let her know you had a panic attack."

"Okay."

"I'm coming home early."

"You don't have to—"

"I wasn't asking for permission. I'll be home around lunch time."

"Okay."

"Call me if you need me, okay?"

"Okay."

The call ends and I put my phone down on the counter to take off my clothes and throw them into the hamper. My fingers brush under the stream of the shower to test the temperature of the water. Once I'm and the water is covering me, all of my walls come down and the sobs wretch from my chest. I don't even know why I'm crying, but I can't seem to stop.

Daph knocks on the door, "Liv? I have your clothes."

"Thank you." I choke on a sob.

"You good?"

"*Mmhmm.*"

"No, you're not."

I've never been able to hide the way I'm feeling from her, even when we were kids. Mom used to tell us that twins were special because they could feel what the other was feeling.

"I don't know what's wrong or why I'm crying."

"What you just went through with Holt is hard, *plus* being pregnant?"

"Beck wants me to call my therapist."

"I think that's a good idea. I'll be just outside if you need me, okay?"

"Thanks."

She leaves, closing the door behind her, and I finish my shower. Once I've done my entire routine and get dressed, I walk into my bedroom to call my therapist.

An hour emergency therapy session and an almost three hour nap later, I find myself curled up on the couch with my sister. She hasn't tried to press me on the conversation or ask me what we discussed and for that, I'm grateful. The moment I sat down next to her, she covered me with a blanket and turned on an early 2000's romcom.

According to my therapist, panic attacks can be normal after what I went through. Even if I feel like I'm okay, my nervous system is still healing in its own way. She said I need to prioritize myself and my mental health.

Well, her exact words were, "If you were on an airplane, and it started to go down, you would put the oxygen mask on yourself first. You cannot take care of other people if you don't take care of yourself first." So, starting today, I am going to prioritize myself and if that means vegging in front of the TV, that's what I'm doing.

There's a knock on my door and my sister hops up to answer it. She looks over her shoulder and smiles at me suspiciously, so I feel like it's probably Beck.

Derek walks through the door first and kisses my twin on the top of her head. Beck follows after him, but he comes bearing gifts. He's holding two bags from Taco Me Up and I can smell the burrito bowl the moment he walks in through the door.

"I figured you were hungry." Beck sets the bags down on the counter. He rummages through them and fishes out my bowl. "I also called the mechanics and your car is ready, so Derek and I picked it up." Derek grins and pulls the keys out of his pocket, setting them on the counter before he gets his burrito out of the bag. Beck hands me my food, taking a seat on the couch next to me.

"But I haven't paid."

"I took care of it."

"You didn't have to do that."

"I *wanted* to."

"I can take care of myself."

"I know you can, Freckles." He tucks a strand of hair behind my ear and kisses me gently on the lips. "But I want to take care of you, too."

I can feel Derek and Daphne staring from the kitchen, so I peak over Beck's shoulder. They immediately jump and pretend like they're eating their food. I bite into my bowl and groan as the first bite hits my tongue.

"That good?" Beck asks. I nod, rolling my eyes for dramatics. "I have a couple names." I practically choke on my food.

"Go on." I force down the bite.

"Sadie?" I shake my head. It's not the worst name I've ever heard, but it just doesn't *feel* like her name.

"Parker?"

"You didn't like Maisie, but you like *Parker?*"

He shrugs and I can't help but laugh. Not because of the name, but because of how different our choices seem to be. How are we ever going to be able to decide on a name?

20

Olivia's Twenty-Five Weeks Pregnant

It's no surprise that Skarred has taken a serious back burner recently.

I've photographed a couple more shows for Wrecked Youth and any free time I do have, I'm spending with Olivia. I think Derek knows the conversation is coming, but I don't think he knows when to expect it. Tieran has already left the band has been traveling for his apprenticeship at work. We've texted here and there, but we seem to miss each other most of the time.

Aside from photographing and spending time with Olivia, I've started working on a secret project at work. When I found out that I was going to be a dad, I decided on building the crib. It wasn't until last week that my dad saw what I was doing and decided he wanted to help. We did countless hours of research to make sure whatever we decided to build was up to all of the safety standards. Then we found the perfect design, a mid-century modern crib made from a combination of both hard maple and walnut wood.

So far, my dad and I have cut out and milled fifty-four spindles to be used in the frame of the crib. And we have cut and edged all of the railings, which are made of the hard maple. Once it's all done, it will be two-toned and I think will look really fucking cool with however Olivia decides to decorate the nursery.

I sit in front of the warehouse for practice. It feels like so long ago that this was the highlight of my life. I was this lost man who only found peace at the bottom of my beer can waiting to wail on my drums and lose myself in the music. I wasn't addicted, no, I wouldn't ever allow myself to get that far, but I didn't have a purpose.

Now, with Olivia and the baby, I do.

Derek and the guys have found someone to replace Tieran, and tonight is the first night he's going to practice with us. I think Derek said his name was Walker or something, but I can't remember.

I pull out my phone to text Olivia, just to let her know what time I'll be home.

Me: Hey. I'm at practice, but I'll try not to be too late.

Freckles: Okay.

Three little dots.

Freckles: The bed seems so cold without you.

That makes practice feel like it's going to be even longer.

We've spent the last few weeks switching off between her place and mine. I don't even know how that happened, really. After everything with Holt, she slept at my house and now we're just together every night. I wake up to her perfect ass pressed against me and a rock hard boner every damn morning. I've been patient, honestly waiting for her to just make another move. I don't want to push her to do anything she's not ready to do or anything she's not ready to be, especially after her panic attack.

I'll wait forever for her.

I walk up the walk towards the door that leads to the warehouse. Sounds of cheering echo out into the night.

"What's all the fuss about?" I ask as I come into the room. I've never seen Derek as excited as he is right now, so now I'm even more curious than I was a second ago.

"That was Thirteenth Avenue's manager, and they want us to fucking open for them tomorrow!"

"Cool, where's the show?"

"Roswell Falls."

"That's like four hours from here?"

He looks at me questioningly.

I shrug and take a deep breath. "Look man, I'm down to do this one but we're going to have to find my replacement soon."

"What the hell do you mean, Beck? You're one of the founding members."

"Yeah, and so was Ti. I've never been super invested in us going big anyways."

I feel bad, don't get me wrong, I do. This has been Derek's dream since we were teenagers. It's just never been mine.

"You're joking. Right? Shit is just starting to happen for us."

"I know and I'm sorry. I really am. I'll stay with you until you find a replacement, but Liv only has a few months left. I can't travel like this again." I can tell he's frustrated, pissed off even, but since he's stopped drinking and doing drugs, he's a lot less hotheaded.

"Can we talk more later?"

"Yeah, sure."

"Let's get a quick practice session in and then head out. The manager said he got us a couple of hotel rooms down the street from the place."

"Wait, we're leaving tonight?"

"Yeah, they need us there for sound check and everything tomorrow. It's going to be a whole process."

"Let me just call Liv."

"Sure. Do whatever you gotta do. We're going to start practice in five."

I throw him a thumbs up and walk towards our couches. The phone line rings a couple of times before she answers. It's very obvious that I woke her up from sleeping.

"Beckett? Is everything okay?"

"Hey, yeah. I guess we got a gig that's out of town, so I'm not coming by tonight and I think I'll be gone tomorrow night, too."

"Both nights?" She sounds disappointed, which makes me feel like an ass.

"Yeah. I'm sorry. I know it's last minute. Derek is pretty insistent on us going tonight."

"No problem." She yawns. "I'll miss you and the way you snore."

"I do *not* snore."

"Oh, you absolutely do snore. But it's like my white noise now." I roll my eyes when Derek shouts my name. "He sure is bossy, isn't he? I'll let you go. Text me when you get to the hotel?"

"Will do."

We say our goodnights and I hang up the phone. I ignore the imaginary daggers that Derek's currently throwing at my head as I walk past him to my drum set. I offer him an exaggerated shrug, rolling my eyes towards Hayes as I take my seat. I settle in behind my drum set and twirl my stick between my fingers before counting us in.

I DRIVE myself to Roswell Falls because I absolutely *refuse* to be in Derek's creeper van with the guys for four hours. The manager of Thirteenth Avenue booked us two hotel rooms down the street from the venue; each room has two beds. Derek and Watson, not Walker, share a room so Hayes and I are sharing the other. By the time I take a shower and hop into my bed, Hayes is already fast asleep. My phone's backlight illuminates the space around me when I pick it up to let Olivia know I made it. It's well past midnight, so I'm sure she's asleep.

> Me: I made it to the hotel, Freckles. Goodnight.

I put my phone on the bedside table and lay back in bed. I tuck my arm behind my head and stare at the ceiling, hoping that sleep claims me quickly. My phone vibrating surprises me, so I grab it and see a text from Olivia.

Freckles: Are you alone?

I raise my eyebrows.

Me: Not really. Hayes is in the bed across the room.

Freckles: Oh. That's no fun.

Me: What's no fun.

Instead of a reply, I get an image. She's propped up on her side wearing one of those sexy silk pajama sets she always wears. One of the straps is falling down her arm, exposing just the smallest amount of her full breasts. Her bottom lip is between her teeth. *Fuck.*

Freckles: I wish you were here.

Me: Fuck. I wish I was there too.

Freckles: What would you do to me if you were?

I let out a quiet laugh. For some reason, I never saw Olivia as the sexting type, and most definitely not the one to start it. My lip curls into a sly smirk.

Me: I'd start by kissing your neck and kiss my way down until I take your nipple between my teeth.

Freckles: I think I'd like that.

All I can think about is how much I'd like that, too. I get up and go into the bathroom. I'm hard as fuck and in desperate need of some kind of relief.

> Me: I'll finger your tight pussy and kiss my way down your body until my tongue circles your clit.

> Me: You'll be begging for me to fuck you.

Freckles: Oh, will I?

She's feeling sassy. I fucking love it.

> Me: You absolutely will.

> Me: When it finally gets too much, I'll tease you with the tip of my cock.

Freckles: Hmm.

Freckles: Then what will you do?

> Me: I'll slide in slowly at first.

Freckles: And then?

She responded faster than I expected. I push my pajama pants and underwear down to my knees, imagining how Olivia felt wrapped around me as I move my hand over my cock.

> Me: I'll go faster and harder. You'll be screaming my name.

> Me: Are you wet for me, Freckles?

Freckles: Yes.

> Me: Prove it.

The three little bubbles pop up and disappear. I slide my hand up and down my shaft, tightening the grip I have on myself while I wait for her reply. What I wasn't expecting? A photo of her pleasuring herself with a small pink toy. *Fuck.*

Freckles: Now your turn.

I snap a quick photo of my length before I stroke fast and tighter, the sensation building in my gut. It doesn't take long for cum to spill out over my hand.

I *need* to see her, so I decide to facetime her.

"Beck?" she answers in her room. It's dark, with only the backlight of her phone showing her face.

"I want to watch as you cum, Freckles." I can see the redness of her face, even in the darkness. Her breathing is heavy, and I can hear the faint sound of buzzing in the background. "Eyes on me." She lifts her eyes to meet mine through the screen of the phone. "*Hm.* Good girl."

She bites her lower lip and lets out a moan, my name escapes as a whisper, as she rides out her orgasm.

"I'm sorry." She buries her face into the pillow.

"For what?"

"I..." She takes an audible breath. "I don't really know. I guess, for texting you all sexy too early in the morning."

"There's literally no such thing as texting me sexy too early. Please feel free to do it more."

She laughs. "I might be able to actually sleep now."

"Why couldn't you sleep?"

"I don't know if it's my hormones, but I've been uhm—"

"Horny."

"Yeah, *that*, all day and night. I thought about seducing you when you got home, but then you went out of town."

"Tell me more."

"When do you get home?"

"Not till Sunday."

"Dang, okay."

"I can say fuck it and come home Saturday after the show."

"I don't want to ask you to do that."

Little does she know, I'd do anything to make her happy.

"If I decided to do it on my own?"

"I wouldn't be opposed to being woken up."

"Noted. Goodnight, Freckles."

"Night, Beckett."

"I...Talk to you tomorrow."

I love you.

I'm able to stop the word vomit before it escapes. I've never uttered those three words to someone besides my family, but I *wanted* to say them.

I'm in so much deeper than I thought.

ONCE WE END the show the next day, I opt to just go home and not stay the night in the hotel again. I literally couldn't stop thinking about getting home to Olivia and the drive flies.

I unlock the front door to her apartment with the key she had made for me and walk into the dark room. Daphne is in Roswell Falls with Derek and the guys. Since I left, Hayes and Watson are sharing a room to give Daph and D some privacy.

There's a dim light coming from Olivia's room. I make my way quietly through the apartment and to her bedroom, pushing the door open the rest of the way. She's lying on the bed, on her side, with one leg bent upwards. Her silk nightgown is raised up above her ass and I am surprised to see that she's wearing no panties.

I run my fingers along her bare leg and follow up the curve of her body. She stirs and rolls over on her back, her eyes flutter open.

"Hey. You came home," she mumbles.

"It looks like you were hoping I would," I whisper softly, allowing my lips to barely graze the top of her ear.

"*Mmhmm,*" she hums and melts into me. Her fingers trace the hem of my shirt. "Why are you still wearing all these clothes?" She lifts my shirt up over my head and tosses it across the room. Her hands shake as she fumbles with the button of my jeans. I lean up on my knees to help unbutton my pants and take them off, tossing my denim and underwear across the room with my shirt.

"You sure?"

She smirks and raises a brow, raising her hand to behind my neck. She grips tightly and pulls me down to her. Her lips meet mine gently, but I can feel the hunger behind it, and I know she wants to consume me the same way I want to consume her.

Her moan vibrates against my lips. My hand slides up her inner thigh to the hem of her nightgown. I pull it up and over her head, throwing it into the pile of clothes. I run my fingers down her neck, her nipples pebble as I make my way down her torso, until I slide a finger into her wet pussy.

"*Hm.* Already so wet for me, Freckles." I lean down and kiss her neck.

I leave a trail of kisses down her neck and collarbone, taking her nipple into my mouth and sucking softly before I continue my descent. My mouth reaches her sweet pussy and I lick her clit in a long, gentle stroke.

"Oh, Beck. I'm already going to—" she moans.

"Fuck. I could listen to the sounds you make all day."

"Lay down," she demands.

Fuck. I like bossy Olivia.

"You're the boss."

Olivia tosses her leg over me and grabs onto my hard cock, lining my tip to her entrance before stopping and looking at me, almost like she's realizing something.

"Oh, shoot. I don't have a condom."

"I'm clean. I haven't..." I clear my throat. "I haven't been with anyone since you."

"Wait, really?"

"Really, but can we talk about this *after*."

"Of course. So, you're—"

"Absolutely okay to do it without a condom."

She shudders as she slides down my length.

"Fuck Freckles, you feel so good."

I grab onto her hips and guide her hesitant movements, keeping them slow while she adjusts to me. Her head falls back when she begins to move, her rhythm getting faster. I release the grip I have on her hips to move my hands up to her breasts, teasing her nipples.

"You take all of me so well." Her pussy clenches around me at the praise and she moans my name as she rides. And fuck is she riding me. I sit up slighting, running my tongue up her body. She trembles above me and tosses her head back again. My name escapes her lips in a breathy moan. Her hands hold onto my shoulders and her nails dig into my skin.

"Is this what you were thinking about last night? What you've been needing?" I suck her nipple into my mouth and between my teeth. Her hips grind into mine, over and over, while her whimpers fill the room.

"Yes."

"Use me. Take what you need," I whisper as I nibble against the soft skin of her collarbone. My heart is beating so fast I think I'm going to explode. I fall back onto the bed and dig my fingers into her perfect ass.

"Grab onto the headboard, Freckles." She looks up at me and her eyes grow wide. I meet her thrusts, going deeper and harder with each one until I can feel my own release is near.

Olivia's moans get louder and louder with every thrust until she comes completely undone around me. She moans my name, again, but this time it's not a whisper. No, it's loud enough for the neighbors to hear and fuck me if it's not my favorite sound. My vision blurs as I empty myself inside of her, filling her completely. I ease her off of me and onto the bed beside where I was just laying. I nudge her legs apart and lick my way up her thighs.

I glide my tongue up her pussy, relishing the sweet tang of our cum combined. Her hips buck when I swirl my tongue around her swollen clit.

"Beck," she moans as I drag my tongue up her slit once more. Reluctantly, I pull myself back and lay on the spot next to her. I could taste her all night long, but I know she's going to be exhausted tomorrow.

"So." She adjusts to look up at me. "You really haven't been with anyone else?"

"I'd never lie to you about that, Freckles."

"Can I ask, why?"

Because I love you.

"There's nobody else but you." My stomach twists into what feels like a dozen knots.

"Beck..."

"You don't have to say anything. Just lay with me."

My fingers trace circles onto her arm, she tucks in closer to my side. She grabs my free hand and brings it down to her stomach. The familiar nudge and movement of the baby flutters beneath my palm.

"But I...I do need to say something."

"What's that?"

"I feel that way, too. You're home for me. There's no other way I can describe it. Like you're where I feel safest. You're just...you're home."

I pull her in closer, squeezing her arm gently, before I place a kiss on the top of her head. I don't try to fight the lump that's building in my throat. I've spent most of my life searching for the feeling I have right here, and I don't ever plan on letting it go.

Twenty-Eight Weeks Pregnant

I don't know how, but Beck and I haven't been able to get enough of each other. Especially the last couple of weeks. Really, since that night he came home from the Roswell Falls show. Don't get me wrong, we were together basically every night since the whole Holt *incident*. But whatever is happening now is different. Could it be that we basically both told each other that we love each other without actually saying it? Absolutely most likely.

I know twenty-eight weeks is technically early for a baby shower, but I need to make sure I have more than enough time to get everything ready. Planning and organizing are guilty pleasures of mine.

Unfortunately, we still haven't able to come up with a name. But regardless, my sisters and Gracie are very understanding and not too upset about not being able to order any of the custom stuff they want.

All I know about the shower is that I have to wear baby pink and Beck has to wear red.

My makeup is already done, so all I need to do is curl the last couple of pieces of hair and put on my dress. I found the cutest pastel pink midi dress that has loose sleeves and a ribbed top. It's been hard for me to find clothes that I actually like right now, and I have to pee so darn much that I've basically been living in dresses.

I finish my hair and get up to change. A quick pain shoots down my leg, which I've been told is normal and it's called sciatica? Well, guess what, Dr. Floris? Sciatica freaking sucks. I throw my pajamas into the dirty clothes hamper and put on my dress. It's hot for May, so I'm glad I went with a cotton blend.

There's a knock on my door and then a second later it cracks open.

"Knock, knock."

"Hey Mom, you can come in."

My mom turns the corner and smiles. "Wow. You look gorgeous, Livy."

"I don't *feel* gorgeous." In fact, I feel like a whale and I'm barely even into my third trimester. I think every single part of me is swollen. I sit on the edge of the bed and Mom sits right beside me.

"Ah. I understand how you feel, sweet girl. I won't say that whole *once the baby is born, you'll forget about it* bullshit because you won't forget. You'll never forget, but it'll be worth it." She gently pats my leg.

There's another knock on my door, but it doesn't open.

"Is it safe?" Beck asks from the other side.

"Everyone's decent," Mom replies and then leans down and whispers. "Not that he hasn't seen you naked."

"Mom!"

"What?" She laughs and the door swings open. Beck is in jeans, his black checkered vans, and a red button up shirt. His tattoos are all exposed, including the rose on his neck, and I have to remind myself to calm down.

Mom slaps her knees and stands up. She hugs Beck as she walks past him. Just before she leaves, she turns and mouths *I like this one* and points towards Beck.

Me too, Mom.

"You look beautiful," he says when she disappears.

"Well, you don't look too shabby yourself."

"Do you want to just forgo this thing and stay home?" He wraps his arm around my lower back and pulls me on close, leaning down to whisper into my ear. "I'll make it worthwhile."

"Tempting." *So freaking tempting.* "But Daphne will kill us if we miss it."

"After then?" He pulls back and smirks. My cheeks heat up instantly and I nod, taking my bottom lip in between my teeth. "We better go cause it's almost time. We're taking your car though cause your Ma is driving with us."

I grab my purse off the bed and head into the living room. A bouquet of sunflowers is sitting on my island in a vase. I look over at Beck who just shrugs and goes to open the door. Mom walks out first and I follow, getting up on my tiptoes to kiss him as I pass.

"Thank you for the flowers."

"You're welcome." Beck kisses me again and shuts the door once we are all out into the hallway.

He comes to my side, lacing his fingers between mine, and joins in the conversation with my mom. To be honest, the moment his hand touches mine, I forgot what we're even talking about.

Daph and Gracie rented out an event hall that a local brewery owns. Thankfully, it's only a fifteen minute drive to it because by the time we get out to the car, I have to pee again.

There's a sign outside the door that says, "Welcome to Beck & Olivia's berry sweet shower". It's on a light pink background with small strawberries and bows scattered around the writing. We walk into the venue and it's so freaking cute I want to cry. The tables are covered in a light pink and white gingham tablecloth with red vases that are filled with pink and red carnations and baby's breath.

"Hey!" Gracie struts around into the room holding the most adorable vintage heart shaped cake. "What do you think?"

"I'm obsessed. I love it." My eyes burn with the onset of tears.

"Everyone helped. Blaire, Celeste, Mattie, and your mom. It was really important to everyone that it was perfect for you guys."

Excitedly, they show me around the rest of the venue. The caterers, who are making tacos and rice, are cooking in the venue's kitchen and the girls have put together games, gift baskets for the winners, the cutest little favor baggies filled with grandma strawberry candy, and so many other small details.

It all makes something in my heart squeeze tight. I try to stop the tears, I really do, but before I know it, I'm a sobbing mess. Beck rubs the small of my back with his palm to try to soothe me. I look over at him through my tear filled eyes and my heart just feels full.

"Okay." I take a deep breath and wipe my tears away with a napkin Gracie hands me. "No more tears."

"It's party time," Daphne shimmies with a devious smile and directs me towards the photo backdrop. When I turn around to pose, Gracie is dragging Beck to stand next to me. "A picture of mom and dad."

Beck guides me close to him and wraps his arm around me. It seems like everyone there is snapping pictures of us. We finish and everyone disburses to a table. That's when I realize that I *never* scheduled a maternity photo session.

My heart drops into the deepest pit of my stomach.

"Oh no."

"What's wrong?" Beck grabs onto my arms gently and searches my eyes.

"It's not a big deal," I murmur. He raises an eyebrow. "I forgot to schedule maternity pictures. It's probably too late to get it done with the photographer I wanted."

"I mean I can take them for you." Beck shrugs and puts his hands into the front pockets of his jeans. "I'm not a professional photographer, but I take photos for bands sometimes."

"You'd do that?"

"For the mother of my daughter, I'd do literally anything." He kisses the tip of my nose and sits down in a chair. I ignore the audience making *aww* sounds to the side of us.

The guests begin to trickle into the room and soon Beck and I are surrounded by people. I don't know if I missed the "please touch me" sign that's apparently on my stomach, but to them, it's front and center. My coworkers and closest friends haven't even touched me this much. Shoot, even Beck didn't grab at my stomach until I forced him too and it's *his* baby!

Eventually everyone finds a seat and the food is served. Each bite of the tacos is the best bite I've ever had. I was even more excited when Beck came from the kitchen with a bowl of guacamole and blue corn tortilla chips.

"Have you ever seen such a beautiful thing?" I ask and scoop some guac onto my plate.

"Actually, I have." He leans down and whispers in my ear. My breath hitches as he runs the tips of his ringers across the exposed skin of my back. Even just the smallest touch of his skin sends electricity through me.

Thirty Weeks Pregnant

WE OPTED to open all of our baby shower gifts in private, so Beck has taken a majority of them to his new house. He's already got the keys, but because he's been painting so much, he wants to wait until it has time to air out before I join him there. We haven't talked about what is in the future for us, but I know we're going to have to have this conversation soon.

I made Gracie quite literally the happiest person in the world by asking her to do my hair and make up for my maternity photos. I've picked out two outfits: baggy jeans and a white button up and a sheer robe with a matching bra and panty set. The butterflies in my stomach are on tornado warning thinking about Beck being the one to take my photos. Which doesn't make any sense at all since he's already seen all of me more than once.

"Ready, bitch?" Gracie walks into my room with a big bag

full of makeup in one hand and a curling iron in the other. "I've been waiting for you to willingly let me do your makeup since *forever.*"

"You've done my makeup before, Grace." I plug in the curling iron and set it down on the top of my vanity.

"Yeah, but not willingly!" She shimmies and runs her fingers through my hair, pinning half of it up into a claw clip she grabbed from my vanity. "Are you so excited?"

"I think so?"

"Nervous?"

"Definitely. It feels like such an intimate thing."

"Babe. He's literally been *inside* of your most intimate parts. I don't think you can get more intimate than that."

"I don't know how else to explain it."

She picks up a strand of my hair and twirls it around the barrel of the curling iron. Her eyes meet mine through the mirror and she smiles, slightly tilting her head to the side.

"You got it bad, don't you?"

"What do you mean?"

"I mean you and Beck."

I shrug.

"It's just us here, Liv. You can be honest."

"I've got it so bad."

Gracie smirks and bounces from one foot to the other.

"What?" I protest.

"I've just been waiting for you to admit it." She finishes curling the first layer, lets my hair down, and sections it again. I don't know why I didn't let her do this earlier; I'm loving that my arms are not getting exhausted. "So, are you moving into his place? Are you guys dating? What's the sitch?"

"We haven't talked about any of it."

"Like *anything*?"

"I mean we've talked about the baby, obviously, but nothing past that."

"*Hmph.*"

"What was that? *Hmph?*"

"I just think you guys need to have these conversations. You guys are about to have a baby together." She moves onto the final layer.

I know she's right. Beck and I do need to have these scary conversations, sooner rather than later, but I can't help but feel...scared that if I try to push something on him that he's not ready for, I'll ruin what we have right now. Sharing a baby is one thing but bringing up the potential of being an *actual* couple with someone who doesn't date is terrifying.

"Close your eyes," Gracie demands and brings an eyeshadow brush to my lids. "I'm not doing it super dramatic, but just a little something to bring out your beautiful eyes."

"Thanks for doing this."

"After our lifetime of friendship, I don't know why you forget I'd do absolutely anything for you. You're my person, Liv." Even shut, my eyes begin to sting with incoming tears.

My chest tightens with her confession. Have Gracie and I been friends for forever? Yes. But she isn't normally one to be so open with how she's feeling. She'd kill someone for me before ever admitting that I'm one of the most important people in her life out loud.

She moves on to eyeliner, then mascara, before putting on blush. I'm grateful that she didn't put anything heavy on my face because I want to still feel and *look* like myself.

"Okay. I'm done!" she announces and I open my eyes to look at my reflection. Gracie is standing behind me with her arms crossed with a smile that looks like she just won the lottery. "You are already one of the most stunning humans I've ever seen, but damn, I did good." I run my fingers over the loose curls that cascade down my shoulders. She's pinned back one side, smoothing it out and using a bobby pin to keep it in place behind my ear.

"Wow, you really outdid yourself, Gracie."

She smirks and rolls her eyes exaggeratingly. "Do you want me to drive you to the studio?"

"If you want to. I can get a ride home from Beck after." I get up off my vanity chair and grab my clothes off my bed.

We walk out of my bedroom and into the kitchen. I sort through my cabinets to find my tumbler so that I can fill it up with ice and water. Summer has *officially* come to Dryer Hill, and I am actually dying because it's so hot.

I head up the stairs to the address Beck gave me for the studio. It's in Old Dryer Hill, like the most original buildings he town has. The wooden planks groan and creak beneath my feet as I walk to the stop of the stairs. I open the only door on the second floor and walk into a very bright room. One of the walls is nothing but windows while one of the other one is an off white color. A loud noise comes from a hallway off to the left.

"Beckett?" My voice is shaky as I call out his name.

"Hey, Freckles." He comes around the corner and his lips curl into my favorite cocky grin. He's wearing a button up that he keeps open, his sleeves are rolled up just to above his elbow expose all of his tattoos. My hormones are *really* getting out of hand because I could literally jump his bones right now. He lifts up his camera and raises a brow. "You ready?"

"Where do you want me?"

"Right there." He points at the big white wall I noticed when I walked in.

Beck walks over to where I'm standing up against the wall, unbuttons my pants and folds down the front some, and unbuttons my white shirt just enough for my stomach to hang out. He leans down and kisses the top of my exposed belly softly. Heat travels up my neck and I know I am crimson. He directs me into a pose and snaps a photo. His camera *clicks* what must be a dozen times as he moves closer and in different spots around me.

After two more positions up against the wall, he grabs a tripod and sets his camera up. He lines it up just right and comes to stand behind me. "I want a couple of photos with us together, is that okay?"

I nod.

I would absolutely love that.

He wraps his arms over my shoulders, draping them just over my breasts, and leans in close. I put one hand on the top of my stomach, one on the bottom, and lean into him. His camera *clicks* in the distance, but my heart is drumming in my ears. His hand glides up the front of my neck and pulls me towards him. Our lips meet and dizziness consumes me. I'm sure he hears my heart beating because if I didn't know any better, I'd think it's about to break through my chest. It's not like we've never kissed before, but there's something about this moment, something about the level of intimacy, that makes everything around us disappear.

At this moment there's only him, only us.

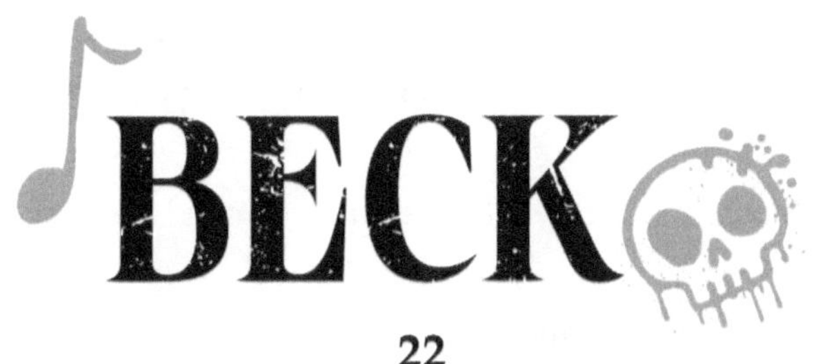

BECK

22

After we finish up with Olivia's photos, we're both *starving* and I can't think of a better thing to eat than Messina's. I pull into a parking spot and shut off the truck. Her brows are creased and she's chewing on her bottom lip, so it's not hard to see that her brain is focusing really hard on something. I'm not sure if I should press her on it or just wait and let her tell me when she's ready.

I take her hand as we walk into the pizza place, leading her up to the register so that we can order. The tables are all lined with the cliche white and red plaid tablecloths and the smell of tomato sauce and yeast hangs thick in the air. I wouldn't be lying if I said that I was happy we're finally over the burrito bowl craving and happy to be on to other foods.

"Beck!" Dante hollers, throwing his hands in the air. He comes around the counter and embraces me. "And who is this?" He raises his brow and tilts his head in question.

"Dante, this is Olivia. Olivia, this is Dante. He owns this fine establishment."

"Nice to meet you, Dante." Olivia sticks out her hand to shake his, but Dante pulls her in for a hug instead. "*Oof.*"

He pulls her back and smiles. "What are you with this guy for, eh?"

"He feeds me." She shrugs and throws a smirk in my direction.

Dante looks at me and then gestures to her stomach, almost like he's saying *yours?* I nod once and his smile somehow grows even bigger. "You're gonna be a daddy!" He pulls Olivia and I both into another hug. "Congratulations! Pizza is on me tonight. You want the usual?"

"Just a medium pepperoni, Dante. We're gonna eat it here. But you're gonna let me pay you."

"Can I order a salad bar please? I love a good salad bar."

"Your money is no good here, alright?" He walks back around the counter and looks through the kitchen window. "Medium pepperoni pizza."

He gives us two cups for the soda fountain and a plate. Olivia goes over to the salad bar, and I get our drinks. Me, a Dr. Pepper and her, sweetened iced tea. I pick o one of the many empty tables and sit down. I realize I haven't checked my phone basically all day, so I pull it out and look through my notifications. There's a couple here and there, but I pull up the band group chat which apparently popped off.

> Derek: Practice tonight.

> Hayes:

> Derek: We booked a show in town tomorrow, so we need to be spot on.

> Derek: Got confirmation there will be a manager looking to sign there.

Watson: Fucking cool!

Derek: Anyone hear from Beck?

Hayes: Nope.

Watson: Not me.

This conversation, and the missed phone calls from Derek, are all from a few hours ago. There's no doubt that Derek is pissed, so I press on his name and call him while I wait for Olivia.

"You're alive?" he chides.

"Sorry, man. What's up?"

"You gonna be at practice?"

I look around to find Olivia. She's bouncing back and forth while she makes her salad, and I have to choke back a laugh.

"I told you I'd be there until you find my replacement. Maybe you can talk to this manager about finding a new drummer."

"Why do you want to quit so bad?"

I take a deep breath and rub the bridge of my nose. I *really* don't know how to make it easier for him to understand.

"I have shit that's just more important, D. I don't want to miss out on my kid's life by spending time at practice or playing shows."

"But you'll be there tonight?"

"Yes. I gotta go."

I hang up as Olivia slides into the booth. She's frowning. "Is everything okay? You look irritated."

"Just Derek. I need to disappear or something."

"We could always go on a babymoon."

"A what?"

"You know…" She stirs her salad around and pops a crouton in her mouth. "A babymoon! It's like a vacation before the baby comes."

"Where would you want to go, Freckles?" I take an olive from the edge of the plate and throw it into my mouth.

"That's so easy! Seal Point Cove."

"The little beach town that's like almost five hours away?"

"That's the one! We went a handful of times when I was a kid and teenager. Some of my favorite childhood memories were made there."

"Noted."

"So, we need to talk."

My stomach drops straight out of my ass. "What's up?"

"We need to agree on a baby name."

I run my hand down my face. Fuck. I thought she was going to say something stupid like we need to just be friends. *But… what are we? What does she even want to be?*

"Okay. What else is on that list of yours?"

"Juniper?"

"Absolutely not." I take a drink from my cup. "Josephine?"

"What? No." She scrolls through the list on her phone. "Autumn?"

"No."

"Jade?" I shake my head no. "Hm. Sawyer?" I stop and look at her. Slowly she smiles and clasps her hands in front of her chest. "Really?"

"I don't hate that name. I actually really like it."

"So, do we have our daughter's name?"

"I think we do." I nod and lean onto the table.

"Now she needs a middle name."

I try not to groan. Not because it's not important, because it is, but it took us *weeks* to agree on the first name and now we need a second? Dante brings the pizza to the table and sets it in between us, letting us know it's very hot and to be careful before talking away.

"Sawyer Rose?" She blows on her pizza and takes a bite. I think about it for a second and decide it's actually beautiful.

"I like that one."

"See, that wasn't so hard." She smiles and shimmies in her seat. "Sawyer Rose Haven."

I try not to choke on my pizza, but I fail.

"Haven?"

"Yes?"

"You want to give her my last name?"

"Why wouldn't I?"

"I guess I just assumed you'd give her yours." Her face turns a dark shade of pink, and she tries to fight the smile that is appearing despite her efforts. "What?"

"I mean," she clears her throat and adjusts herself in the seat. "Would it be unrealistic to hope that maybe one day we'd all have the same last name?"

I'm stunned.

Absolutely stunned.

She's thought about fucking *marrying* me?

"No, Freckles. It's not unrealistic."

AFTER WE EAT, we head back to the apartment. Olivia is in the kitchen putting her lunch together for work tomorrow, so I have my laptop out and I'm scrolling through hotels in Seal Point. There's a ton that are in town, but I'd really like to find something beachfront. When I'm all out of hotel options, I pull up a vacation rental property website.

I find an apartment within the first page. It's a single level two bedroom, one bathroom rental. There's a patio that leads straight onto the beach. On the patio are two chairs and a small table. Immediately, I imagine Olivia and I sitting there and watching the sun go down. I book it for next month without a second thought.

"Hey, Freckles?"

"Yeah?" She doesn't lift her eyes from where she's cutting up some kind of vegetable.

"I booked us an apartment for the weekend."

"You did what now?"

"For your babymoon thing." She scurries around the island and stands in front of me on the couch.

"You did? Really?"

"See." I spin the computer around and show her the booking. She closes my laptop and puts it on the coffee table.

Olivia moves to straddle my lap with her legs spread wide across me. I've never been so grateful for dresses than I am at this moment. I run my hands up soft thighs and the tip of my finger over the inner band of her panties. Our lips meet and immediately our tongues are dancing as my hands roam her body.

I grip on tightly to her hips and whisper as we try to catch our breath, "I've been thinking about you all fucking day, Freckles." My dick strains against my jeans as her lips travel down the side of my neck.

Olivia moves off of my lap, nudging my legs apart before

she gets on her knees on the ground between them. She looks up at me through her thick lashes and takes her bottom lip between her teeth. *Fuck, she is sexy.* Her eyes don't leave mine as she tugs my jeans and underwear down to my ankles. She teases the tip of my cock with her tongue and tentatively runs it up my length before she takes me into her mouth. I grip her hair tighter than I mean to and guide her pace so that I don't cum before I've had a chance to *really* enjoy this moment.

Her moan vibrates against my cock and my head falls back. She glides her tongue along the underside of my shaft and takes me into the deepest part of her throat, gagging slightly as it hits the very back. I look down to watch, surprised when I meet her tear filled eyes.

"I need to be inside of you."

She whimpers at my confession, swirling her tongue around the tip of my dick before releasing me from her mouth.

"I don't know if I can be gentle right now," I say in warning.

"I don't know if I want you to be."

Fuck.

I move her to the couch and flip her over, accidentally ripping her panties when I pull them down. I line the tip of my dick to her pussy and rub it along her entrance. "Is your pussy aching for me, Freckles?"

"Yes."

"How bad do you want me to fuck you?"

"So bad," she whimpers and drops her head forward, pushing back towards me. "Please."

"I love it when you beg." I grip one hand onto her hip and guide my cock into her with the other. She lets out a loud moan when I thrust into her hard and fast. I grip onto her hips and lift her so that I can get as deep as possible. Her pussy tightens around me, and she starts to meet me thrust for thrust.

"You feel so fucking good."

"Beck, I'm going to—" I slam into her, taking her even deeper.

"Come for me, Freckles." She pushes back into me.

I suck two fingers into my mouth and reach around, circling them over her swollen clit. Her moans fill the air as her pussy throbs against my cock. A deep groan escapes the base of my throat, my own release nearing. I thrust into her and ride out both of our orgasms as I empty myself inside of her.

She falls onto the couch, landing on her side. I sit down at her side and pull her into me, leaving a soft kiss on her temple. We sit in silence for a moment to calm our heavy breathing.

"Come on. I think we need a shower after that one." I pull my pants up and help her to her feet, guiding her towards the bathroom. I start the water and help her lift the dress up and over her head before taking off of my own clothes. "You okay?"

"Yes! I'm more than okay. Just need a nap now."

I help her step into the shower, the steam curls around her as she steps into the water. She lifts her head back into the water and fuck if she doesn't look like a fucking goddess. She turns around to let the water run down the front of her body and I come up behind her, moving her wet hair from one side of her neck to the other. A soft gasp escapes her lips as I nibble along her skin. I run my hand down her chest, pinching her nipple softly before continuing over her stomach. Her head falls back against my shoulder as I continue to softly bite her neck.

The tips of my fingers trace along her slit. "You still want more?" I whisper against her ear. She arches into my touch as I slide two fingers into her entrance. Her arm reaches around and grips onto the back of my neck. Her moans echo off of the tiles in the shower. Her knees threaten to buckle, but I hold on tight as another orgasm rushes through her.

We finish our shower with no other, *erm,* interruptions and curl up on the couch before I have to leave for practice. My fingers run lazily through her damp hair.

"Hey, Freckles?"

She hums lazily, probably half asleep.

"Can I ask you something? It may seem super lame, especially since you're having my baby."

"Now I have to know, so please ask away."

"Do you think that maybe you'd want to be my girlfriend?"

I've never had one before, so I don't know how to ask. Am I supposed to ask?

She practically leaps off of the couch and onto my lap.

"Really?" She kisses me. I laugh against her lips and nod my head. She breaks our kiss and looks at me with a huge smile "Abso-freaking-lutely I do."

And just like that Olivia Connoly is my fucking girlfriend.

23

Thirty-Four Weeks Pregnant

I have never looked forward to summer break as much as I have this year. Last week I closed up my classroom for the summer and now I can just relax. I say that word loosely, *relax*. I'll be doing nothing but prepping for the baby for the next few weeks, but for today I'm going to at least attempt to relax.

Beck left early for work, still widdling away on his super secret project, so I have a slow-ish morning. I woke up and went back to the yoga studio for class. My therapist has helped me work through my panic attacks, which have been coming less frequently. I get one every once in a while, but *nothing* like that first one. After yoga, I'm home, showered, and decide it's the perfect time to go get brunch with my besties.

Me: Brunch?

Gracie: Hell yeah

Daph: Meet you in 15?

Mattie: It's a slow day. Charlotte will probably
let me leave!

Mattie: She said absolutely.

Gracie: Savor?

My mouth immediately begins to water when I think of their amazing French toast.

Me: Yes. Please!!

I throw on one of the only dresses I own that doesn't make me feel like a tent and braid my hair so it's out of my face. My feet have grown at least half a size, which means I slide on a pair of sandals before I grab my bag and head out the door. Savor is only down the street from my apartment building and I decide to just walk it.

I regret it almost immediately.

It's too freaking hot.

Sweat runs down my neck, making my hair to stick to my skin. You know where else I sweat? My butt and crotch. I'm absolutely *not* made for being pregnant in the summer.

Note to self: our next baby will absolutely not be a summer baby.

I hail a cab and slide in breathlessly. He takes one look in the back seat and doesn't question why I'm taking a two minute taxi ride instead of the ten minute walk. I sit back and try to cool down before I get to the restaurant.

Gracie and Daphne are already at a table when I walk

through the doors. Immediately, they wave me down, I greet the hostess and make my way towards my sister and best friend.

"Look at that belly!" Gracie exclaims as she hops up from her seat, leaning down to rub on and kiss my stomach. She's one of five people who are allowed to do so without asking. The others are my sisters, Mom, and Beck, obviously.

"I can't believe you still have like five more weeks to go," Daph says.

I pull out my chair and sit down. Nodding in agreement. I *also* can't believe I still have five-ish weeks to go. It's not likely I'll have the baby earlier, with her being my first, but I wouldn't be mad if she decided to come before than thirty-nine or forty weeks.

"I'm here! I'm here!" Mattie's purse lands on the table with a *thud*. Granted, I don't know if the huge thing she carries around can be considered a purse. It's more like a small suitcase and is full of god knows what.

None of us have to look at the menu, so by the time the waitress comes over to greet us we already know what we want. Ordering the waffle stack with a side of bacon, well done, and hashbrowns was the easiest choice I've ever had to make. The girls all order a mimosa, while I just ask for sweet tea. These days, just about all citrus gives me heartburn. Which is unfortunate because I love citrus.

I listen to the updates about their lives and realize it's been a while since we've all gotten to sit down like this. Mattie is beyond happy with her job and has decided to go back to college so that she can become an editor. My big sister heart is soaring with how proud of her I am. Gracie and Daphne share their stories about the other members of Skarred and how much *fun* they're having with them. Almost in unison everyone turns to me, staring at me and waiting for me to interject.

"What?"

"Don't act like you know we aren't *dying* to find out what the fuck is happening with you and Beck? You guys are like officially dating?" Gracie puts her chin into her hands and waits for me to respond.

I open my mouth to speak, but snap my jaw shut. I'm *so* beyond excited to be with Beck, and of course they already know he asked me to be his girlfriend, but I'd be lying if I said I wasn't a little anxious about their opinions. After all, they have hung out with him and his bandmates for years.

"I think what Gracie means to ask is, are you guys serious or..." Daph encourages me to continue.

I look down to my stomach and back up to them. "I mean, kind of?"

"I mean, obviously you guys have Sawyer, but you know what we mean."

"We love you and we just don't want to see you get hurt. You're literally the first relationship he's ever had, Liv. That's a big deal."

"What exactly is your point?" My tone probably comes off more irritated than I mean it to, but I stand my ground.

"I'm just protective of you, that's all." Daphne shifts in her seat. "I'd hate to have to square up with him if he hurt you or the baby."

"He's not going to hurt me," I say with my whole chest, releasing a sigh to force myself to relax some. There are zero parts of me that don't believe that statement.

"We know Beck's a good guy, we just have our concerns." Gracie leans forward on the table.

"Which is understandable, but we have developed a really solid friendship. It's solid enough that, if for some reason, we don't work out we would be able to co-parent. At the end of the day, it's about having a relationship for Sawyer anyways, regardless of what kind of relationship that is."

The waitress drops off our food and my stomach twists in hunger. The first bite is pure heaven. I let out an audible moan when it finally hits my lips. The conversation continues around me, but I'm in my own bubble with these darn waffles.

My plate is practically licked clean before someone brings back up Beck and our relationship.

"So." Daphne clears her throat. "how's the sex?"

I choke on my tea.

"We're all thinking about it. You've been *apparently* drooling over him since high school. So, how is it? Everything you've ever dreamed of?"

Amazing.

Otherworldly.

Mind-blowing.

But I don't say literally any of that. "It's fine."

"You're a lying bitch!" Gracie exclaims loud enough for people's heads to turn.

"Gracie!" I scold.

"Sorry, but you can't just say it's *fine* and expect me to not call you out on your bullshit. I need all the details."

I can feel the heat creep up from my chest and up to my cheeks. Daphne squeals and kicks her feet beneath the table, but Gracie looks at me with her mouth gaping open.

"Oh, my fucking god."

"What?" My eyes grow big.

"You're in love with him. You're in fucking love with Beck!" Gracie covers her mouth with the palm of her hand.

There's no use in saying it's not true.

I am head-over-heels so freaking in love with Beckett Haven.

AFTER BRUNCH WITH THE GIRLS, I head back to my apartment and take a nap. Everything, and I literally mean everything, drains me. When I finally wake up, I grab my phone from the side table and check my texts.

> My Hot Baby Daddy: My place tonight?
>
> My Hot Baby Daddy: Time to start packing.

I check the time and see I slept basically the entire day away. It's already almost five, so I know Beck will be home soon.

> Me: See you soon.

I'm not sure if it's just the honeymoon stage, or what, but the butterflies in my stomach swirl around at the thought of seeing Beck. Even though it's been less than a day, not even a full twelve hours.

Once I have everything packed and ready for a night at Beck's. I head down to the garage. My phone connects to my speakers, and the sound of my podcast fills my car. The current episode is of a murder that took place in New York in the 1908's.

After the short drive, I pull up to Beck's house and put my car in park. I let the episode come to a stopping point before turning off the ignition.

I walk up the stairs to the front door, knock three times, and wait patiently for the door open. My hands are folded on top of my stomach, and I chew on my bottom lip while I sway back and forth. Blaire opens the door with a scowl; her face softens when she sees it's me.

"Hey! Beck's getting Messina's. Come in!"

I smile and cross the threshold, into the living room. There're boxes piled up around the living room and lining the hallway. Blaire sits back onto the couch, pushing play on the TV. I set my duffle bag down onto a pile of boxes and join her on the couch.

"What are you watching?"

"The newest season of *You*. Have you seen it?"

A smile slowly spreads across my face. "Of course I've seen it! I loved last season." I settle back and grab a dark gray throw blanket from across the arm of the couch.

Halfway through the episode, Beck walks in the front door with a bag and a pizza box. He closes the front door and stands in the walkway, staring at us for a second.

He shakes his head. "She's convinced you to watch this shit?" He comes up behind where I'm sitting on the couch and I tilt my head back to look at him, resting the back of my head on the cushion. He smiles softly and leans down to kiss the top of my nose before walking into the kitchen. My eyes follow him through the archway, stopping when they clash with Blaire's.

"I've literally never seen him like that."

"Like what?"

"In love."

I don't even attempt to hide my smile.

Beck rejoins us hands us both our plates before announcing he's going to take a shower. He mumbles something about all of the wood dust gets into his hair and disappears down the hallway

Blaire and I watch the rest of the episode and not before long, Beck comes back. He takes both of our plates and puts them in the kitchen. The faucet turns on and the sound of running water and porcelain plates clinking together flow into the room. After a few minutes, I am immediately aware of his presence, and so is Sawyer because she jumps on my bladder like it's a trampoline.

He sits down on the couch next to me, grabbing my legs and draping them over his own. His hands are rough and calloused, but his grip is gentle as he rubs my calves down to my feet. It feels so good that I lay my head back and close my eyes.

Thirty-Five Weeks Pregnant

THE DRIVE to Seal Point was nice. *I think.*

It seems I slept for almost all of it. Which stinks because I downloaded a new book on my e-reader that I have been desperate to read. The car comes to a stop and Beck put it in park, gently nudging me awake. I wipe the drool away from the corner of my lip with the back of my hand and groan.

"Why didn't you wake me up?"

"I don't think you would have woken up, Freckles. You were snoring."

"I was not."

Beck's lips curve into a mischievous grin and he lifts up his phone, pressing play on the screen. The sound of me snoring immediately begins to flow out of the speakers. I can't help but burst out into laughter.

"Okay. So, I snore a *bit.*"

He turns off the car and opens the door. Waves crash against the shore in the distance and the brisk, salty air flows with the wind. The sun setting on the horizon in between our rental and the house next to it, bathing the sky is rich oranges. The view, even from here, is beautiful.

We make the short walk up the path and Beck enters the code into the lock. The device groans and snaps into its place, allowing us to open the front door.

In true coastal fashion, the entire house is decorated white and cream with hints of blue and green. The porcelain wood floor is a neutral gray. We walk into the living room and the entire wall is a series of windows and a sliding glass door that leads to the back porch.

"I think the bedroom is this way," Beck announces and walks down a short hallway with all of our luggage. By ours, I really mean my rolling suitcase, duffle bag, and his one small overnight bag.

The bed is set in between two windows that open up to the beach. It's made with white sheets and a light blue comforter. On either side of a small bedside table, both decorated with seashells and lamps. I turn to face the entryway to the bathroom that is right next to a closet that's doors are a full length mirror.

Beck sets the luggage in the corner of the room and comes behind me. He moves my hair from one side of my neck, to the other, and leans down until his lip presses against the top of my ear. "I've been thinking about you all day." His voice is husky, laced with lust.

I lean back, arching into him, as his hand trails up my thigh where it disappears beneath the hem of my dress. His finger teasingly traces the edge of my panties for a moment, and I know I'm going to come unglued when he finally touches me. My head falls back and rests on his shoulder.

"No, Freckles. I want you to watch." My eyes open and meet his own in the reflection. "Good girl."

His praise makes me blush.

I watch as he guides my panties down my legs and around my ankles, steadying me as he helps me out of them and throws them somewhere in the room. He raises back to his feet and pulls my dress up over my head, tossing it away. I'm mesmerized by him and how his eyes hold contact with mine the entire time. The tip of his finger trails up my spine, causing goosebumps to cover my body. He unclasps my bra and lets it fall to the floor before where I stand.

"Fuck." He moans into my ear and reaches around to take my full breasts into his hands. A sudden wave of insecurity rushes over me when the light reflects off of the silver lines that now cover my thighs and stomach.

He leans down and nibbles on my neck, taking my skin in between his teeth and putting more pressure. The pain sends a shot of electricity to all of the right places. I moan, fighting against the urge to close my eyes and lean into him.

"Don't leave any marks," I manage to whisper.

"Why not? I want everyone to know you're mine."

You're mine.

Something about the possessiveness in his tone makes me feel hot all over.

"You are a fucking goddess, Freckles. Now, let me worship you." He comes to drop on his knees in front of me, pushing me back to where I'm sitting on the bed. *Beck is on his knees. For me. This can't be happening.* He runs his hand up an ankle, slowly up my calf, and stops just beneath my knee.

"Watch," he commands, tilting his head towards the mirror behind where he sits.

I can feel his eyes burning holes into me as I watch him in the reflection, teasing me. He leaves small, gentle kisses up my thigh. His tongue glides up my slit and he moans, sending a sweet vibration up my clit and throughout my entire body. I weave my fingers into his hair as he sucks on my swollen, and *very* sensitive, clit. My moans fill the air as my orgasm rocks through me.

He stands, cutting off my view of the mirror, and I watch as he takes off his clothing. First, he lifts his shirt up and over his head. My eyes wander down his body, looking over the tattoos that cover him. I've begun to memorize them all. Slowly, he unbuttons his pants and drops them, and his underwear, to the floor. My eyes travel further down, and I gasp when I see how *hard* he is. I still can't wrap my head around the fact that I do *that* to him.

My mouth waters, freaking *waters.*

I adjust myself onto my hands and knees, motioning for him to get on the bed behind me. There's literally no ounce of hesitation as he walks around the bed and positions himself on his knees behind me. I watch his hand in the mirror, running up my side before he moves it over my chest. It emerges at the base of my neck and up just below my jaw. He leans down, cranking my head back gently and applying slight pressure to where his grip is.

"You want to watch while I fuck you this way?" I nod to the best of my ability.

I don't even realize his other hand is on my hip until he tightens his hold.

Slowly, and I mean almost agonizingly, he enters me. He pulls out at the same pace, slamming back into me. It's rough, but in the most delicious way. My head wants to fall into the cushion of the bed, but he holds it up to watch.

He releases his hold on my hip and moves it around to rub circles on my clit. I arch my back, our eyes meeting in the reflection. He takes his bottom lip in between his teeth and picks up his pace, holding my gaze as he thrusts harder and deeper into me. His eyes are darker than I've ever seen them. They're filled with a lust I've never experienced. A lust for *me.*

"Look at you." He pushes into me hard and fast, pulling out slow before pushing into me again. "So fucking beautiful."

My vision blurs as waves of pleasure crash around me. With one final deep, hard thrust, Beck begins to tremble, one final moan escaping his lips as he fills me. He groans and pulls me out of me.

Beck takes my face into his hand and kisses me gently. "I'm going to start a bath."

I nod, trying to steady my breathing and calm my racing heart.

After a short time, he comes back into the room and holds his hand out. I lace my fingers with them and he guides me into the bathroom where a *huge* bathtub awaits. He helps me in and slides behind me. I take his hand and place it on my stomach where Sawyer is bouncing around.

As much as I don't *love* the feeling of her moving inside of my stomach, I do like that this is something Beck can experience with me.

BECK

24

After our quick session, Olivia takes a catnap. She literally can't keep her eyes open for longer than a couple of hours anymore it seems. While she naps, I unpack and lay out a dress for her to wear to dinner tonight on the foot of the bed. The restaurant we're going to isn't fancy, so it's just for comfort. I know she can't stand to wear much else right now.

I sit down next to where she lays in the bed and scroll aimlessly on my phone while I wait for her to wake up. After what feels like only ten minutes, her eyes flutter open.

"How long was I out for?" She yawns.

"Not long."

She lifts her hands above her head and stretches.

"I'm starving."

I scoot off of the bed and grab my shirt for dinner. "The restaurant is right across the way. We can walk along the water if you want."

"That sounds so beautiful." She rolls off the bed and walks

over to where her dress is laid out. "I feel like I could go back to sleep. I'm so exhausted."

"I can just go pick dinner up? We don't have to go out."

"No, I *want* to. This will be like our first real date."

Guilt tightens my chest. Shit, I guess this will be like our first date.

"I mean there's been—"

"Just taco bowls and movie nights," she reminds me.

I rub the back of my neck and grimace. "Shit. I'm sorry. I guess I should have taken you out earlier."

Olivia smiles and saunters over, wrapping her arms around me. She places her chin on my chest and looks up at me with soft eyes. "I don't wish that things were different, Beckett. However it happened, we are here now."

I lean down and kiss the tip of her nose. "Ready for dinner?"

"Yes. I'm starving," she responds and slides on her sandals.

We walk across the back porch and onto the beach's white sand. She wraps her arm around mine, squeezing lightly as she pulls me close. The setting sun reflects off the calm water and I let the moment sink in. Like *really* sink in. I'm walking along the edge of the water with Olivia Connoly by my side, pregnant with my baby, no less. *Fuck.* The universe has a way of making things happen when you don't expect it.

We talk about her birthing plan as we walk, which I didn't even know was a thing. She desperately wants to labor at home for as long as she can. It is also *very* important to her that she gets her epidural. Suddenly, she stops dead in her tracks and as serious as I've ever seen her, she says, "But if the doctor even jokes about the husband stitch, punch them."

I nod and make a mental note, even though I have no idea

what a husband stitch is. And it definitely sounds like something I shouldn't look up.

We get to the restaurant and onto the outdoor seating area. We are brought to one of the tables near the edge of the patio. The tables are set with a small bundle of white flowers in vases with a couple of small LED candles in the center.

"Everything sounds so good!" She turns one of the pages in the leather bound menu. "And they have a really nice selection of allergy safe options."

The waitress comes and takes our drink and appetizer order. Olivia's hair blows in the wind as she watches the waves crash in the distance. I don't know what it is. It could be the color of the sunset or the lights that are strung across the top of the patio, but fuck, she's radiant. I wonder if this is what people mean when they say they're glowing. But whatever it is, I'm obsessed.

"What?" She raises a brow and tilts her head slightly.

"Nothing."

"Obviously it's something. You're basically staring."

I'm head over heels for you, Freckles.

"You just look beautiful tonight, that's all."

"Beckett Haven, are you flirting with me?"

I place my elbows on the table and cross them beneath my chest, leaning over as much of the table as I possibly can. "So, what if I am?"

Blush creeps up her face and floods her cheeks with a deep pink. "I think I like it."

"That's good. I have no intention of stopping anytime soon."

She tucks a loose strand of hair behind her ears and sucks her bottom lip in between her teeth.

I almost ask her to move in with me right then and there,

but I don't. There's a way I want to do it, and it isn't on our first technical date. No, I want to show her everything I've been working on. I need her to know I'm serious about this, about us.

I DIDN'T WANT to go home from our slice of heaven, but it's time to move all of the way into the new house.

I've had the keys for a while, I just needed to make sure that everything was perfect. I don't have too much stuff and I'm letting Blaire keep a majority of the furniture since she's staying there. It was almost easier for me to buy new furniture and have it delivered than it was to take the old stuff from our shared house.

I stand in the center of the living room and can't help but feel pride. I've heard from enough people in my life that I wasn't going to amount to much. More people were surprised than proud when I graduated from high school. Well, except Mom and Dad. They cheered loud enough for me the day I walked across the stage that I didn't notice who *wasn't* cheering.

Now, here I am. I'm standing in the house that I bought by myself, for my family.

My family.

I walk down the hallway and into the room I decided is Sawyer's nursery. The crib I made sits against one of the walls. In basically no time at all there will be a baby, *my* baby, in that bed. I close the door and walk into the room next to it.

For the last few weeks, I wasn't even sure what this room

would be. I had thrown around the idea of it being a guest room and even a game room. But neither of them felt right.

After I was done building the crib, I was left with some scrap pieces, and I wasn't sure what exactly to do with them. Until, that is, I overheard my sister and Olivia talking about art.

Similar to me, Blaire loves to create art and she's damn good at it. Unlike me, who can't paint a fucking blob, she creates the most stunning pieces. She and Olivia share a love for painting and have bonded over that love. Once I heard Olivia say she wished she had somewhere to paint, I knew the spare room had to be her office and studio space. Have I asked her to move in? No, but I want her to have a space if she says yes when I do. Which is happening today.

Back to the project with the excess wood.

Once I decided the spare room would be for her use, I got to work. Using whatever I had left over, plus some additional wood, I built her an easel, a stand for her paint, and storage for the room. Then, I asked Blaire for help. There was no hesitation in her accepting my request. In fact, she named her task *Operation: Liv's Birthday.* So, with my card, and no budget, she set off to the art store only to come back three hours later with five bags of art supplies.

I lean against the door jam, arms crossed across my chest, looking into the room. The easel is in the center, with a stool and a small stand. One of the walls has a window and the other has the storage compartments I built. Everything is stained a light yellow-brown and she can paint the rooms, any of the rooms really, whatever color she wants.

"Knock, knock." Olivia's voice flows through the hallway.

"Hey!" I hurry into the living room so that she doesn't start to wander.

"Am I too early?"

"No. You're right on time." I smile and kiss her.

My stomach twists and turns in anticipation. I'm trying to not weigh in on the possibility that she's going to say no, but the little voice in the back of my head is toying with me.

She's going to say no.

"So, what is this super secret thing you've been working on that I *finally* get to see?"

I walk around and cover her eyes with my hands. I lean down to whisper in her ear, "Do you want the surprise or your birthday present first?"

"You didn't have to—"

"*Tsk. Tsk. Tsk.* Don't finish that sentence, Freckles."

"Sorry. Let's do the surprise first."

"Good choice."

Still covering her eyes, I guide her down the hallway towards the nursery. My stomach is in knots as we come to the door. I suck in a deep breath, let it out slowly, and lower my hands.

"A door?"

"Open it," I whisper and lift her hand to the doorknob.

She turns the knob and pushes the door open, gasping immediately when she sees the room. Her hands go up to her mouth and she turns to look at me over her shoulder. I nod and motion for her to go in.

"I wasn't sure what color or decorations you wanted to put on the walls, so I'll leave that all to you." Olivia runs the tip of her fingers over the crib and walks over to the chair my mom picked out, she sits in it and rocks back and forth. She looks around the room as she rubs her stomach. "So?" I lean against the door jam.

"I'm obsessed with it. It's gorgeous. Especially this crib. I've never seen anything like it before." I look down at the ground and laugh. "What?"

"I made it. Well, my dad helped."

"You made it? That's amazing, Beckett!"

My chest fills with pride at the compliment, especially because it came from her lips.

"If this is my surprise..." She pushes off the arms of the chair and springs to her feet. "Then what's my birthday present?"

"Do you want me to cover your eyes for this one?" She shakes her head, so I reach out to take her hand instead.

I guide her back to the other end of the hallway, towards the room I've made her studio, and stand in front of the door.

"Another room?"

"Another room."

Olivia opens the door and walks through the threshold. Unlike seeing the nursery for the first time, there's no big reaction. She stands in the center of the room and doesn't move for a moment, almost like she's taking it all in.

"Freckles?"

Her shoulders rise and fall as she takes a deep breath. She turns around, with silent tears streaming down her face, and attempts to respond. "Mine?"

"Yeah. This is yours."

"Why?"

"Because...I wanted you to have a place to go. Your own place. You can do whatever you want with this room. I know you wanted—" I'm cut off when her lips crash into mine. I wrap my arms around her lower back, pulling her into me as much as I can around her belly. Her arms wrap around my neck, and she groans into my mouth. She pulls back and I lean to rest my forehead on hers. "What was that for?"

"This is just the sweetest thing anyone's ever done for me." I lift my hand and wipe away the tear gliding down her left cheek. "The wood for the easel is the same as the crib, isn't it?"

"It is."

"I don't know how to say thank you for everything."

"Move in with me." I blurt out, immediately regretting my loose tongue.

"What?" She pulls back and I curse under my breath. Leave it to me to go and fuck up a good moment.

"I mean, you don't have to. I just thought it might make it easier."

"Do you *want* me to move in?"

Yes. Please. Absolutely.

"Only if you want to."

Olivia takes a deep breath and pulls out of my arms, bringing her hand up to her mouth. "Can I think about it?"

"Of course. You don't have to answer me anytime soon. I shouldn't of asked like that—"

"Yes."

"Huh?" I stand there, completely in shock of what is happening right now. Is she really saying what I think, what I *hope*, she's saying?

"I want to move in."

I stare at her like she grown horns or something.

Olivia just said she wants to move in with *me*, and while that's exactly what I want, I'm still beyond surprised. She smirks and tilts her head. I open my mouth to respond, but just as quickly snap it shut.

"What's wrong?"

I shake my head and pull her into me, letting her warm scent drift up and engulf me in the best way. "I just didn't expect you to say yes," I murmur into her hair.

"You didn't?"

"No, but I was hoping you would."

She pulls back from the embrace and gets up on the tip of her toes. I bend down to place my lips on hers, moving my hand to cup her jaw. Despite how many times I feel her soft lips against mine, I'm still thinking about the next time I get to kiss her.

We stand in the middle of the hallway, getting lost in each other.

The is *our* home.

Olivia

25

Thirty-Eight Weeks Pregnant

Each day I feel more and more like a beached whale.

Even though Beck has assured me many, many times I'm not, I don't believe him.

The sole purpose of our adventure today is to get everything we need for the hospital bag and the rest of the stuff for Sawyer's diaper bag. My sister gifted us the most perfect backpack diaper bag that I have ever seen and I'm antsy to fill it up.

I force myself out of bed, doing my best to avoid all of the boxes scattered around the room. Making the choice to move in with Beck was one of the easiest decisions and came at the most perfect time. Daphne and I were at the end of our lease and now that her and Derek are getting more serious, I think that getting a place together is in their near future.

After digging around in one of the boxes labeled *clothes* for about ten minutes, I am left completely out of breath. Luckily, I did find the dress I was looking for. I take off my pajamas and throw them into the dirty clothes hamper in the corner of the room. They land with a soft thud as they hit the bottom. I grab the dress and sit on the edge of the bed, trying to find the energy to put it on.

I've never been this tired in my life and I know once she gets here, I will only be even *more* exhausted. It's not even just the exhaustion that's kicking my butt, but the aches and pains that I feel every second of the day and the constant need to pee. I take a deep breath and remind myself that it's only going to be a couple of more weeks.

The door to the bedroom swings open and Beck leans against the doorframe. "You okay?" I nod and move off the bed to stand on my feet.

"I'm just ready to not be pregnant anymore, honestly."

"But you make the prettiest pregnant person ever." He helps me pull the dress down around my swollen belly.

"You're biased."

"You are not wrong. I am absolutely biased. But I'm still right."

I shrug and throw my hair up into a messy bun. I know the second we walk out of the house I will be completely saturated with sweat, so I want to be somewhat prepared. Even though there's literally nothing that will prepare me for what it's really like.

"Ready to go?"

"Yes!" I exclaim, feeling nothing but excitement about getting to finally go shopping for everything we need for the hospital. I'm surprised by myself and the lack of preparation I've done for Sawyer and the hospital stay.

We walk out the front door and to my car. No matter how

many times I have seen it since we've installed it, the sight of the car seat base hasn't gotten any less weird. Beck scrolls through his phone for a second before backing up out of the driveway. I recognize the introduction to my favorite podcast as it fills the car.

"I didn't know you listened to them."

"I don't." He looks at me from the corner of his eye with a smirk. "But you do."

Swoon.

His hand moves to my leg, and he squeezes my knee so gently that I barely notice it. Beck has never made me feel anything but safe, so his hand on me is comforting and I welcome it.

I STAND in the diaper aisle, looking back and forth between two different brands of soap. *What makes one better than the other?* I grab the two bottles and look to Beck in hopes that maybe he can read my mind and give me some insight, but he just shrugs.

"I literally have no idea."

"That brand is just the generic version of that one," a voice from behind us says. We both turn to look over our shoulder and I smile to the stranger.

"So, they're the same thing?"

"Essentially, yes. But that one is half the price."

Beck takes it out of my hand and puts it in the cart already filled with stuff for my hospital bag. I printed a list off the internet and went through it to see what I would use and what I wouldn't, but there was just so much. I didn't even realize that there could be so much to possibly need.

"Thank you," I respond to the nice stranger and put the other soap back on the shelf.

"Your first?" she asks.

"It is." My hand automatically goes to the top of my stomach. The woman has two younger kids in the cart, so I compliment them in hopes to try to spark some kind of a conversation. "They're so sweet." I wave at the little girl with short blonde hair in pigtails.

"Oh, thank you." She turns to them and makes a silly face. "She just turned three and this little guy..." She tickles the younger child in the seat. "Just turned two."

We talk for a few minutes in the diaper aisle and just when she's about to leave, she grins. "You're going to get *a lot* of advice, but my biggest for the two of you?" She moves her finger between Beck and I. "Remember you guys are a team and it won't be fifty-fifty. There's going to be days where one of you can't give it your all, just give it your 'some' and lean on each other. You guys will be okay."

I fight against the lump in my throat and nod. It was like she's seeing me, really *seeing* me. Every fear I have about my relationship with Beck and every fear I have about becoming a mom is on full display.

We turn the corner and walk right into the baby clothes section. I turn to look at Beck, who's already shaking his head in understanding. Does she need more clothes? No, absolutely not. Am I still going to buy some? You bet your butt I am. I can't help it when they make the little clothes so stinkin' adorable!

First, I find a cream sleeveless romper with a cherry and polka dot pattern. Of course she needs that in two sizes. Then I find a brown and ivory striped romper that looks like overalls, and I basically melt into a puddle right there.

I must have blacked out because next thing I know there's at least ten more outfits and a couple packs of bows in the cart. Beck just leans onto the cart, watching me with a softened expression.

"Okay, I'm done." I shrug and put another romper into the basket.

"You sure?"

"I think so, yeah."

"I don't think she could *ever* have too many white short shirt things."

My head falls back as laughter erupts from me. Beck smirks, unsure of what I could possibly find so amusing.

"The *rompers* are not white; they're cream and ivory."

"Oh, sorry." He throws his hands up dramatically. "The *rompers* are a necessity in every color, shape, and style."

"They absolutely are."

Beck walks around the cart to where I'm standing at the end and takes my chin between his thumb and pointer finger. Gently, he lifts my chin so that our lips meet. "Whatever makes your heart happy, Freckles," he says against my mouth.

My body suddenly feels hot and there's an ache forming between my thighs. I need to get Beck home *immediately* or I'm going to end up pulling him into a dressing room.

I basically sprint to check out, cringing at the total when the cashier finishes ringing everything up. I dig around my bag to find my wallet, but before I have a chance to pull it out Beck is already paying for everything.

"You didn't have—"

"She's my daughter, too." He raises an eyebrow and smirks at me.

That smirk.

WE GET BACK to the house and I nearly scream at him as he slowly unpacks the car. He carries everything except for the box of diapers inside, which I decide to get, and then I close the trunk. The walk to the house feels like torture because everything is *overly* sensitive and I literally want to do nothing but feel him inside of me right now, but I don't tell him that. No. Instead I let my face become flush and there's no way to hide how I'm feeling.

We place our haul in different areas of the nursery and Beck walks to the living room. He sits on the couch and rests his elbows on his knees before running his hands down his face.

"I've got to tell you something."

My heart sinks.

"Shit, no. It's not anything bad."

"Well, don't start out like that next time," I grumble.

"Sorry. It's just about Skarred."

He sits back on the couch, and I stand between his legs, waiting for him to tell me whatever it is that's eating at him this way.

"I've made the choice to leave the band. It's been over for a while and I told Derek some time ago, but I'm just waiting on my replacement."

"You...you didn't quit because of me, right?" I chew on the inside of my cheek, guilt tightening my chest. I know how much he loves music and I would hate for him to give it up for me.

"No, not at all." He leans back forward and runs his hands up the back of my thigh. I inhale deeply at the warmth in his touch. "I just don't love it anymore. Not like I love other things."

"What other things?"

"Like you."

My eyes grow wide. *What did he just say?*

"Wha—"

"I love you, Freckles. And not just because we're going to have a baby together. It's only been you since high school. Since that first day you sat next to me in class."

"Since...since high school?" My eyes widen.

"I didn't know it then, of course." He tightens his hold on my thighs. "I was young and stupid, but yeah. I think I've always loved you."

Beckett Haven loves...me?

His hands slide up and graze the underneath of my butt. I'm suddenly even more desperate for his touch than I already was. His fingertips trace the lining of my panties, and I lean into him. He slips a finger beneath the fabric, sliding it slowly along my slit. As if a muscle memory, my hips move forward. A sound of approval escapes his throat, and I let my head fall at the sound of it.

I could come undone right then and there, but the moment he starts circling my clit with the lightest touch...I'm done. My thighs begin to tremble beneath his hold. Slowly, he slides two fingers inside of me and I moan in approval at the intrusion. I grip onto his shoulders so that I don't fall when my knees eventually give out. He curls his fingers deep inside of me with slow, deep strokes. I can *feel* his eyes on me as my orgasm ripples through me.

He pulls down my panties and quickly takes off his own pants. I don't even care to see where they end up, all I can think about is him inside of me *now*. I climb onto the couch, straddling him so that each of my legs are on the outside of his. He pulls my dress up and over my head, tossing it somewhere in the room.

I line his tip up with my entrance and slowly sink onto him. I'm so sensitive that I'm basically about to orgasm just by the sensation of him stretching me. His hands dig into my hips as he guides my pace, slow at first.

"Kiss me," he commands. He slides his hand up my spine and grips the back of my neck, bringing my mouth down to his. My lips part for him and his tongue intertwines with mine. He kisses me hard, taking my bottom lip between his teeth.

"Oh, Beck." I sigh. His lips trail along my jaw and down to my neck.

I pick up my pace, frenzied even, as my orgasm becomes undeniably close. The couch groans beneath us as we move together. My back arches as I shatter around him. He moans, grabbing onto my hips and thrusting into me, deep and hard, one last time as he fills me with his own release.

"*Fuck,*" he hisses. I lay my forehead on his, the sound of our breathing fills the space between us. "I love you, Freckles. I don't expect you to say it back, but I do."

"Beck." I take a deep breath and try to steady my racing heart. "I love you, too."

He grabs my face and pulls me back so that he is looking into my eyes. He searches between them, his own full of desperation, almost like he's terrified I'm lying. For a moment, even if it's brief, I can see his walls coming down and I think he's finally letting me all the way in.

26

I'm still waiting for Derek to find a replacement drummer, but he is dragging his feet. I know that he doesn't want to lose another founding member of the band. I get that, I do.

I haven't been showing up to practice and because of that, there haven't been any shows. Randomly, Derek texts the group chat and says we need to have a "band meeting" at the warehouse immediately. So, for once, I leave work early and now I'm sitting in the parking lot. I don't even know why I'm here, but all I want to do is be home with Olivia. I pull out my phone and shoot her a text.

> Me: Just thinking about you.

Three bubbles pop up immediately.

> Freckles: I'm going to take a nap. My stomach has been hurting off and on.

Freckles: My mom said it sounds like it's the start of labor.

Shit.

Me: Do you need anything?

Freckles: I'm okay, thank you *heart*

Me: Keep me updated.

Me: I love you.

Freckles: I love you :)

I smile down at my phone before sliding it back into my front pocket. Realization quickly hits me that *fuck* I'm going to be a dad any day. That was something I never expected to happen in my life. Did I want it to happen? Sure. I had thought about it once or twice. But never in a million years did I think it would be happening with Olivia. I had given up hope that a future like this was even in the cards for my life, but here it is.

The ground crunches beneath my boots as I jump out of my truck and make the walk across the parking lot towards the warehouse. I know I won't be able to concentrate much on whatever it is Derek called us here for. My mind will only be able to be on Olivia. Daphne is sitting on the couch, beaming with excitement when I walk into the warehouse.

"Hey, Daph."

"Beck!" She jumps up and wraps her arms around my neck. Judging based on the look on her face, she knows what is going on. "How's my favorite brother-in-law?" I raise my brow at the title. "I mean you practically *are.*"

"Ready to know what was so important that I had to leave work early to be here."

"Go over then!' She smiles and motions for me to join the guys.

I roll my eyes and meander beside Derek, who looks like he just won the lottery with the smile that's plastered across his face. He turns around and throws his hands in the air. "Beck! Finally!"

"What's up, man? You made it sound important."

"Now that you're here, I can tell everyone." He closes his eyes and inhales deeply. "We're getting *fucking* signed!"

The guys cheer from where they stand around Derek, patting him on the back and giving each other high fives. I'm in shock. Not that they got signed, no, Skarred is great, and I always knew the band would go places.

But where does this leave *me*?

"D. Can I, uh, talk to you in private?" I step to the side, running my hands down my face. I can't believe this is happening.

"What's up, man?" D joins me and the others talk loudly about their plans.

"I just thought I was fairly clear with you about where I stood." I cross my arms across my chest.

"About what?"

What the fuck does he mean, *about what?*

"That I'm done with the band, Derek."

He looks confused, as if we haven't had this conversation several times at this point. It's taking everything in me to not scream at the smug look on his face.

"I guess I just thought since we got signed—"

"No. That changes *nothing* for me, Derek. Getting signed

doesn't matter to me. What does matter to me is Olivia and Sawyer. Making sure I am there for both of them every day. Making sure I show up *every day*. I refuse to miss any part of my daughter's life." He takes a step back. "You've had plenty of time to find my replacement, D. I'm out." I turn and start walking towards the exit. "Congratulations on getting signed."

"You turn your back on me now, Beck. You're dead to me."

I stop dead in my tracks and turn around to look at him. "Start digging my grave then, Derek. I love you and Skarred, man, but I love Olivia and Sawyer more."

I give Daphne a hug and leave the warehouse. I refuse to allow myself to feel any guilt. Am I happy for Skarred? Fuck yeah, I am. But my priorities are different, and there's nothing that could take me away from Olivia or Sawyer.

As IF I was on autopilot, I drive to my parents' house. Their house has been my safe place for years now, and thankfully it's just around the corner from mine and Olivia's, so I can just swing by for a quick talk before going home.

I open the door and announce my arrival.

"Ma?"

"Beckett, is that you?" She pops her head out of the kitchen. "Hi baby, what brings you by?"

"I just came to talk to Pop. Is he here?" He's a man of few words, for sure, but he is the best person for advice or words of confidence when I need them.

She nods and pulls me in for a hug, patting me on the shoulder. "Yeah. He's out in the garden."

"Thanks." I kiss her temple and walk through the kitchen. The old wooden floor creaks beneath the weight of my steps. I open the back door and walk down the newly replaced stairs that lead into the yard. The summer wind smells like freshly cut grass and newly bloomed roses.

"Hey, kiddo," Dad calls from his spot.

"Hiya, Pop." I sit down in the chair next to him, an old metal table separating the two chairs.

"What's going on?"

I shrug and stare out into the area around me. He's not oblivious that I came here for some form of advice or confirmation. To be honest, I'm not even completely sure what I came here for. I just know I needed to talk to my dad. In the center of the yard is an old tree that still has a tire swing attached to one of its thickest branches. When we were first placed here, Blaire would make me push her on it for hours.

"Skarred is getting signed. Derek just told me."

"Well, that's good news. Congratulations." He adjusts himself in the chair. "So, does that mean a record and a tour, all of that?"

"I suppose." I run my hand through my hair and take a deep breath. "But I told Derek I'm out." I can feel the weight lift off my shoulders at my announcement. There's something about saying it out loud to my dad that makes it feel all the more real.

"Oh? Why is that?"

"I...I want to be the best possible dad and partner that I can be. I can't do that if I'm on the road or in the studio. Especially during the first year of Sawyer's life. I don't want to miss anything."

A smile tugs on the corner of my dad's lips. "I'm proud of you, son. You've come so far. I have absolutely *no* doubt that you'll be an amazing dad and partner." I fight against the lump that builds in the base of my throat, but the onset of tears burns my eyes anyways.

"Beck!" My mom's yell echoes through the kitchen window into the yard. She looks more stressed than I have ever seen her. Panic instantly fills me and causes my stomach to practically fall out of my ass.

"Celeste, honey, what is it?" My dad jumps to his feet, looking like he's ready to go to battle to protect her.

Mom brings her hand to her heart and tries to catch her breath. "Olivia called and said she couldn't reach you." I pull out my phone from my pocket and try to turn it on. The screen remains black until a small empty battery symbol pops up. *Shit.*

"What's wrong?" I ask and start moving towards the door, barely giving my mom enough time to actually reply.

"Her water broke." My heart sinks. "Gracie was at your house, so she took her to Dryer Memorial." I'm almost to the top of the stairs when she follows up with, "She left all the bags at home!"

I run through the house and practically levitate into my truck before turning out onto the street. My nerves are on overtime. I quickly plug my phone into my car charger, cursing myself for letting it die.

I'm going to be a dad.

I'm going to be a fucking dad.

I pull into my drive way and throw the truck in park, not even waiting for more than a second before I turn it off and hop out of it. I run inside and open the coat closet by the front door, pulling out the hospital bag and diaper bag, and put them by the front door. I've never been more thankful for how prepared for everything Olivia is. Before I leave, I walk down the hallway so that I can grab Olivia's favorite blanket and her car keys. The car seat is in her car so I should *definitely* take that instead of the truck.

My mind feels like it's running a hundred miles per minute.

Sawyer's nursery door is open. I stop and look into her room, leaning up against the doorway. I'm giving myself one minute, just one, to brace myself for the change that's happening. The moment I walk out of the house, our life will never be the same.

Olivia

27

Thirty-Nine Weeks Pregnant

I sit in the waiting room, scared to death. Everything is about to change.

Everything.

I've had nine months to wrap my head around being a mom, but somehow, I forgot about the fact that I was going to have to actually give birth to her. Gracie shakes her knee while biting on her cuticles before hopping up and walking across the waiting room towards the nurses station. Again. I keep telling her that I'm okay, but every single time I make a noise or have a contraction, she panics.

I'm grateful that she chose today to stop by for a random visit. She hasn't seen the house yet and wanted to finally get a tour. I'm even *more* grateful that my water broke while I was on the tile. I would feel so bad if it broke on the carpet that Beck just installed.

Beck.

I hope he gets here soon. I don't want to do this without him.

The anxiety in my gut rises and my chest tightens. Another contraction spreads from my lower back to the front of my stomach. I have to remind myself to breathe as the pain radiates through me. None of the birthing videos or classes prepared me for how much this hurts, which is a-freaking-lot.

"I think she hates me." Gracie sits back down beside me.

I nod, breathing through the pain until it finally subsides.

"She doesn't hate you. She's obviously overwhelmed, Grace. It's after hours and there's a lot of people in the emergency room waiting right now."

"Is it a full moon?" I look at Gracie with a puzzled expression. As a teacher, I know there's power behind that statement, but I was shocked to hear her question what phase the moon was currently in. She shrugs and continues. "I don't know. I know that full moons make the emergency rooms really full or something."

I let out a small laugh and adjust myself. Not only is this chair incredibly uncomfortable, but there's an insane pressure on my tailbone. It might very well be my least favorite part of all of this.

"Olivia Connoly?" a nurse in pink scrubs calls my name. Gracie helps me to my feet and over to the double doors. "Hi. I'm nurse Lorraine. I'll be the one taking you over to labor and delivery. I'm so sorry you had to wait!" She nods to the wheelchair next to her and both her and Gracie help me into it. Just in time, too, because another contraction rushes through me. I check the time on my phone to keep track, but a text from Beck steals my attention.

My hot baby daddy: I'm on my way.

My hot baby daddy: I love you, Freckles.

Relief seems to calm the anxiety that is raging inside of me. At least a little bit.

We get to a set of metal doors and the nurse stops and uses her badge to scan us into the department. The doors open slowly, revealing a long hallway. Beige walls are lined with professional photographs of newborn babies. There's a thick, stale, clean smell that fills the air as I'm pushed towards a row of doors, some close and some open. I've never been a huge fan of hospitals and even though I love the reason I'm here, it doesn't help ease my anxiety any.

The wheelchair comes to a stop at room twenty-two and Lorraine helps me to my feet. "This will be your room for the next couple of days. Put your gown on and I'll be right back to hook you up to everything."

"Thank you." I turn to her and smile.

"You're so welcome!" She closes the door behind her, and I grab my nightgown off the foot of my bed before going into the bathroom. I've had to pee for the last twenty minutes. I really thought I was going to burst in the waiting room. I would have *loved* to use the bathroom in the emergency room, but the line was ten people long almost the entire time we were waiting.

As soon as I sit down, another contraction hits, this one hurting worse than the last.

Remember to breathe, Olivia.

Right. Breathe.

When it finally ends, I change into the birthing gown. I look in the mirror and turn to the side, admiring my belly one last time before she's in my arms. Then, I make a mental note to have Beck braid my hair when he gets here.

"I was about to send in a search party," Gracie announces when I walk into the main room. "I was scared you gave birth in the toilet or something."

"I had a contraction when I sat down. Then I had to actually change."

At first, the bed is a little intimidating. There're several machines surrounding it and the closer I get, the more anxious I feel. I crawl onto the bed and pull the blanket up to my thighs. My butt is hanging out of this gown and no matter what I do, the gown refuses to stay closed.

"Ah crap." I groan and let my head fall back onto the pillow.

"What's wrong?"

"I forgot my blanket at home, and I never packed it."

The door to my room opens and nurse Lorraine walks in. "I found someone wandering the halls and I think he might belong to you." She winks.

Beck comes barreling in behind her with our bags *and* my favorite blanket. I could cry right now. He drops the bags next to the couch and rushes to my side, making sure to cover my legs with the blanket. I've never seen such a concerned look on his face as the one he's wearing now.

"You're here."

I feel like I can breathe again.

"I'm here." He kisses the tip of my nose and rests his forehead on mine. The nurse starts to pull different medical items out of the drawers and lays them across my lap. I breathe through my contraction while Gracie kisses me on my forehead, nodding to let her know I love her too.

"I'm going to take my leave now. I love you so much. Beck, take care of our girls. Okay?"

"Always." She hugs Beck and then waves as she leaves the room.

The nurse finishes putting the monitors on my stomach and slides in my I.V. She talks to Beck and I during all of it, asking us about the baby's name and if I have a birthing plan, but towards the end of the conversation I check out and let Beck do the rest of the talking.

"I hear we're having a baby!" The doctor enters the room and stops at the foot of the bed. Per instruction, I scoot to the edge for a cervical check. Everyone in the room, including myself, is shocked to find out I'm already at seven centimeters.

The nurse and doctor both jump into action. Lorraine rests her hand on my shoulder and lets me know she's going to find the anesthesiologist to get me the epidural immediately.

After everyone leaves the room, the nerves *really* hit me.

We're having a baby.

AFTER I GOT MY EPIDURAL, I was finally able to sleep some. I only get about an hour worth of a nap in, but it's something. Beck is sitting on the couch, scrolling through his phone, when my eyes finally flutter open.

"Hey." My voice is hoarse. He tosses his phone down, jumps up off the couch, and grabs my cup with ice chips in it, moving the hair out of my face before feeding me one. "I forgot to ask you to braid my hair."

"I will do that right now." He rustles around in our bags for my toiletries. He finds my hairbrush and a couple of ties and when he returns to the bed, he brushes my hair the best he can with my limited mobility. His fingers twist the strands of hair as he effortlessly creates my braid.

"Oh. I meant to ask. How was that band thing that Derek was so adamant about that had to happen immediately?"

"It was okay. I told Derek he needed to find my replacement like yesterday and that I was done for good."

"How are you doing with that? I can't imagine it's easy." He drops my braid and sits on the edge of the bed.

"I'm good. I'm at peace with my choice."

I bite the inside of my cheek. I'm scared to ask my next question, but I *need* to know. "You didn't quit because of me... right?"

"What? Not completely, no. Obviously, it did make me want to push for it harder, but I have been done with Skarred for a long time. *Years.* You and Sawyer are my life now, Freckles."

My cheeks warm and I open my mouth to respond, apologize really. But the monitors start to go crazy, and several nurses and the doctor fill the room within seconds. Beck jumps off the bed and stands at my side, grabbing onto my hand.

Panic fills my chest.

"Olivia, honey, the baby is in distress, and we need to see what's wrong."

I might puke.

Tears blur my vision. I'm unable to verbally respond so I just nod. I don't know why I can't speak, but I feel like my mouth is frozen. Beck's grip on my hand tightens when they transition me on my back. The nurses help put my legs in the stirrups, and the doctor disappears beneath my sheets.

"Okay, Olivia, it's time to push now. So, on this next contraction I need you to push." I nod with tears streaming down my face in hot streams. "Now."

Beck places his hands between my shoulder blades to help keep me up as the nurses bring my knees to my chest. I try so hard, baring down harder than I've ever done before. I literally can't feel *anything* so I'm just hoping there's some kind of progress.

"And relax."

I sit back and look at Beck. I'm not sure if he's trying to fake like he's calm, but he smiles softly and raises my hand to his mouth.

How am I already drenched in sweat?

"Here comes another one. Push. Push. *Push.*"

My vision blurs and I feel lightheaded. The doctor looks to the nurse and sighs. Nurse Lorraine pops her head out of the door and within seconds the room seems to flood with more people. My brain starts to feel fuzzy and I'm not sure if it's my anxiety, but my lungs feel like I can't get enough oxygen.

The doctor says something to everyone in the room and turns to me, her eyes softening.

"Your baby is in distress. We need to take you in for a c-section, right now."

BECK

28

*S*urgery.

I don't even have the time to attempt to process what's happening. One of the many nurses hands me teal blue a package wrapped in plastic and directs me to dress quickly. I open the clear bag and pull out its contents: booties, a hair net, and some kind of long sleeved overall situation.

I throw everything on in record time, but when I finally lift my attention to Olivia, they're already wheeling her out of the room. I hurry after them and follow everyone down the hall. We enter a small corridor with two doors across from one another at the end.

"You have to wait here until they're finished prepping her for surgery. It'll only be a few minutes," a nurses says, holding her hand up to stop me from going in.

I want to yell.

I want to push my way into the room.

But I don't. I can't.

I pace back and forth in the small room. I swear it's taking longer than a few minutes. The skin of my lip is raw and the metallic taste of my blood dances on the tip of my tongue. My heart is going to pound out of my chest if I don't get in there soon. My finger nails leave crescent shaped imprints in the palms of my sweaty hands. There's a small window on the door that allows me to see some movement, but I can't find Olivia when I try to peek through it. My cuticles are being bitten down to nothing while I wait to be able to be by her side.

After what feels like a lifetime, the nurse opens the door and calls me into the room. I rush to a stool at Olivia's head.

She's strapped onto boards attached to the surgical table that force her arms out. She lets her head fall onto the side and tears stream down her cheek. I wipe them away from her soft skin.

"Hi, Freckles. We're going to meet our baby soon."

"I'm...so...scared." Her jaw rattles as she shivers.

Lorraine disappears and comes back seconds later with a blanket, draping it carefully across her chest. She smiles softly at Olivia and returns to her place at the surgical table. She stands right by the curtain that blocks our view of anything below Olivia's chest.

I run my hand over the top of Olivia's head, smoothing out the little bit of her hair that shows beneath the hair net and moving it out of her face. I don't want to speak because I know my voice will tremble and not because I'm cold, no.

I'm scared, too.

So fucking scared.

But I can't let her know that.

I can't let her know. Not right now anyway.

My heart is beating in my ears. It's so loud I can't hear

anything else in the room. So when the doctor announces something to us, Olivia nods, but I have no idea what's been said. She grimaces and I want to help her. I want to take all of this pain away. But there's nothing I can do.

I'm helpless.

Useless.

A sudden wail rings out in the room and the tunnel I've been trapped in dissipates from around me. I look up to see the doctor holding a crying Sawyer above the curtain. Just enough for us to get a quick glimpse before they rush her away.

They lower her back beneath the curtain and towards a table in the corner of the room. Lorraine lowers herself down to my level and whispers, "You can go to your baby. I've got mama."

I gaze down at Olivia. I don't want to leave her, but she smiles softly and nods. "Go to her, Beck. She needs her daddy."

Daddy.

My knees shake as I rise to stand. I've never been as nervous as I am now, walking to meet my daughter for the first time. The nurse cleaning her turns to me and grins. "She's eight pounds and four ounces and twenty inches long."

My cold black heart seems to grow three sizes right there, like I'm the fucking Grinch or something. She is literally the most perfect thing I've ever seen.

The nurse wraps her up and hands her to me. I haven't held a baby since Blaire, and that was lifetimes ago, so I feel like a fish out of water. She's so tiny, but fuck if I don't already love her more than I ever thought I was possible of loving someone. Tears sting my eyes, and I do absolutely nothing to stop them from running down my cheeks.

Two days later and Olivia is dying to be home. She has been walking every couple of hours, pacing back and forth in our room until she needs to sit back down. I'm in complete awe of her and her strength as I watch her push through and attempt to breastfeed Sawyer. A lactation specialist has come in twice in hopes to get her to latch, but it's not coming as natural as Olivia had hoped.

We made the choice not to have family visit us in the hospital. After we called and let everyone know that she was born and filled them in a little bit about her entry into the world, nobody gave us a hard time about our request. Not that I thought anyone would. We have a really good group of people around us and I know we're going to have to lean on them even more right now.

Sawyer stirs in the hospital bassinet, so I pick her up. Olivia couldn't wait to dress her in one of the floral footie pajamas she bought, so that's what she's currently wearing. And shit if she didn't look so cute. Carefully, I head back to sit on the couch and curl up with the baby in my arms. Looking at her sweet little face almost feels like an out of body experience.

I'm not exaggerating when I say I never thought this life was something I was going to be able to experience. I was always too scared to let anyone in. Every one night stand, every hookup, was kept at an arm's length. I never got to know them well enough to even know their middle name, let alone have a baby with them. But Olivia has always been different.

Subconsciously, I knew that if it wasn't with her, I didn't want it with anyone.

The door lightly opens and Lorraine joins us, waving apologetically as she puts hand sanitizer on her hands and grabs gloves.

"I hate doing the late night or early morning patient checks because I hate waking them up," she whispers, standing beside the bed.

Olivia's eyes flutter open and, with the help of Lorraine, she sits up slightly. They run through the series of vitals that she has to have done every couple of hours and Lorraine hands her a weird tube thing and asks her to blow. She explains to Olivia how she needs to do it every so often to prevent complications with her lungs.

She finishes her check and says her goodbyes and lets us know who the next nurse on shift will be. Once she closes the door behind her, Olivia's head falls onto her pillow, and she smiles softly.

"She's pretty damn cute, Freckles," I say, watching Sawyer.

"Yeah, she is."

"How are you feeling? Do you need anything?"

She shakes her head and settles back into the bed, pulling the blanket up to her shoulders. "I'd like to go home."

"Lorraine said they'd probably let you go home tomorrow afternoon."

"Yeah, but that's not right *now*. I want our bed and our shower."

I let out a small laugh and Sawyer startles in my arms. *Whoops.*

"Should I try to feed her?"

I shrug.

"I'm like this close to giving up my breastfeeding attempt." She holds up her fingers to show me for effect.

"I support you in whatever you decide to do."

She grins, keeping her eyes on me with Sawyer for a minute before breaking the silence. "Did you ever think we'd end up here? Like this?"

"I think I always hoped. I had a huge crush on you in high school. You were probably the only girl I ever really liked like that."

"You're joking."

I shake my head and bring my attention back to Olivia, whose mouth is hanging open.

"I had a huge crush on *you* in high school," she admits.

My eyes widened in surprise. "There's no way."

I can't imagine that high school Olivia ever thought anything positive of me. I was a shit kid. I always ditched, smoked and drank during school, and literally didn't give a shit about anything besides music. I was the textbook definition of a troublemaker.

But not Olivia. No, she was kind, selfless, and full of love.

She was, and still is, everything I'm not.

"Every girl has a crush on the *bad boy* once in their life. You just so happened to be mine."

"Now we're here." I look down at this perfect life Olivia and I created together. I'm still not able to tell exactly which one of us she takes after more, but I hope it's her mama.

"And now we're here."

Olivia's eyelids are heavy, and I watch as she tries so hard to keep them open.

"Sleep, Freckles. We will be here when you wake up."

She smiles softly and her breathing turns heavy as she falls back to sleep.

"It's me and you, kiddo," I murmur to Sawyer, running the side of my finger gently over her full head of light blonde hair.

Olivia

29

We've been home for four days. I sit in the rocker that's in the corner of the nursery, this stunning nursery that Beck and I just finished decorating when Sawyer decided to make her appearance.

Nobody talks about what happens when you come home with a baby.

Not really, anyways.

They don't talk about the loneliness seems to call out to the darkest cloud so that it can hang over your head. Or the exhaustion that seems to invade every single one of your thoughts. Or the darkness that seems to swallow you whole.

Family has been dying to come and see her. I haven't been ready and have told them as much. Which everyone has been *so* understanding about.

My mom and Celeste have taken turns dropping off hot meals at the front door. And if Gracie isn't dropping off coffee, Daphne is. Nobody has pushed us to see her, but I can tell they're getting worried.

Beck knocks on the door of the nursery and slowly swings it open. "Hey. Why don't you sleep some while she's down?"

I shrug and continue to stare aimlessly at literally nothing. I'm screaming internally, but on the outside I'm silent. I don't know what I need. Sleep? A shower? Food?

"I need to shower," I say.

"Let me help you."

He comes to me and brings me to my feet. It feels like both of my legs are weighed down with bags of sand as I drag myself to the bathroom. Beck sits me on the toilet and starts the shower. He doesn't speak as he brushes through my matted hair, or when he pulls it back into a braid, or even when the tears start to flow down my cheeks. Carefully, he pushes my arms out of the sleeves of my nightgown and pulls it up and over my head.

I avoid my reflection in the mirror. I'm still not in the place where I can see my incision without feeling...I don't know what I'm feeling. I step into the shower. The water nips at my skin as it cascades down my back. My back is sore, which the doctor said will happen during the healing process.

I know Beck's standing right outside the door. He hasn't really left my side since we came home from the hospital if he can help it. I want to call out to him. I want to tell him that I've never felt like this in my life. I've never felt so alone, so *empty*.

I'm not supposed to feel empty, right? I just had a baby. I'm supposed to feel happy and whole.

"You okay?"

My suspicion is proven correct when he pops his head through the cracked door.

"Fine."

"Okay, well. I uhm..." He rejoins me the bathroom. "I called your therapist. If that's overstepping, I'm sorry. You have an appointment via video call in like 15 minutes."

I want to be angry.

I want to cry.

I want to yell and tell him I don't need it.

But I know deep down, I do.

Beck helps me bathe the parts of my body I still can't reach. He's gentle, not scrubbing too hard with the loofah as he lathers soap onto my skin. He pulls the shower head down and rinses my body clean before turning off the water and helping me dry myself off and get dressed.

I want to tell him how much I love him, but all I can manage is thanking him. Afterward, he sets me and the computer on our desk in the bedroom, kisses the top of my head, and leaves the room.

Within a few minutes the laptop starts to ring with the incoming video call from my therapist. I'm not even aware when I answer it.

"Olivia. Hello!"

We exchange pleasantries, but I know she's itching for me to divulge more. I want to, but why am I so hesitant? Why do I feel so...embarrassed?

"I...I'm just tired."

"That's expected after what you've gone through. You labored and then had emergency surgery. Your body is healing twice as hard right now."

I shake my head. "I don't know if it's just that. I feel like I'm fighting a battle with myself. I want help, but I don't want it."

"This is the part you can't prepare yourself for. The overwhelming sadness, right? You feel like you're underwater and no matter how fast you swim, how hard you fight, you can't reach the surface. Can we touch on that more?"

"I'm just...I'm just so angry."

"Olivia. There is no one way that you should feel. You can have bad moments and happy moments. Whatever you're feeling at this moment is valid. What you'll be feeling tomorrow is valid. My job, right now, is to make sure you are safe. You're a planner by nature, and nothing went according to your plan. You are *grieving* the loss of that experience."

I nod, not even attempting to hold the tears back as they slide down my face and soak the top of my shirt.

"It's okay to be angry. You have to allow yourself time to grieve, time to feel everything. Just remember you don't have to do it alone. You have an entire village of people who love you. Lean on them. Lean *into* them for support. May I recommend something?"

"Of course, please."

"Paint. You have that beautiful studio. Go paint."

I wrap up my therapy session and hang up with my therapist before emerging from the room. Beck leans back on the couch and I can see his face from the end of the hallway.

"Hey. How'd it go?"

"Good." On my way to the living room, I pause by my studio, eyeing it. I don't even know if I can sit on the stool seven days postpartum, but I kind of want to try.

I've always found joy in painting, but what if I can find healing in it too?

"Hungry?" Beck asks.

"Kind of."

"Want me to order Messina's?"

I lean up against the wall and take a deep breath. "Messina's sounds great, but make sure it's enough for visitors. I think we can slowly introduce people. I'm not saying both of our families at once, but maybe like two or three people at a time."

"You sure? Everyone's cool waiting."

"I'm sure." I look over my shoulder at the door of my studio. "Sawyer sleeping?"

"Out like a light." He holds up the video baby monitor. "Are you going to take a nap?"

"No. I think I'm going to go paint."

"Okay." He nods with a look on his face like he's excited but doesn't want to seem *too* excited. I smile and turn to go down the hall and towards the door of my studio.

The smell of fresh wood hits me the moment I open the door. I haven't been able to spend much time here, so everything still smells brand new. I close the door behind me and head to the stack of canvases, grabbing a medium size one.

Once its set up, I sit there staring at the blank canvas for a minute, letting myself really *feel* everything. The disappointment, the grief, the anger. I let myself feel it all, dipping my paint brush into paint and letting it all out of my canvas.

I LOSE TRACK OF TIME, but when I finally emerge from my studio Beck is paying the pizza delivery man. That painting session made me feel...lighter.

"Gracie, Mattie, and Daphne are coming over. They'll be

here in a few minutes." He put the pizza boxes on the coffee table. "I figured you'd want them over first."

Gratitude fills my chest. Sometimes it's like he knows me better than I know myself.

"I'm going to go wash the paint off." I lift up my hands to show him the different shades of red and gray that cover my skin.

One the way to our bedroom, I crack Sawyer's door slightly to peek inside. She's still taking one of her many mid-day naps. Which is good because once some of her aunts get here, she will become the center of everyone's attention. I go through my bedroom and into the bathroom, making a mental note to finish decorating every other room in the house.

After washing off the paint that freckles my skin, I take off my shirt and toss it into the hamper. Our closet is somewhat organized, so finding a shirt is pretty easy. The voices of my sisters and best friend travel down the hallway and into my room. Excitement builds up in my stomach for the first time in a week and I have to refrain from skipping down the hallway.

"Biiitch!" Gracie exclaims when she catches sight of me.

"Livy!" Daphne and Mattie yell together. The three of them surround me and wrap me in an embrace. I welcome the physical show of affection from my sisters and my best friend. I'm not sure who starts it, but before I know it the four of us are sobbing.

At some point during the embrace, Beck leaves the room. When he returns, he announces his arrival by saying, "And here is the newest member of girl's night." They all turn and squeal with excitement.

"She is perfect," Gracie cries.

"Literally the most perfect thing I have *ever* seen," Daphne agrees.

Mattie just stands there sobbing, tears streaming down her face as she tries to mumble something. The three of them run off into the kitchen and bathroom to wash their hands, knowing I absolutely want them to have clean hands before touching Sawyer.

In the living room, I find my place on the couch and Beck follows to hand me the baby. He kisses the top of my head. "I'll leave you guys to it. If you need me, I'll be in our room."

"Love you."

"Love you more, Freckles."

One by one, they all come into the living room. None of them try to pry the baby out of my hands or demand to hold her, which I appreciate more than they will ever know.

First, I hand her to Daphne. There's something about my twin, the other half of my soul, being the first person to hold my child that feels poetic. While Sawyer's with my sister, Gracie disappears into the kitchen. A minute later she comes back with a tumbler full of ice and water and a stack of paper plates. She opens one of the pizza boxes and puts a piece of pizza on one of the plates, handing both the tumbler and the plate to me.

"Eat," she demands.

I know there's no use in fighting her. If I was to *try*, she would absolutely force feed me.

Sawyer takes turns being held by each one of her aunts, who all named themselves until she's old enough to name them. Daphne requested Auntie D, Mattie asked to be called Aunt Mattie, and Gracie wanted Gigi. I try to explain to her that's a grandma's name and she refuses to accept it.

About an hour passes and they all leave. Each of them saying they don't want to overstay any welcome. I'm *exhausted* after they're gone, but really everything drains my energy right now.

"Let's wait a couple of days before letting anyone else visit," Beck suggests, and I nod, sitting on the edge of the bed. He crawls behind me and rubs my shoulders. "You doing okay, Freckles?"

"Yeah. Seeing them made me feel a little bit like myself again, but I just need to find a new sense of normal. Maybe I need to get out of the house."

"Do you want to go out on a walk tomorrow? We can after Sawyer's six a.m. feeding?"

"Actually, I think that sounds really nice."

Beck helps me lay back onto the pillow pile we had to make since I still can't sleep completely flat on my back yet. He sits up against the wall next to me and takes my hand in his. Gently, he rubs the pad of his thumb along the top of my hand.

"Thank you."

"What for?"

"I don't know. Being so patient with me, I guess."

Beck lifts my hand to his mouth and kisses it a couple of times. He lays his head against the headboard, gazing at me with such a tender look in his eyes. A smile plays on the corners of his lips before he chuckles. "Freckles, we are a *team*. It's us against the world."

He puts an arm behind my neck, pulls me into his side, and kisses my temple.

BECK

30

Olivia is starting to finally be able to move easier and now that we're forming our new normal, her dark cloud is a little less black. She's still in therapy weekly until her therapist says otherwise. She's been spending a lot more time in the studio and has even started to talk about the possibility of showing people her work.

Nights have been hard the last week, so we've spent the last few nights tag teaming our little night owl. I look at Olivia sleeping on the couch with our daughter sleeping in the bassinet next to her. *Fuck.* Loving her is like...is like breathing. It's easily the most natural thing I've ever done.

My phone vibrates in my pocket, and I'm surprised to see a text from Tieran.

> Tieran: I am the worst friend, ever.

> Tieran: Congratulations on the baby! I can't wait to meet her.

Me: No, man. You've been busy with your schooling and stuff. Come by whenever! We're always home these days.

Tieran: How's like twenty minutes?

Me: Perfect! See you then.

I slide my phone in my back pocket and head into the kitchen. There is a sink full of bottles and dishes that are calling my name.

"I was going to do those, I swear," Olivia whispers from the couch. The water fills the side with the stopper, and I shrug.

"Rest. I got this."

"Do you want me to make something for lunch? As much as I love Messina's, I don't think I can do pizza again."

"Your mom brought over a chicken Caesar pasta salad, so we can just eat that."

"That does sound good."

Now, at almost two weeks old, Sawyer has met her entire family.

I expected it would be emotional for everyone, but I didn't expect my dad crying. A couple days after the girls all came over, we invited our parents and Blaire over to meet Sawyer. Both of our moms brought enough freezer friendly food to last us two weeks.

"Tieran texted me."

"Oh?"

"He's coming over in like fifteen-ish minutes. If that's okay?"

Immediately, I realize I should have asked first.

"Yeah, absolutely. I have therapy around that time anyways."

I nod, pushing the bottle cleaner into one of Sawyer's

bottles and scrubbing the inside of it really well. I'm excited to see my best friend. He's been one, if not the most, supportive friend I've ever had.

Olivia comes up behind me, wrapping her arm around my waist, and lays the side of her face flat on my back.

"You okay, Freckles?"

"*Mmhmm,*" she hums into my back. The vibration from the sound travels up my spine. I drop the bottle and turn around, pulling her into my chest.

"There's no escaping now."

The doorbell goes off and she looks up at me and chuckles. "Saved by the bell." I kiss her forehead and release my hold on her.

She disappears down the hallway and closes the door behind her. I dry my hands off on a towel before going to open the door. Tieran smiles and throws his hands up in the air.

"Beckkk!" He wraps his arms around my shoulders and pulls me into a hug.

"Hey, Ti. Come in." I move aside and gesture for him to come into the house.

"Man. This place is awesome! Where's your bathroom?" I point him towards the door in the hallway. He disappears into the bathroom, shutting the door behind him.

I walk around the couch and pick Sawyer up out of her bassinet.

"Hello, daddy's sweet girl." She's awake, looking around all bright eyed.

"There's a sentence I never thought I'd *ever* hear Beckett Haven say." Tieran sits down on the couch next to me. "But fuck if it doesn't look good on you, dude."

"Yeah?"

"Absolutely." I lift Sawyer up and hand her to Tieran. He places one of his hands gently at the base of her head and scoops her up with the other. "Dude."

"I know."

"You made this human."

"I did, in fact. Granted, Olivia did all of the work."

"How's she doing?" He bounces the baby softly in his arms, staring at her.

"She's as okay as she can be." I respond, unsure of how much to actually divulge. It doesn't seem like it's my place to talk about things she's struggling with. "It's an adjustment."

"I can only imagine. Did you hear about Skarred?"

"Yeah. Derek finally got what he wanted."

I sit there, watching my oldest friend hold the newest love of my life and I realize so did I.

I just didn't know that *this* is what I've wanted all along.

IT TAKES a couple of weeks after the fact, but eventually Derek does apologize for the way he acted when I said I was out. Everything happened for Skarred *really* fast. Once they officially signed all of the paperwork, the label was able to find my replacement and they were in the recording studio within a couple of days. Today, they're packing up to leave for the first part of their tour and I'm going to go see them off. Since Daphne and Derek are dating, she's going to go with them. So, we are having everyone over for breakfast before they leave.

Olivia has been cleaning the house in a frenzy since Sawyer

woke up at five. I've tried helping, several times in fact, but she is in the groove. Music fills our house as she moves from room to room. I go into the kitchen and start breakfast. I may not be a baker like her, but I can cook a mean breakfast.

I start on the country potatoes, cutting up the onions and bell peppers to sauté them on the stove. Once they are in the pan, I cut the potatoes into bite size pieces and add them to the mix. I put the bacon on a baking sheet, stick that in the oven, and get started on the scrambled egg mixture.

There's a knock on the door and it opens slowly. Daphne comes in first, followed by Derek, Hayes, and Watson.

"The party has arrived!" Daphne sings and raises two bottles of champagne. Everyone follows her into the dining room off the side of the kitchen. "Cups?"

I point to the cabinet where we keep everything other than our coffee mugs. Every bit of oxygen leaves my lungs when I catch sight of Olivia. She's wearing a bright yellow dress that hugs every curve on her body in just the right way. She sidles up next to me, putting her hands on the edge of the counter, the corners of her lips curve slightly.

"Can I help you with anything?"

"Almost done here."

I move to stand behind her, careful not to push her against the counter as I lower my mouth to her neck and leave a trail of kisses on her exposed, soft skin. She lets her head fall back, granting me greater access. *Fuck.*

"Hey. We know how Sawyer was made. She doesn't need a brother or sister just yet." Daphne laughs and snags open the fridge. She grabs the orange juice and wiggles her eyebrows at us before joining the others at the table. Olivia turns around, resting her back against the counter.

"I love you." She wraps her arms around my waist.

"I love you too, Freckles." I lower my mouth to hers, kissing her gently.

Olivia takes the bowl of fruit she cut earlier this morning to the table and I pull the bacon out of the oven and place it on a paper towel covered plate. It doesn't take long to finish the rest of the breakfast preparations and I finally have the opportunity to sit with everyone.

The guys are chatting about the tour and everything they hope to experience. Derek talks about everything the manager has planned for them, from meet and greets to podcast interviews. I'm happy for them, truly I am. But there's no place I'd rather be than home.

Once breakfast is all finished, Daphne and the guys team up to do the clean up while Olivia and I take a break on the sofa. She protested, but I sat down with no hesitation. She's next to me, pressing herself into my side. I wrap my arm around her shoulder and pull her closer to me.

"Do you regret it?" she murmurs.

"Regret what?"

"Not going on tour with the band." She traces circles onto my chest and continues. "I thought you would have changed your mind and decided to go with them."

"You didn't really think I'd leave my girls, did you?"

She shrugs, chewing on her bottom lip.

"Freckles, I am so fucking in love with you I couldn't leave even if I tried."

"Yeah, but the band—"

"But the band, nothing. I'd search for your face in every crowd." She lays her head onto my chest. I kiss the top of her head. "My place is right here, with you and Sawyer. There's literally nowhere else I'd rather be."

When the chaos of the band is ready to leave, we put Sawyer into her stroller and take short walk to their bus. The summer breeze is gentle beneath the trees that line the street. It's already pretty warm so I welcome the shade from their leaves.

We wait on the curb as the band loads their instruments and luggage into various compartments. Daphne sticks her arms out at Olivia, who returns the gesture and pulls her sister into a hug.

"You have to call me every week and tell me how the trip is going," Olivia demands.

"Only if you send me daily pictures of Sawyer."

"It's a deal."

One by one they wave at us and disappear through the door of the bus. We watch in silence as they roll out onto the street. I take Olivia's hand and together we start the short trek back to our house. She may not believe me, but I'd choose her over anything any day.

This is where I'm supposed to be.

EPILOGUE

Olivia

*D*eciding on a first birthday theme was one of the hardest choices I have ever made. Not really, but you know what I mean. There are just too many cute designs and I fell in love with every single one I found before deciding: Sawyer is Onederful. There is so much yellow and orange *everywhere* that I think Beck is going to ban the color from our house from here on out.

I am just about to finish up the balloon arch that I'm stringing along the picture backdrop when I hear my sister come into the backyard through the side gate. "Livy!"

"Daph!" I drop what I'm doing, ignoring the couple of balloons that pop as I embrace my sister.

Skarred has been on tour off and on for the last ten and a half months and they haven't been staying in Dryer Hill for longer than a couple of days before leaving again.

With the help of the internet, the band grew in popularity at a crazy fast rate. They've just gotten home from the United Kingdom this week and I haven't had a chance to see my sister yet.

"Do you need help with anything?"

"*Erm.* I don't think so, but Mattie and Mom are inside with Gracie. Go say hi!" I wave to Derek, who has found the group of guys standing at the base of our deck. No doubt talking about the grass, which has become one of Beck's favorite conversation topics.

Such a dad.

I turn to face the party and can't tamp the feeling of accomplishment. There's a small bounce house for anyone who decides to use it, which by the looks of it, it's just going to just be the adults. The tables are decorated with white and yellow gingham pattern tablecloths and bud vases full of baby's breath. I wanted to keep it simple, but beautiful, and I think I succeeded.

A hand wraps around my waist, pulling me against a hard body. "You look absolutely beautiful, Mrs. Haven."

"Not Mrs. Haven, yet." I wiggle my hand in the air. My engagement ring sparkles in the sunlight.

"Eh. Semantics. You will be soon enough." He kisses my cheek.

"Mama!" a small voice calls to me, I turn to Sawyer running away from Gracie, straight towards me. I pick her up and swing her around in the air. "Gigi get me!"

"Oh no. Do we need to get Gigi back?"

She nods her head and giggles, lifting her hands up to pretend like she's a monster. We chase Gracie around the backyard for a couple of minutes, until Beck announces it's time for pizza.

I sit Sawyer in her highchair while Beck hands her a plate with a small piece of cheese pizza. Not long after, he hands me a plate with a slice of pepperoni.

"For baby, and mama."

"I no baby!" Sawyer protests.

"Daddy's sorry, pretty girl. You are *not* a baby. You're a big girl."

We sit down at the table right next to where Sawyer is, joined by all of our friends and family. Everyone talks about the memories they made with her for the last year, but I can't help finding myself thinking about everything even before that.

"Cake! Cake!"

"I think someone wants cake." Celeste laughs.

"I'll go get the cake and candle."

I walk into the house and pull out the smash cake I had made for Sawyer. It's frosted with white frosting, decorated with orange polka dots with a yellow vintage fringe. It's honestly one of the cutest cakes I've ever seen even though it's so simple. I put the singular candle in the middle, light it, and head back outside.

Everyone sings *Happy Birthday*, which Sawyer apparently doesn't like.

Immediately, everyone begins to whisper it instead of singing and that seems to calm her down. I put the cake in front of her and go to her side with Beck on the other

As the song ends, three of us blow out her candles together.

ACKNOWLEDGMENTS

I'm not exaggerating when I say that I have the best village, but we're going to keep this short and sweet.

Thank you...

Hubs for never EVER trying to stop me from chasing this crazy dream of mine.

Keona for being the best cheerleader and best friend turned family. I couldn't do this crazy world without you.

Tori for stepping in as my alpha reader and absolutely killing it.

Kate for being literally everything I could ever need or want in not only an editor, but a best friend.

My author group chat (Kate, Katie, & Britt) for always listening to my ideas and supporting them no matter what.

My beta team for loving my characters as much as I do.

My readers for supporting me and sharing my work with others. No matter what book you found first, thank you for finding me.

My family for supporting me and always cheering me on loud enough so I can't hear those who aren't. Especially my sissy, since she's the only one who is allowed to read my books. Sorry mom & dad.

Lastly the biggest thank you to therapist, Stephanie and her insane amount of support and wisdom.

ABOUT THE AUTHOR

Katarina Martinez lives on West Coast with her husband, three kids, and three dogs. She is currently a full time college student, stay at home mom, and indie author.In her spare time she enjoys to camp with her family and crack open a good book with a nice iced vanilla latte. She enjoys reading literally anything she vibes with. If she isn't reading, she is listening to audiobooks, podcasts, or blasting her early 2000's playlist because let's be honest... it was never a phase.

She hopes you get as much joy from reading her books as she gets from writing them.You can connect with Katarina on TikTok and Instagram at @authorkatarina, in her facebook reader group {Katarina's Reading Group}, and in her Discord.

ALSO BY KATARINA MARTINEZ

Binding Fate

Rewrite Coming Late 2026

Midnight Duology

Midnight Whispers Available Now

Book 2 Announcement Coming Soon

Dryer Hill

It Could Be You Available Now